RENEE HARLESS

Cover Design by: Renee Harless
Photographs: Shutterstock

Website: reneeharless.com
Facebook: authorreneeharless
Instagram: renee_harless
Twitter: Renee_Harless

More Books by Renee Harless

The Stone Series
Stone Shattered
Stone Unhinged
Stone Mended

Welcome to Carson
Coming Alive
Coming Together

RENEE HARLESS

This book is dedicated to my kids. I hope that

one day you have the chance to find the person

that makes you complete.

Love with all you have.

RENEE HARLESS

Welcome to Carson, Book One

RENEE HARLESS

Prologue

AVERY IS LATE. SHE is so late that she is tempted to take an unscheduled absence and just clock in for tomorrow. Luck is on her side, though: her boss' car isn't yet parked in the employee lot.

Wasting no time, Avery rushes through the sliding glass doors at the physician's office and shoves her items into her locker. Melanie, her friend and coworker, appears behind her in the break room and props herself against the locker adjacent to her own.

"So, I have a thought, but I want you to hear me out."

Turning to face her, Avery can see that Melanie is doing little to mask the anxiety on her face – crinkles are knitted between her brows and bite marks of worry are on her lips. She does this when she's concerned about her. Melanie knows that a year later, Avery is still struggling to get over her fiancé's death, as well as trying to make peace with the horrible life she attempts to keep buried in the past.

Forcing a smile, Avery asks her to continue.

"I think you need to move away."

A gasp explodes out of Avery's mouth at the suggestion.

A year after Declan's passing; Avery continues to find she is just wandering through life, masking the pain she still feels inside at the loss of her almost-husband. Though there have been a few moments of happiness - a new neighbor that loves to have Avery over for dinner with her two sons – and of course the event that she never saw coming: Max and Melanie's wedding. That one definitely took everyone by surprise. She supposes that in a way, Declan's death illuminated the true meaning of living your life to the fullest, especially for their two friends.

"Hold on, Avery. Don't get upset, I think it would be good for you. Everything here reminds you of all that you've lost. You need a fresh start."

Taking Avery's hand in-between her equally small ones, Melanie garners more of attention.

"Look, my cousin Nikki lives in this adorable town in North Carolina. She needs a new roommate since hers just up and left, and I think you two would get along great. She works as a receptionist at a private practice in her town. When I mentioned what you do, she said they were actually hiring a medical assistant for each of the physicians at her practice." Pulling Avery closer, she wraps her in a tight hug. "This is your chance, Avery. You can be someone new where no one knows what you've been through."

Avery takes a moment to consider Melanie's proposal. The idea isn't a bad one really; it's actually something she had been tossing back and forth in her own mind for quite some time.

"You really think I should do it?"

"Max and I don't think you have anything to lose. And I really think you could be happy there. We all want you to be happy, Avery."

Absorbing her words, Avery asks if she can let her know by the end of the day. She wants to make sure she has taken adequate time to decide if this is what she really wants – no, *needs* to do.

This new concept is so distracting that during her daily workload of patients, Avery is admittedly surprised when she reaches the end of the day without severely harming anyone.

When at last Avery finds Max and Melanie standing by the water dispenser at the end of the shift, she tugs Melanie into her arms before saying, "How soon can I move?"

RENEE HARLESS

Chapter One

*W*ALKING THROUGH THE DOORS that open up to the small and cozy waiting area, Logan is greeted by a sultry smile from the receptionist, Nikki. Her come-hither stare sends electric pulses straight to his dick and he knows it won't be long before he's banging her in the staff bathroom. They've been circling each other for a few months, since the day she started at their practice.

One of the other physicians in their group greets Nikki "good morning," capturing her attention and Logan scoots along to his office. Glancing down at his schedule, he grunts when he looks at the full day of appointments and the group interviews for some medical assistants. He can deal with the appointments, but he's not really in the mood to deal with egotistical hopefuls who think that they know more than he does. That's what had happened to the last few interviewees that had come in: not a single member of the practice felt like the "help" these new-comers could offer would actually benefit the practice.

There are a total of five doctors making up this small office in the middle of the tiny town of Carson, North Carolina. After finishing his residency two years ago, Logan joined almost immediately. Much to his relief, Logan is no longer the newbie: Charles came on a year later. The rest of the team is comprised of the three original owners who founded the family medicine practice. The office handles everything from yearly physicals, to sports medicine, to gynecology. Luckily, Logan doesn't have to worry about the latter, as that was Charles' specialty during his residency. Being the closest physicians in a hundred-mile-radius of this rural countryside, they've seen a significant increase in patients since the new manufacturing plant opened up eighteen months ago - hence the need for the extra help with triaging patients before a doctor can see them.

Reaching for his white coat where it had been draped along the back of his chair, Logan winces at the pain in the over-tired muscles along his upper arms and chest. He may have overdone it at the gym with his friend Austin. After his horrible encounter with Rachel during his residency, Logan has really become a gym rat. If he's not at work (or fucking), he's at the gym working out. Unfortunately, these distractions do little to keep the painful memories from rushing forth like water from behind a broken dam. Even now, four years later, a brief recollection can leave him frozen in his chair.

Logan shakes his head to clear away thoughts of Rachel, wincing as he pulls on his jacket. He takes a seat in the chair, flipping through the patient charts that are placed before him as he prepares for his scheduled appointments. As he scans the last file, Nikki knocks gently on his open door. Leaning against the frame, the blonde hair twisted over her shoulder adds the finishing touch to her preppy look of a white polo shirt and tight khakis.

"Hey, handsome," she says huskily, quickly running her tongue against her lips.

Knowing he needs to remain professional - the other doctors are sitting in the offices just next door, after all - Logan replies simply, "Hey, Nikki. What's up?"

"I was just wondering if you or anyone else has chosen your MA yet?"

"No, not yet. I'm hopeful, though, after seeing some of the resumes that I've reviewed for the candidates who are interviewing in the next few days."

"Do you think it would be possible to squeeze in one more interview at the end of the week?"

"Um, I don't know, Nikki. Have you checked with everyone else?"

"Yeah, Charles is the only one with an appointment scheduled after hours. He says he trusts y'alls judgment. My cousin Melanie asked me about the opening."

"Is she the one interested? If I remember, she was actually pretty competent and it would be nice to have someone who doesn't question me at every turn."

"I don't know actually. She didn't say if it was for herself or Max."

"Well, I guess go ahead and schedule it. I'll make sure we're all happy with our choices."

"Ok, thanks," She murmurs with a coy smile, sauntering further into the room. "So...what are you doing later?"

"I'm meeting Austin for drinks at Horizons. Why? Are you interested in something?"

Her eyes skim down to his chest, drinking him in for a moment before looking back into his eyes and replying, "Yeah, something. Maybe I'll see you there."

Winking at her, Logan adds, "Looking forward to it," as she walks sultrily away, hips swaying, and back into the hall.

Sitting in their small conference room at the end of the day, Logan shuts his eyes as he leans back in his chair and waits for the others to arrive their interviews. The next candidate is the one Logan is hoping to snag. Judging from her resume, she seems like she'd be an incredible help. As a woman in her mid-sixties, she moved here to be closer to her grandchildren. With thirty-five years of experience in the medical field and having worked singularly for private family medicine practices, he is cautiously optimistic. It doesn't hurt that her references rocked as well.

The two candidates he interviewed last week had spent the entire time ogling him.

I mean, really? Who makes come-fuck-me eyes to their potential boss? He wonders.

That's why he's glad that three of the four interviews will be with hopefuls who are older or male. The exception, of course, will be for Melanie or Max. Luckily, they're not only married but Melanie is also Nikki's cousin, so he doesn't think there will be a problem.

As the other doctors make their way into the room, Logan throws a look at Nikki as she ushers in their interviewee. He winks at her as she exits, hoping she got the message that he's definitely interested in her showing up at

Horizons later; it's all he has thought about during his full day of appointments.

Mary Bell introduces herself to the group, full of confidence, and spends the next hour answering all of the physicians' questions with competence, while also asking a few great ones herself. Logan really likes her; she is the type of person he always wished his mom would have been. Mary possesses that intangible ability to make a person feel at ease when she is around, and Logan knows her calming presence speaks of a great bedside manner that will make her an invaluable asset.

Once she has left the room with promises of follow-up calls, Logan immediately stands and shouts that he wants her. Dr. Fields, his mentor and one of the original owners, laughs and complains jokingly.

A unanimous decision to hire her is made quickly and Logan hustles out of the room, making a mental note to contact Mary first thing in the morning. Locking his closed office door, he chucks off his coat as he walks towards his small closet. Logan always keeps a few "after hours" outfits in there - just in case. Since he is meeting Austin at the bar in approximately thirty minutes, tonight will be one of those occasions.

Removing his shoes and slacks, he replaces them with some dark denim and worn-out black boots. Logan rolls up the sleeves of his blue button-down to his elbows, then quickly glances at himself in the full-length mirror that is kept in the office just for such times. Satisfied with his appearance, he grabs his wallet and keys and heads out of the office.

As he steps through the door into the local bar, Horizons, he scans the room for his buddy Austin, his senses are assaulted by the smell of cheap booze and cigarette smoke. Every time he inhales that malignant odor, the first wave of recognition always triggers the last memory of his father.

Logan can't help but stand stock-still as visions cloud his mind.

It was the night before he left for college. He had decided to bring home a girl from a few trailers over, planning to have some fun since his dad wasn't around. He was a good-looking kid who got laid any chance he could - ever since he turned fifteen - and he wasn't about to waste such a golden opportunity: Logan was gifted with smarts, after all. Kelly may not have been much of a looker, but she had a nice rack and a tight pussy that he could barely wait to get lost in.

The two of them had hardly made it through the door before he had her pressed against a wall, her panties torn away from beneath the skirt that barely covered them. After delving his fingers into her wetness, Logan made her come quickly. The next thing he knew, she was clawing at his pants, begging for his dick. Moving over to the couch in the midst of silence, Logan donned a condom and sat her atop his thighs, shoving his dick into her harshly. Her moan quickly turned to screams of ecstasy, but before he had a chance to get his load off, his dad comes stumbling into the trailer drunk, high… and angry.

Shoving Kelly off quickly, he watched as she scooted out the door, pushing down her skirt from where it had been bunched at her waist.

His dad hollers angrily, "Whatcha doin' boy?"

Jostling his dick back into his pants, Logan turned to follow Kelly out the door, but before he has a chance to make a

quick escape his dad's clammy hands twist around his arm,
tugging him into the wall.

"Where the fuck are you going? Who do you think you are
fucking some girl in my house, you son-of-a-bitch?"

His angry words had Logan cowering in the corner: the
smell of cheap booze permeated through his father's skin. He had
been told that he was a handsome kid, but Logan was scrawny in
comparison to his father's shadowing figure. His hits had been
known to leave bruises on Logan's skin for weeks and he had never
been as angry as he was in that moment.

The incessant name calling and hateful words continued
as Logan's dad switched to beating his face and kicking his
abdomen. Kelly was his godsend that night, calling the police after
she left, otherwise, Logan was sure he would have been dead. His
father was escorted away in handcuffs while Logan was left to deal
with a broken nose and three shattered ribs.

Logan never saw his father again and word is that he was
killed in jail.

A quick shake of his head forces the memory back
into its vault, and Logan turns to view the pool tables where
he finds Austin pressed up against a hot redhead,
attempting to show her how to make a trick shot, though
Logan can tell that really he is just enjoying the feel of her
massive tits on his arm.

Heading towards the bar, Logan orders a beer and
makes his way in their direction. During his trek, his phone
buzzes in his pocket. It's a text from Nikki, letting him know
that she's on her way. Answering the text to confirm that
he's here, Logan continues along his path and shoves Austin
just as he helps his conquest make her shot. Originally
furious, thinking that a drunk had stumbled into him,

Austin pulls his fist back until he realizes it's Logan and then he pulls him in for a man hug. He briefly introduces Logan to Tiffany, who licks her lips as she glances up and down his body before returning her attention to Austin. Finished with the game, he and Austin move back to the bar and Tiffany follows like a lost puppy, staking her claim while perching herself in the chair next to his.

By the time Logan is on his third beer, he finds himself fending off woman after woman while he waits for Nikki to arrive. It really is amazing what a woman is eager to do, just to garner the attention of a good-looking man… or a free drink - sometimes it's hard to tell.

Nikki finally shows up, an hour after she had initially messaged, saddling herself onto the stool next to his - obviously making it known that she is here with him. Unfortunately for her, Logan's not exactly a patient man and he doesn't like having to wait.

"Hey handsome. Can I get a drink?"

"Hey, Nikki. Where've ya been?" Logan asks, betraying a bit of irritation by lifting his eyebrow in her direction, but trying to restrain the anger in his voice.

Brushing off his attitude, she gesture up and down her body, making sure his eyes follow her manicured hand as she showcases the skintight, red dress that barely covers her pert ass. Enough of her cleavage is hanging out that Logan can easily determine she isn't wearing a bra. Nikki dressed to get his attention, as well as every other man's in the bar.

"Enough said," Logan replies to her display, "Though it really wasn't necessary."

With a humph, she grabs the drink the bartender sits in front of her and takes a large swallow.

"You're not really good with words, Dr. Chamberlin. That's not really what a girl wants to hear when she spends extra effort to look sexy."

Killing his mood with her whiny tone, Logan turns in her direction and stares at her.

"Babe, I appreciate the effort, but Horizons isn't that kind of bar. You'd look just as sexy in jeans and a t-shirt. And you probably wouldn't have attracted all the attention of the old men across the way."

Looking around the bar, she notices the aforementioned men whose attention she's garnered and then turns back to face him, a large smile on her lips.

"Well, at least my efforts are appreciated by someone; though I do take your last statement as a compliment, so I won't hold your lack of admiration against you. Now, can we pick up from where we left off earlier?"

With a shake of his head, Logan chuckles and replies, "Sure thing, babe. Do you know how to play pool?"

"Not really, but I'd love for you to teach me," Nikki says, stroking her hand up and down his arm.

Getting the attention of Austin and Tiffany, a difficult task considering they are busy sucking on each other's faces, Logan asks if they want to join them for a game. The couple agrees and they all head towards the pool table for a friendly match.

Teaching Nikki how to play pool may not have been Logan's wisest decision. The way her body brushes against his hips has caused his dick to take major attention to her lack of attire. Standing against her, he directs her cue to take a shot as she wiggles her behind against his tightening jeans. Noticing Logan's hardening member pressed against her backside, she takes her hand that is holding her pool stick and strokes it up and down. With a sensual glance over her shoulder, she licks her lips before bending forward and taking her shot.

Wrapping his hands around her hips, Logan pulls her even closer and places his lips right below her ear, kissing her softly before nibbling on her skin. Luckily, her blonde hair had been pulled to the opposite side while they played the game.

"You ready to get out of here?" Logan asks her, rubbing his hands back and forth along her hips.

Turning in his arms, she licks her lips before grabbing his hand.

"Like you wouldn't believe."

Following Nikki back to her place, they pounce on each other once she closes her front door and the two topple over the edge of her couch. Without taking a moment to check out her apartment, her dress finds its way to the floor and they become a tangled mass of arms and legs on her furniture.

Before they have a chance to take it to their desired point, Nikki's phone rings. At first they ignore it, but then it begins ringing persistently again and she apologizes before answering. She moves into the kitchen to take the call and Logan finds himself looking around her apartment and taking note of the mess that she has laying around.

Seriously?

Logan's not OCD, but he likes things to be in their rightful place and the sight of Nikki's apartment instantly removes the hard-on he was sporting. He can't help but wonder how someone can live in this filth.

Nikki wanders back in moments later and begins apologizing profusely, explaining that they're going to have to end the night early since her cousin is on her way. She pouts through the entire statement, which isn't nearly as attractive as she assumes it is. Logan can't decide if it's the mess or if it's the outside-of-work meet-up, but he finds himself less and less attracted to Nikki the longer he stays in her apartment.

"It's alright, babe," he tells her. "I don't think this was a good idea."

"Yeah," she replies, grabbing an oversized shirt from the floor and tugging it over her head. "You're probably right." After a deep breath she asks timidly, "It's not going to be weird at work is it?"

Logan shakes his head.

"Am I going to get fired?"

Approaching her slowly and placing his hands gently on her shoulders, Logan looks down into her eyes and shakes his head.

"Don't be silly, Nikki. We couldn't replace you if we tried. You're a great receptionist. We'd be lost without you."

Releasing a deep breath, she seems to relax under his hands before leaning her head against his chest.

"Thanks for tonight, Logan. Sorry I'm kicking you out."

"No sweat. I'll let myself out while you wait for your cousin."

As he descends the steps outside Nikki's apartment, Logan notices a large moving truck pulling into the complex. He takes a second to watch the new tenants pull into a spot before he sees Melanie – whom he has met a couple of times during her visits to Nikki - jump out of the passenger seat. Waving his hand as he walks in her direction, not wanting to frighten her in the dark at this late hour, she startles at first, then relaxes and rushes towards Logan upon recognizing him.

"Logan, it's so good to see you. I feel like it's been ages."

Returning her hug, Logan smiles broadly and returns the greeting.

"Sorry to rush off, but we have a lot to do. I'm sure I'll see you soon," she says.

Moving towards the driver's side of an older sedan that Logan hadn't noticed, he sees her bend down to talk to a man whom Logan assumes is her husband, before looking towards something in the backseat. Before he heads off, Logan offers to help them move whatever they need, but she tells him that they have it taken care of and advises him to drive safely. Taking them at their word, Logan turns back towards his car and heads off into the night.

Stopped at a traffic light outside their complex, he steals a glance back at Nikki's apartment and watches them move around inside, feeling like he's some sort of creeper. But what gains his attention first is watching Nikki gasp, then bring her small hand to her mouth, looking completely shocked at whatever she's being told by Melanie. The second thing Logan notices is a dark swash of wavy brown hair. Even from this distance, he can see it shining like a beacon from the light in Nikki's apartment. The captivating hair is attached to a petite frame being carried by a large man.

A boisterous car horn alerts him to the light's change and Logan moves forward, whizzing past the sparse traffic in their tired little town.

ONCE AVERY MADE THE decision to leave and head to North Carolina, everything seemed to happen at lightning speed. One day she was at work, the next she was turning in her resignation (much to the disappointment of her supervisor) and packing up her tiny dwelling. Melanie has been by her side since Avery decided to take this journey, counseling her through all of her breakdowns while she packs.

"Who did all this stuff belong to?" Melanie asked when she walked into the guest room that is stacked full of boxes.

With a deep sigh, Avery responded, "Everyone that I ever loved."

"Do you want to talk about it?"

After taking a moment to study Melanie, Avery decided that she needed to tell someone – that she couldn't keep the grief in and let it continue to suffocate her.

"You may want to get comfortable, it may take a while."

"I've got nothing but time," Melanie replies gently.

How little did she know that time was never on Avery's side.

"I remember…I remember how the sheets of paper rattled within their tight grasp in my trembling hands," Avery begins as the memories play in her mind.

As she closes her eyes, she continues to relay the visions verbally to Melanie, but Avery is so lost in the recollections that she finds her consciousness transported back to the moment.

The thick, cream-colored cardstock sat heavily in her palm. The papers have finally been signed: it felt like she has been waiting forever for this moment. It had taken eighteen years to get to this point.. well, really six considering the age difference, but now Avery felt like her life had a purpose and she couldn't begin to fathom how their lives would change.

She would be hers to take care of – fully; not that Avery hadn't been taking care of her already, but her life would now rely solely on her.

In Avery's eyes, her six year old sister was utter perfection – could do no wrong. The deep red of her auburn hair starkly contrasted the blue of her eyes; eyes that captivated and pronounced her innocence at first glance. She was wise beyond her years, already coming to terms with the vile hatred their family felt towards them.

Growing up, Avery was treated as utter scum and filth since her mother had shown up pregnant at the age of fifteen. Her grandparents' wealth masked the shame they felt, and they hid her mother away until Avery was born: an unexpected surprise by one of the staff, Avery's mother claimed.

Yes, staff. The mansion, which sat atop a hill, looked out over eighty acres of land and the city below, and housed at least fifty employees.

Three stories of brick and mortar, grandiose columns, and wraparound porch were all it took to fool everyone.

This façade of a home was nothing but lies. From the time Avery turned two and could push a broom and pan, she was made to work the grounds. Ignored by her actual family, she tried clinging to anyone that showed her maternal care. All of the servants ignored her out of fear from their employer and shoved Avery out of their way most days - except for one, Mila. A Slavic immigrant, Mila came to work for Avery's grandmother as a caretaker to her dying husband, Avery's grandfather. She made sure Avery always had food to eat, clothes to wear, and a warm bed in which to sleep. She was also the one who disclosed, in secret, Avery's placement in the family: she was not a slave, but a child of old money.

Avery's grandfather died when she was twelve, right around the same time her mother announced another pregnancy and engagement.

When baby Aria was born, their mother and grandmother took pleasure in her arrival. It was like night and day to how Avery had been treated, but she couldn't find it in herself to be jealous. She loved Aria. She was the most beautiful little baby Avery had ever seen; pale skin, eyes that matched the sky at mid-day, and a swatch of red hair. Unfortunately, at her grandmother's insistence, Avery wasn't allowed to be near Aria. Her grandmother claimed that her shallow soul would taint the child. But Mila, who then became Aria's nanny, made sure to sneak Avery into the baby's room daily during the early morning light.

When Aria turned three, Avery's grandmother found a note from their mother saying she was running off with her second husband and her trust fund, planning to never return again. Her grandmother, whom Avery guessed was disgusted by this, turned against Aria. The abuse became both mental and physical. The staff seemed to always turn a blind eye to the beatings so Avery took it upon herself to try and contact local help. The police laughed in her face the day she snuck away and went to the police station. They couldn't seem to fathom that a sixty year-old woman *of her social stature could raise a fist. Dejected, Avery dove head first into research regarding child abuse and child turnover.*

She knew that if she could get her grandmother to sign over the parental rights to Aria, which their mother had given to her own mom upon her disappearance, then Avery could become her legal guardian. With this in mind, she pushed along for the next three years until her eighteenth birthday. Avery prayed that one day her grandmother would decide to ignore Aria, as she had her, but it seemed the longer their mother stayed away the more furious their grandmother turned. There were weeks at a time when Aria would have to miss preschool due to bruises on her face or arms.

Mila did her best to keep them upbeat and to keep the girls from their grandmother's wrath, but one person could only do so much against a self-proclaimed goddess.

Yet, even as Aria took beating after beating, she still remained this cheerful beacon of light in Avery's life. Love wasn't strong enough a word for what she felt for Aria. She was unaware that we were sisters, but she knew that Avery helped take care of her. At the time, it had been enough for Avery.

On Avery's graduation day she also turned eighteen, double the reason for her joyous outlook. No genetic family was in attendance, for obvious reasons, but Mila had come along with Aria to watch her cross the stage. Tears sparkling in her kind eyes, Mila proclaimed that she couldn't have been more proud of her. Avery's mind reeled and couldn't even settle on the achievements of the day. No, she was completely sidetracked by what she had planned for the following morning.

The next day, Avery stood in front of the cold dark room that was her grandmother's office. The papers from the attorney shook in her hand; a pro-bono case she was lucky enough to receive from a school-mate's mother. The knock on her grandmother's door echoed in the hall like a taunting laugh. She entered when commanded, but Avery didn't utter a word, just laid the papers in front of her grandmother.

"What's this?" her grandmother asked harshly, the wrinkles on her face scrunching closer together and resembling crepe paper.

"I want Aria. Please. I'll take her away from here and you won't ever hear from us again. I swear," Avery pleaded.

The pounding of her heart raised her body's temperature, staving off the chill of the dungeon-like room

"You'll never return? You'll take yourself and that bastard sister away?"

Avery cringes as the word "bastard" floats through the air - a term she has become far too familiar with.

"Yes, I promise. Please," she begs again.

Without any further argument, her grandmother signed the papers beside the noted tabs and handed them back to Avery.

"Good riddance," she proclaimed as Avery rushed to leave, closing the door behind her and resting against its cool wooden details.

Avery sighed deeply and shut her eyes as triumph and adrenaline coursed through her veins.

A rapid succession of coughs from inside the room jolted her back into reality. Avery turned on her heel, heading down the hall and then up the stairway.

Shoving the papers into a manila envelope that Avery left resting on her bed, she rushes to find Mila and Aria in the cavernous home.

Locating them in the garden, Avery wraps her arms around Mila excitedly as she rushes to tell her that they need to leave as soon as possible. Mila, the guardian angel that she is, decided that she was joining the sisters in their escape.

Mila is able to find them a small apartment in Savannah, Georgia, close to the community college that Avery received a scholarship to attend. The gratefulness pours from Avery in the knowledge that Mila is joining her on this journey - not because she can't take care of Aria, but because Mila had stowed away her earnings from Avery's grandmother, thus allowing them a nice financial cushion.

Avery began school immediately, taking summer courses towards her career choice as a medical assistant. Mila and Avery also located jobs as housekeepers for a local motel. Mila opted to work the night shift, allowing Avery to work the early morning shift. This gave her time to get one or two classes in a day.

In the blink of an eye, two years whizzed by. Avery and Mila were celebrating her adorable sister's eighth birthday. Seated at a local pizza place, on the rare occasion that both Mila and Avery were free from work, Aria looked blissful as she blows out the candles on her small pink cake. A smile grew on Avery's face as she gazed at Aria, whose hands were working happily to remove the wrapping paper on the present Mila handed to her. The package of books under the cheap paper sent joy through Aria and though she didn't think it was possible, Aria's smile grew wider as she read through the titles of the newest sorcery novels.

Avery startled when a large hand came to rest on her shoulder.

"Avery, right? I think you're in my anatomy course."

Shocked, she turned to look into the chocolate brown eyes set on a boyishly handsome face. His eyes remain locked with hers, waiting, and then Avery remembers that he asked her a question.

"Uh, I'm sorry, what?" she replied shyly.

Smirking, he repeated himself with his hand still gently resting on her shoulder, "You're Avery, right? I think we're in anatomy together."

"Um, yes. I think so," she murmured hesitantly.

Unsure what this handsome man's name is, Avery searched her mind for a hint, but came up empty. She pays notoriously little attention to people outside her tiny circle.

"Nick," he said, answering her unspoken question and finally removing the hand that had sent small sparks tingling through her shoulder.

"Nick, that's right. You sit at the lab table across from me. This is Mila and my sister Aria. We're here for her birthday. Would you like to join us?" she inquired while extending pleasantries, noticing the boyish face was actively seeking her attention.

"That's ok, I'm just here to grab a pizza before heading to a study group," Nick replied nervously, shuffling his feet. "Actually, since you're here, do you think you'd like to go out sometime? Maybe dinner?"

Blushing profusely, Avery turned away and glanced toward Mila, who sat with her hand over her heart and a smile on her face, gazing in Avery's direction. She nodded her head upon seeing the question in Avery's eyes.

Looking back in Nick's direction, he graced her with a small smile and Avery responded with a tiny grin of her own.

"Sure, that would be nice. What did you have in mind?"

"Are you free tomorrow?"

"I usually work in the early morning, but maybe we could do something earlier in the evening?"

"Why don't you give me your number and we can get together around three?"

"That sounds perfect," Avery answered, a smile still plastered to her face as she repeats her home phone number. "Thank you, Nick."

"No, Avery. Thank you," he delightedly replied. Nodding towards Avery's sister, he said, "Happy birthday. You all enjoy your night. Bye, Avery."

Waving back as he turned around, she mirrored his expression, "Bye."

As soon as their impromptu visitor had left, Mila gushed about Nick while Aria divulged her appetite on the cake. Both excited and nervous about this pending date, Avery is flooded with emotion. She's had a boyfriend, been on a date and shared a few kisses with boys she went to high school with, but nothing she would consider meaningful. At this point in her life, she couldn't help but think that those romances she had read in the fairytales when she was little were just that: fairytales. Avery had no desire to find love, but something meaningful that would fill her heart with joy. And Avery could already tell by the nervous flutters in her stomach that any relationship with Nick would be meaningful.

Nick and Avery met at a local diner the next day and after just an hour's conversation, she found herself completely taken by him. He was charming and sweet, a boy any mother would be proud to call her son. They had similar interests in music and movies, literature, and hobbies. He is someone that, in her past, she had never expected to find. But in that moment, sitting across from him and feeling this mutual attraction, Avery felt that the possibilities were endless.

She never expected to fall so hard or so fast. Avery could tell that Mila was worried. She was afraid that Avery was completely wrapped up in her first real relationship and unable to understand her feelings. But Avery knew. She knew after two months of dating Nick that she was in love with him. He was exactly what she had expected for herself, nothing more, and nothing less.

A year after Nick and Avery began dating, Mila became very ill. Avery often found herself waking in the morning to her incessant coughing fits. Avery begged Mila to see a doctor for three weeks straight before Nick finally carried and strapped her into the barely running car so they could take her themselves.

Aria was in school when they finally got Mila to a physician and learned the terrible truth. Mila had stage four lung cancer and severe heart disease, due to years of smoking and undiagnosed high cholesterol. It was a hard fate to swallow. To add fuel to the roaring fire of pain, the doctor announced that he doesn't even know how she has made it this long. With a sorrowful glance, he informed them that he didn't think she had much time left, then discharged her back to their home.

Mila passed away two weeks later in her sleep, which was a great relief to the family. Nick and Aria didn't witness her suffering. Avery, on the other hand, had decided to stay up with Mila the previous night because she somehow knew this would be her last night. Avery's gut had churned all day, like rocks rolling around in her stomach, and she knew that something terrible was bound to happen. That night, under Avery's watchful eyes and the small room blanketed in darkness, Mila recounted to Avery all the memories she had of her growing up, and Avery shared with her the ones she remembered so fondly. Both of their favorite memories were those when she would sneak Avery into the nursery to play with Aria in the early morning. The women wept as Mila struggled to take her last breath. In that final breath, she whispered the words that would run through Avery's mind for the rest of her life. The words were so powerful, yet they came from a woman writhing to gain oxygen in her lungs.

As if she was transfixed in another world, staring ahead into the blank space, Mila whispered, "Love hard, Avery. When you feel you have nothing, open up your heart, it's what we all *want from you. Don't turn a blind eye to love. You'll be scared and try to fight against it, but you need to love. You need to embrace it. I love you so much, Avery. You were the best daughter I could have ever asked for. It won't be for long, but love Aria and Nick fiercely, you'll need it."*

With tears in her eyes, Avery whispered to Mila her words of love. She watched as Mila closed her eyes and took her last gulp of air, the pressure in the room squeezing Avery's lungs in response.

Sitting in the church after Mila's burial, Avery decided to withdraw from her classes for the time being and take care of Aria. Luckily, any savings Mila had were left in Avery's name so she had enough to live on for a while when supplemented with her small part-time job as a housekeeper.

Spending time with Nick and Aria helped to heal her broken heart. It was like losing more than her mother, she was her everything. All she ever knew. The only person to ever show Avery affection and love until meeting Nick.

Nick and Avery grew closer after Mila's death and after a full year of dating and living together, he proposed with a beautiful solitaire diamond ring. Nothing large or extravagant, but enough to show how much he loved her. Avery's world finally seemed brighter after accepting his proposal and she spent her downtime dreaming of being his wife.

A few mornings after the surprise proposal, Avery was sitting at the kitchen table, planning their small affair. Nick suggested that Avery enroll herself back in school since he would be graduating in a few weeks. Excitement radiated through her, and the two contacted the school advisor straight away to reinstate her scholarship and enroll in classes for the summer. After tallying up her credits, Avery would have a little less than a year remaining.

Poring over wedding magazines, glancing at bridesmaids dresses with Aria, Avery's phone rang from across the room, startling them both. She answered the phone to an automated message reminding her of Aria's dental appointment in the morning.

"Crap," Avery said out loud to no one in particular as she stomps her foot in frustration.

"What's wrong, baby?" Nick called from the bedroom.

"Aria has a dental appointment at nine tomorrow morning, but I scheduled that meeting with my financial advisor so that I can sign some papers to reinstate my scholarship. I hate to ask you to take her, you have class."

"It's fine, Avery. We're just meeting in study groups for the final. I'll let my group know I can't make it and email them my notes."

Walking to the back room, Avery wraps her arms around her amazing fiancé and breathes in his masculine scent.

"Thank you." she released him with a sigh. "You're a life saver."

"No sweat. I'm happy to take her. Maybe we can all meet up for lunch after."

"That sounds great. Want to help us look at dresses?"

Laughing, he turned Avery around in his arms and gently pushed her out of the room.

"That's ok, babe. I'll let you girls stick to the wedding dresses."

Returning his laughter, Avery rejoined Aria at the table and they continued their perusal of over-the-top wedding dresses.

The incessant pressing of kisses against Avery's neck and shoulders awakened her from a deep sleep. Moaning into his mouth as he turned her over, Nick wasted no time in removing her small panties and seeking entrance for his hardened member. Sex with Nick is always pleasurable, but this morning it feels different, more explosive, more fevered - like he can't get enough. Avery comes quickly, in powerful waves, at his violently thrusts, and he quickly follows as her body milks him dry.

"That was incredible."

"It sure was. Very unexpected. Any particular reason?"

"Nope. I just woke up, looked over at your beautiful face, and knew I needed to have you."

Giggling, Avery shoved him lightly on the shoulder and moved out of bed, heading for the shower.

After getting herself ready for her meeting, Avery woke up Aria and helped her make some breakfast before she needed to leave for her dental appointment.

Minutes later, Nick asked Aria to get in the car while he says goodbye to Avery.

Standing before her, hands stroking her hair, he stared lovingly in her eyes.

"I love you so much, Avery. I am thankful every day that I ran into you at that pizza shop. You marrying me is going to be the happiest day of my life. I want you to have all the happiness you deserve."

With tears sprinkling her eyes, Avery had to bite back the sobs that wanted to escape.

"I love you too, Nick. So much. I can't wait to be your wife."

Bringing her face to his, Nick kisses her slowly, taking his time to explore Avery's mouth. Breaking away from the kiss before things become too heated, she walks with Nick to the car so that she can also say goodbye to her sister. Pulling her in close, Nick's sweet words from moments ago rang in her head and she held Aria tighter.

He's the best thing to happen to me and my sister, she thought.

"I love you, Aria. Be good for Nick."

"I will. I love you too, sissy. We'll see you at lunch."

With one more hug and kiss from Nick, the two maneuvered into the car and back out of the lot, both waving out the window.

Avery arrived at the meeting with her advisor and they went over the scholarship paperwork, then nailed down her schedule for the summer. As they went through the course list it surprised Avery to learn she only had one more class and an externship to complete. In response to her baffled look, the advisor informed her that some of the dual enrollment courses taken in high school had transferred over and she wouldn't need to repeat them. Avery hadn't realized she was so close to getting everything she had ever wanted.

Stepping out into the bright sunshine on the warm spring day, Avery's ringing cell phone startled her from her reveries.

"Hello?" Avery queried, not recognizing the number.

"Is this Avery Poindexter? Guardian of Aria Poindexter?"

"Yes," she replied hesitantly, chills racking through her bones, "this is she."

"I'm sorry, miss. This is Officer Stewart. I need you to meet me at St. James Hospital, ma'am. There has been an accident."

"Excuse me, what? What kind of accident. Is Aria alright? Is she with Nick?"

Some mumbling goes on in the background, but Avery can't hear what is said.

"We can explain everything when you get here, miss. I'll meet you in the hospital atrium."

Waving her hands frantically in an attempt to hail a cab, Avery asked the driver to speedily take her to the destination, her heart beating profusely along the way. A sinking feeling spirals in the pit of her stomach and she's afraid that everything in her world is about to shatter.

Approaching the hospital entrance, Avery shoved a twenty dollar bill at the driver and jumped out of the cab before the vehicle had even come to a complete stop. Rushing through the automatic doors, she looked around anxiously until she noticed the solemn-looking officer waiting in the corner for her arrival.

Looking in his direction, Avery could see the despair in his eyes.

"Ms. Poindexter?"

Pleading with the officer, Avery cried, "Please, please, tell me she's ok, that her and Nick are ok."

Ignoring her requests, Officer Stewart continued, "Have you seen the news ma'am?"

"No, I've been in a meeting. Please, I need to see Aria."

"I'm sorry, Ms. Poindexter, so sorry, but Aria and the driver of her vehicle were killed in an automobile accident this morning."

"What? No. No, you're wrong. She's at the dentist. Please tell me you're wrong," Avery exclaimed, sinking to the floor as desperate cries wreaked havoc upon her body.

"I'm very sorry, Ms. Poindexter, but we need you to fill out some forms," the Officer said uncomfortably.

Avery couldn't bring herself to remove her body from the cold marble floor, so she continued to let out heartbreaking wails of pain. All Avery could think about is that they're gone. Her entire world had been completely stripped of everything she loved.

A compassionate nurse lifted her into his arms and carried her to a secluded room while another nurse injected her with a sedative. The medication must have been strong, because Avery soon found herself drifting off into nothingness.

Avery woke hours later to numbness she had never felt before; a hollowness encompassed her entire being. The same officer, Officer Stewart she recalls, returns with forms and Avery scratched a non-legible signature across the marked spaces. Within the blankness she heard him speaking to her, telling her about the accident… how an overly tired truck driver was rushing through a turn at an intersection and overturned his vehicle that was carrying heavy concrete highway material. It crushed Nick's and another's cars. Both sets of passengers were killed instantly by the heavy load. In Avery's world of despair, she murmured a silent and fevered prayer that they didn't suffer.

Her sweet sister - she had so much life to live, so much to learn and experience since being whisked away from that hellhole called the Poindexter Estate.

And Nick. He was more than the man Avery loved, he was her best friend. Thinking of her remarkable fiancé brought forth a new level of emptiness. No tears remain, her emotions completely drained.

Avery thought back to his words from this morning and wondered why her happiness continued to get stripped away.

"Holy, cow," Melanie whispers behind her shaking hand. "And then you met Declan."

"I thought Declan was going to be my happy ending, you know?"

The pain still emanating in her chest, she has to rub at the heated spot before she closes her eyes and loses herself in more memories as Melanie cries softly on her shoulder.

Walking into the break room of the small medical practice where she worked, Avery dumped her bag into the locker with her affixed name, shutting the door and exiting quickly, making sure to avoid the looks from her coworkers.

For the past two years, Avery worked at this office and she made sure to avoid conversation with everyone. They know something tragic happened, of that she's sure. There is no point in denying it, but her life ceased to exist the day Aria and Nick died. After a few weeks of one-word answers and a lack of enthusiasm at getting to know the other employees, most of them just gave up interacting with her.

Avery came into the office to do her job and do it well, then she would go home and hide in the apartment she had once shared with her family. Only one person attempted to break through to her. Melanie was a medical assistant for another physician in the practice. She pestered and pestered her until eventually Avery conceded to eating lunch with her every day. Mainly, she Avery would sit there and listen to Melanie ramble on about her escapades the night before.

Avery still blamed herself for Nick and Aria's death. She was supposed to be the one driving Aria to her appointment that day. But, as the saying goes, the past is the past and nothing can change it. It reminded Avery that she needed to start living her life as a memento to the people she had lost.

As Avery headed toward the receptionist desk to see who they had as patients that day, she stopped short at the sight of a tall, lean-muscled man hovering above an employee with a sexy smirk on his face. The older receptionist blushed furiously as she pages another nurse, Max, to the front desk. Avery assumed that's who the handsome man was here to meet.

Then her body's appreciation of the mysterious man sends Avery's heart into over-drive. No one, not a soul since Nick had caught her eye; not that she was ever looking.

When Max came to the desk, they did the typical male handshake-hug combination and the two made quick conversation about meeting up for lunch.

Sneaking up from behind, Melanie whispered in her ear, "What are we staring at? Oh, look at him. Yum."

Turning her head, hoping to shush Melanie, Avery turned back just in time for this sexy guy's eyes to meet hers. She released a gasp from between her parted lips as he continued to stare in her direction. Turning quickly, she headed back towards the break room and decided to wait a few minutes before heading back up front to see the daily patient log, unable to control the fluttering in her belly that arose from the stranger's gaze.

Willing the clock to move faster, Avery let out a heavy breath when five minutes have passed. Walking down the deserted hallway she ran into Melanie with a smack. Melanie smiled as Avery apologized, then handed her a note and sauntered away with an extra sway in her hips.

With shaky hands, Avery opened the note and read the manly scribble.

Hello Gorgeous. I know you felt the spark between us but you ran off so quickly I didn't get a chance to introduce myself. I'm going to call you later and take you out to dinner tonight. I'll pick you up at 7. You can thank your friend for giving me your number. I'm looking forward to it.

Declan

"Melanie!" Avery shouted before exploding simultaneously into nervous giggles. "What am I going to wear?"

Avery anxiously sat on the ratty couch in the apartment she had shared with Nick, Aria, and Mila as she waits for Declan to pick her up. He called while she was on lunch and they chatted for a bit before he asked for her address, mentioning as a side-note for her to dress casually.

Avery's nerves were so high she continued to feel the urge to vomit. Needing a distraction, she turned on the television, but it did little to calm her nerves.

A loud knock on the door startled her from her reverie and she let out a small yelp. Taking a few deep breaths, she walked to the door and hesitantly reached for the handle before opening it wide. The sight that greeted her was nothing short of amazing.

In front of Avery, Declan stood in faded denim that hugged his muscular thighs, a tight black t-shirt pulled tight across his lean muscles, light brown hair styled back into a ponytail.

Images of Jared Leto when he won his best supporting actor award the year before flooded her mind. That's who Declan resembled as he stood at her door.

"You look beautiful, Avery," Declan said as he stepped forward and handed her a bouquet of pink gerber daisies.

Running her hands down the pale yellow sundress she had chosen to wear that evening, she nervously thanked him before inviting him inside while she placed the daises in a vase.

"You have a cute place. How long have you been here?"

"Um, a few years," Avery answered, filling the vase with water from the sink.

After placing the glass on the counter, she stepped out of the tiny kitchen to find Declan staring at the pictures on the wall - the picture of her, Nick, and Aria.

"Your family?" he asked, pointing over his shoulder to the picture as he turned to look at her.

Replying shyly, she said, "Yea," and offered no further explanation.

Taking the hint, Declan stepped closer and put his hands on both of her shoulders, immediately calming her nerves.

"Ready for some fun?"

Smiling graciously at his change of subject, Avery nodded her head and followed him out of the apartment to his awaiting car.

The drive was quiet and Avery was surprised when they arrived at a music festival. She followed Declan as he walked through the gates, then she took a hold of his hand and glanced up at him.

"Thank you. I needed this."

Stopping in the midst of throngs of concert goers, Declan pulled her close and placed both of his hands on her cheeks.

Looking deep into Avery's eyes he whispered, "This is just the start, you're going to be extremely special to me."

Not knowing what to say, Avery smiled and continued to look into his dark chocolate eyes. Leaning forward, Declan pressed his soft lips against hers in a chaste kiss; just long enough to leave Avery craving more of him and his touch.

Stepping back, he brushed his fingers through her hair and took her hand before leading her closer to the stage. He found a deserted spot off to the side and sat down, pulling Avery to sit between his legs. Leaning back, she rested her body against his chest as he wrapped his arms around her.

"Let me know if you get cold, Avery."

"I will," she relented, knowing her body would crave the heat from being wrapped up in him.

During breaks in the music, Declan and Avery talked about their lives. He felt like a kindred spirit, even then, and she found herself disclosing her darkest secrets - the life that at every turn seemed to follow a darkened path. Declan revealed that he, too, had felt his share of loss. His mother died during childbirth and his father passed a few years back of pancreatic cancer. The pain in his voice was just as strong as Avery's when she talked about her own tragedies. They stayed wrapped up in each other through the remainder of the festival and she found sublime comfort in the arms of this stranger who had, just that morning, knocked her so off kilter.

It felt like she'd known him her entire life. How could she feel so connected to someone that she had just met?

When they arrived back at her apartment after the festival, Avery couldn't help but feel overcome by nerves again. Declan must have sensed her anxiety because he tucked her into a tight hug before turning to leave.

Standing at the base of the stairs, he turned back to her and said, "I can't wait to see you again, Avery. Now go inside before I can't control myself any longer."

With a squeak, Avery quickly opened the door and hustled inside, panting as she complies. His heated words left her a quivering mess and she couldn't help but feel the pulsing going on in an area that had been ignored for the past few years.

Her relationship with Declan was easy. The companionship she craved came at no cost with him and he freely gave her his love, never letting her wallow in the hole of self-pity into which she had buried herself. He left notes with Max and Melanie at work when she was helping a patient, or tucked them precariously into the pockets of her scrubs when she was not looking, constantly surrounding her with affection.

Declan moved in with her six months after they both whispered the "love" word to each other. Avery knew that to outsiders it would look like they were moving fast, but they both knew how quickly your life and plans could change.

They even broached the topic of marriage and children one morning. She could tell that Declan was weary to discuss moving forward, knowing that she had been engaged previously to Nick. But Avery told him that it felt right and that she wanted to move on with her life. The past week as they had walked past a jewelry store, Declan pointed at a ring he wanted her to have, but she brushed his comments away.

"I don't need a ring, Dec. I just need you."

While he made decent money working as a personal trainer, Avery knew that both of them wanted to save their money to buy a home.

"Well, you're getting one after we buy a house, ok?"

"Ok," she replied, smiling up into his handsome face.

A few weeks later Avery arrived home from work one night, her instincts on high alert. She rested back on the couch, praying that her premonitions were wrong. Neither she nor Declan carried cell phones, so she couldn't call or text him to make sure he was alright. Turning on the television, Avery flipped through the channels, but nothing caught her eye. Instead, she hopped up off the couch and began working to make Declan's favorite meal – meatloaf and mashed potatoes.

As Avery pulled the meatloaf from the oven, she heard the front door open and then close as Declan arrived home. Stepping outside the kitchen to greet him, she sucked in a breath when she was greeted not by his typically smiling face, but by a grim and somber expression.

"Hey, Dec. Is something wrong?" Avery asked as she wrapped her arms around his trim waist, resting her chin on his chest so that she could look up into his eyes.

Gazing down lovingly at her, he brushed his fingers through her long hair.

"I love you so much, Avery."

"I love you too, Declan. But I have to admit, you're scaring me right now."

"I know, baby. Why don't we go sit down?"

Following his lead, she took his hand as they sat next to each other on the raggedy sofa.

"So, you know how I've been having those terrible migraines?"

Avery nodded in response.

"Well, I went to the doctor today hoping that they could prescribe something stronger than what I can get over-the-counter. It, um..." His voice caught in his throat, and he choked out the next words, "It turns out I have a tumor. A very large one that is pressing everything against my skull."

At first, shock overwhelmed Avery's heart, quickly followed by devastated tears that cascade down her cheeks. Speechless.

What can I possibly say to that? What can I do to ease his pain?

He tucked a piece of hair behind her ear and wiped her tears, but new ones follow even faster than he could wipe them away.

"The doctor says the prognosis isn't good. Because of where it's located, it can't be operated on." Scooting closer, pulling her face into both of his hands, Declan released his own tears that had been begging for exit. "I'm so sorry, Avery. I wanted to give you everything. I wanted you to have my children. I never wanted to leave you."

They cried into each other's arms for what seemed like hours. Avery heard wails of torment bouncing off her thin apartment walls and she realized that they were her own cries of anguish.

"How long, Dec?" she whispered when her eyes could at last produce no more tears.

"He said somewhere between a couple of months to a year at best. I'm so scared, Avery. I don't want to die yet."

Wrapping Declan tighter into the cocoon of her arms, they held each other through the rest of the night and into the morning, not taking any time to sleep, just wanting to be with each other.

After calling into work, for the first time ever, Avery stayed with Declan as they both tried to get a few hours of sleep before heading to see a pain management specialist he was referred to by his doctor. Both so scared, all of their talks of future plans ceased to exist. They only discussed the here and now.

It seemed like the day Declan received his official prognosis his health began to deteriorate quickly. Where he once had lean, strong muscle, he became bone, draped with thinly veiled skin. He had to shave off his beautiful hair so that the probes used on his head by his doctor could affix better during the scans. The chocolate color of his captivating eyes had darkened to a swampy shade of sludge. And the eyes themselves had sunken back into their caverns.

But he was still her Declan.

He was loving and affectionate and still heart-stoppingly handsome.

What Avery wouldn't have given for more time with him.

Six months after his diagnosis, Avery found Declan unable to get out of bed, his muscles too weak from the *deterioration. When his organs had begun to shut down, they had hired a hospice nurse to stay with them, a wonderful gift that Declan's aunt and uncle offered to pay for. After the nurse finished her morning ritual, Avery took her place in the chair beside the bed in the guest room where Declan had been sleeping.*

"Today's the day, baby."

Wiping a tear from her eyes, she stuttered, "Don't say that. You have plenty of time left."

"It is, Avery. I can feel it. Come lay beside me, please."

Getting out of the chair, Avery maneuvered herself carefully onto the bed, so as not to jostle him or the medical equipment too much. Even with as little strength as Declan possessed, he turned himself to face her, placing his frail hand on her face. Avery twisted her face into his hand and kissed his palm.

"I want to say a few things, Avery. Don't say anything until I finish, ok?" he whispered through a crackled voice, mustering what little strength he had left.

She nodded in reply, allowing him to proceed.

"I love you with everything in me, Avery Marie. You would have been it for me. And I know you'll think I'm crazy, but I'm not it for you. And don't get mad," he said, seeing the tension and hurt welling in her eyes, "but neither was Nick. I can see everything so clearly, Avery. You loved us with everything you had, but your soul mate is still out there. You haven't met him, but please, whatever you do, fight for him. I want you to feel everything. I want his love to encompass your world. Don't hold back a piece of yourself. Let him in. It'll be scary, but you've had so much hurt in your life, things from now on can only be good." After his short speech, Declan took a few seconds to stroke away the tears on her cheeks. "I know you'll think I'm crazy, but I swear I dreamt of your family last night. They just stood before me and told me to tell you that they love you and they want you to be

*happy. I want you to be happy. You deserve that, Avery. I want
you to experience true love, get married, and have babies. Even if
it isn't with me like I had wished. I know you'll retreat back to
yourself when I pass, but I need you to live. Live for me, for Nick,
for Aria. But live for you. You only get one chance."*

*Leaning forward he placed a warm, chaste kiss on her tear-
stained lips before resting back onto the bed.*

*"I love you, Declan. I don't want you to leave me," Avery
whispered as he cradled her into his arm, placing her head on his
chest.*

*As Declan drifted off to sleep, she could hear him
proclaim, "I will always be with you."*

*His breath evened out as he fell into a deeper sleep. Rolling
out of his embrace, Avery placed both of her feet on the floor, just
as his heart monitor chimed into an eerie, flat tone.*

*Realizing he was gone, all she could do was fall onto her
hands and knees beside the bed and sob uncontrollably.*

*The hospice nurse, Max and Melanie must have come in
at some point, because Avery woke to find herself in the bed she
used to share with Declan and a bustle of noise coming from the
living room.*

*Collecting as much energy as possible, Avery walked
towards the gathering crowd. Melanie rushed forward and pulled
her into a tight embrace; offering her condolences. All Avery could
do is stare up at the ceiling, willing herself not to cry any longer.
Unsuccessful at her attempts to stop the tears, Max joined into
their hug as they all wept at the loss of their friend.*

*Once everyone has cried themselves out, Avery noticed
two other people in her home and she looked over to Max and
Melanie, raising her shoulder in question and pointing with her
head at the unknown guests.*

Max jumped in and introduced Mr. Allen and Mr. Rockwell, lawyers for Declan's estate.

Estate? she pondered.

After exchanging their condolences, Avery learned that when Declan's father died, he came into a large inheritance from his grandparents. When Declan was diagnosed, he signed a will leaving all of his assets to her, except his car (a classic GTO), which he left to Max.

Opening the letter that listed all of her assets, Avery was taken aback by the number of zeros listed.

"What the hell am I supposed to do with twenty million dollars?" she exclaimed to the lawyers.

Melanie was mid-drink and at Avery's outburst, she spit it everywhere, launching herself into a coughing fit.

"Well," one of the lawyers started, "you can save it, spend it, give it away. Whatever you want. It's all in a savings account, waiting for you."

Avery looked over into the stunned faces of Max and Melanie and found herself only shaking her head, desperately trying to shed no more tears.

"I don't want the money. I just want Declan," she exclaimed as she rushed back to her room to escape the pain and more tears fell down her reddened cheeks.

It was then that Melanie understood completely why Declan's and Nick's things were hard to place in boxes, but the worst was putting away Aria's clothes and toys. Avery hadn't touched anything after Aria's passing and packing up each item unleashed a new form of torment.

Avery was at a loss on how to overcome her grief. Everything she had ever loved was constantly being taken from her. She was even at the point of trying to push

Melanie and Max away because she was afraid that her love for them would cause them some form of harm. After voicing this to Melanie, she hugged her tight and told her that there was nothing she could do to make her go away, Avery was stuck with her for life.

It took a full week to pack up all Avery's belongings and place them into the moving truck, which Max so graciously took care of. He also made sure that her beat-up piece of rust would make the long journey to her new home, though he pleaded with her to spend some of her new fortune on an updated vehicle. They argued and argued, but much to his dismay, Avery wasn't budging. Mila had bought that car when they had finally saved up three-thousand dollars and this was one of the last things that had belonged to her. She refused to upgrade until she absolutely had to.

Staring at the place that she had once called home, now barren and deserted, her broken heart shriveled up and disintegrated into a pile of ash within her chest. The pain pulsating inside her body ached with such a strong abandon that she collapsed into a heap on the living room floor, gasping for air; pleading for the lives she lost. Avery made promises to a God that she had lost all hope in, but that Mila and Declan had prayed to every night. She beseeched Him to offer her some sort of reprieve from this hell He had placed her in, begging for guidance on how to continue along this miserable and lonely life. She cried out to this God for minutes, or hours - time had lost all indication. No answer ever comes. No sign. No proclamation. Just silence echoing against her strangled sobs.

Melanie finds her alone on the floor, imploring an ethereal being for guidance, and sinks onto the floor next to

Avery, wrapping her gently in her arms. Her touch was a loving affection that caused warmth to trickle through Avery's bones.

Stroking her hair as Avery continued to cry onto her shoulder, Melanie whispers, "They'll always be with you, Avery. This is just a place; you'll always have the memories. No one can take those away from you."

Avery's cries began to lessen and she sits back onto her heels, using the heel of her hand to wipe the tears from her cheeks.

"I know you're right," Avery chokes out, her voice soft and scratchy, "I know I need to move forward, but I don't know how; it's so hard."

"I don't think any of us expected it to be anything but hard. But you've been doing great, Avery. Max and I are so proud of you."

Melanie hugs her close again before releasing her so that she can stand up; Avery soon follows.

"Do you think you're ready now?"

Avery takes a deep breath and looks around the desolate room one last time. "Yes, I think I am."

Outside, Melanie piles into the moving truck while Max took the driver's seat of Avery's car.

"I'm sure you'd rather be with Mel, but your car is a bit more comfortable if you wanted to sleep and I'd rather be with your car in case something happens."

With a nod towards Max, Avery slides into the back seat of her car and curls up, hoping to fall asleep quickly.

She wakes to unfamiliar surroundings and has to take a minute before she realizes that she is in her new room, in her new apartment. Before Avery can adjust herself to move out of bed, Melanie comes skipping in, a smile upon her face.

Her curly black hair is artfully styled on top of her head in a messy knot-bun, showcasing her long graceful neck where a classically beautiful face is perched. She unknowingly highlights her toned physique in a black tank top and short gray gym shorts. Melanie truly is effortlessly gorgeous and by the smirk occupying Max's face as he follows behind her, he thinks she is gorgeous as well, amongst other nauseatingly loving compliments.

"How'd you sleep, Avery?" she asks.

"Great, thanks. I can't believe I slept through most of the trip and through the night. I haven't slept that much in well… ever. I didn't mean to take the bed. Where did you guys sleep?"

"Oh, hun, you needed the rest. We crashed on the couch. It was a pull out. Don't fret about it."

"Here's some coffee, Avery," Max says, handing her a travel mug. "Nikki made a big pot before she went to work this morning. She took the afternoon off so she could help you get adjusted since we need to head back around lunch time."

"That was nice of her," Avery says as she takes a large swig, letting the warmth of the drink travel its way down her body. "I'm so thankful for y'alls help. Truly. You didn't have to do this."

"We wouldn't be anywhere else," Melanie replies sweetly. "We're going to start grabbing boxes. Come on out when you're ready."

As they disappear out of the apartment, Avery gives herself a mental talking-to. She reminds herself that this is what Declan, Nick, Aria, and Mila would want for her - that she should enjoy her days.

With her own thoughts inspiring herself, she gets dressed quickly in a pair of black running pants and a yellow racerback tank top. Tossing her long brown hair into a ponytail, she makes her way outside, not pausing to take in her surroundings - knowing that if she absorbs the meaning of her new home, the loss of her old one may overwhelm her.

Max unloads all of her furniture - which isn't much - while Melanie joins her in sorting through the few boxes she brought along. Before they left, Avery had asked Melanie to take the majority of Aria, Mila, and Declan's things to charity whilst she kept a few cherished items and boxed them away for safe keeping. Nick's parents took most of his things when he passed, though Avery managed to keep a few of his shirts.

As Avery places the treasured box in her closet, Melanie suggests she trifle through it one last time and place the items in the fireproof safe Avery had purchased for the move. She wasn't about to take any chances with a new roommate, though she knew Melanie wouldn't have suggested the move if she didn't trust her cousin.

She sits down on the floor facing her closet, a dim light bulb illuminating the space. Opening the stiff cardboard, Avery is first assaulted by the smell of her old home. The smell of old weathered hardwood floors and a hint of lemon cleaner. Why Melanie thought this was a good idea, Avery will never know.

She first pulls out Declan's treasured wrist watch that had been passed down through his family. Avery remembers that towards the end of his life he was no longer able to wear it - so weak that even the soft gold of the band was too heavy for his wrist. Two of his favorite t-shirts come out next and she bring them to her nose, taking in the smell that was uniquely Declan's – sandalwood and male.

After setting those items aside, she unfolds and refolds the shirts of Nick's that she kept and places them beside the box along with Declan's. The small black box containing the engagement ring that Avery hadn't gotten to wear nearly enough beckoned her to reach forward. The squeak of the underused hinges startled her in the silent closet before she gets a chance to admire the small diamond perched atop a band of gold. Avery takes a deep, unsteady breath before closing the box one last time and placing it in the far back corner of the safe.

Next, Avery pulls out the ceramic phoenix Mila had always kept on her dresser. Whenever Avery asked her about it, she always shrugged and reminded her that even when we think we have nothing left but ashes and dust, we will rise again like the phoenix, and come alive with a new spark of life. Instead of placing the figurine in the safe, Avery decides to keep it out as a reminder to rise above her grief.

Finally, Avery finds herself facing the items at the bottom of the box, though they are far from the least significant. She packed three items from Aria's belongings, though she could have found something noteworthy with anything that belonged to her sister - they all held memories for her. Like when they would go to the mall with a few extra dollars and get her a new pair of shoes, or the doll she had admired after seeing one of her schoolmates presenting it for show-and-tell. Aria never asked for anything and she was always grateful for everything she was given.

Avery pulls out a baby onesie first. Unbeknownst to her grandmother, Mila and Avery bought the pale pink material a few weeks after Aria was born. Avery remembers Aria being so tiny that she thought the outfit swallowed her whole, but of course babies grow fast and she only got to wear it twice more. She chuckles aloud at that thought. Next, Avery plucks a small teddy bear from within the depths of the chest. Aria had slept with this bear every night for as long as Avery could remember. Closing her eyes, she swears that the bear still smells like her sister. It had obviously seen better days and Avery knew she couldn't leave it vulnerable to the elements, so she gently placed it in the safe amongst the other items.

Last, but not least, Avery removes the folder of drawings and artwork of Aria's that she collected throughout the years. Even at her young age, Avery knew Aria was destined to be a great artist. She had a knack for showcasing emotions within her pictures. As Avery flips through the cut-and-paste artwork from pre-school, the finger paintings from elementary school, and the penciled sketches she did just while around their apartment, she stops at a drawing that she had forgotten. Though she now remembers asking Aria about it, the youngster only replied that she saw it in her dream and needed to draw it.

Spellbound, Avery unfolds the large piece of paper and rises slowly from her closet, stretching her legs. Resting the drawing on the bed, she walks out of the bedroom to find Melanie.

"Hey, can you come here for a sec?"

"Sure, I'll be right there. We have something to give you before we head out."

Walking back into her bedroom, Avery stares down at the picture before her, drawn in a three-dimensional format. The sketch showcases four angels, none of which has any distinguishable features other than the detailed wings on their backs and the color of their hair. The view comes from behind the angels as they are looking down onto the Earth. That's where you see a girl, who eerily looks like herself, with long brown hair and blue eyes, fire building at the bottom of her feet. The girl is drawn looking onward, past the paper, at people off in the distance - only determinable due to the shadows cast in the drawing. It looks to be a man holding a small hand in each of his own.

Heart racing, Avery looks closer at the angels drawn so carefully in the picture, one significantly smaller than the others, and one with shoulder-length hair.

As Melanie comes into the room holding a small wrapped package, Avery tells her the history of the drawing and asks her what she makes of it.

"I'm really trying not to freak out right now, Mel."

"Don't worry, I am too. There is no way she could have known right? I mean… how could she?"

The girls stare and ponder a bit longer before Melanie speaks again.

"She said she dreamed this?" she inquires, in as much disbelief as Avery is herself. At Avery's nod, she continues, "Who do you think those shadows belong to?"

"I don't know, that part has me the most confused."

With a puzzled "humph", they both go back to studying the picture before a car alarm outside the window startles them back from their innermost thoughts.

"All in all, I think it's kind of cool she had this vision and drew it, as dark as its background may be. If it is all four of them it shows that they're watching over you, because obviously that girl in the drawing is you. It's a bit comforting actually."

"Yeah, I guess you're right. I think I'm going to frame this and hang it up. It's beautiful."

"It really is. She was so talented." Melanie sighs quietly, then shakes her head. "Anyway, we're going to head back in a bit, but we wanted to give you this."

Taking the box from Melanie's hands and shaking it lightly to hear the rattling within, Avery watches a grin grow along Melanie's face as she tears apart the paper and flips over the frame. It's a beautiful shadow box containing a key to the old apartment, Avery's old name badge, her college identification card, and eight pictures.

The first picture is of Mila holding Avery as a toddler. She's looking at the baby lovingly, just as any mother would. Next is a picture of Avery holding a sleeping baby Aria, followed by a picture of the three of them at Avery's high school graduation. Below is a picture of Avery and Nick on the day of their engagement; a photograph of Melanie, her, and Max, taken at their wedding; a candid shot of Declan and Avery at another music festival they had gone to, dragging Melanie and Max along with them. One of the last pictures is of her and Aria outside in the courtyard of their apartment, squirting Nick with water guns as he steps out of his car. Boy, Avery remembers that day; by the time they all came inside they were soaked to the bone, fighting off the chill from the cool night. Glancing at the final picture in the box, Avery's breath is stolen completely from her lungs, like a fist squeezing around her diaphragm. Before her is a seamlessly created photograph of Max, Melanie, Declan, herself, Aria, Nick, and Mila. Gasps of air, like a fish out of water, are the only sounds escaping Avery's lips as she finds herself utterly lost for the appropriate words to describe the impact of this gift.

"This is… wow, Melanie. I'm speechless."

"I hope you don't mind. When we were packing things up, I took a few photos from the albums you had boxed away. And Max spent some time compiling a bunch of them for that last one. He's a bit of an editing whiz."

"It's…it's… extraordinary Melanie. I can't ever thank you enough for this," Avery sniffles as she holds back the tears.

"None of that or you'll have me blubbering, too, and I am not a pretty crier, as you know."

Avery chuckles as she places the box on the bed beside Aria's drawing. She hugs Melanie one last time before they discover Max outside, waiting for them.

"I'll miss you guys. Thank you, for everything."

Max leans forward and hugs her before stepping back and cupping her face in his hands.

"You can do this, Avery. I have the upmost faith in you. You're one of the strongest people I know. Please don't hesitate to call us if you need anything."

"Thank you, Max. I appreciate everything you all have done for me. I'm in a good place right now and I'm excited about the move."

They both hug Avery once more with promises of a visit soon, then she watches as they drive off into the proverbial sunset.

As she steps back from the sidewalk to head towards the apartment, a small set of arms wrap around her shoulders from behind, startling her in their haste.

"I'm Nikki, your new roommate," she exclaims cheerily, not realizing that she has scared the crap out of Avery.

Turning around and stepping back, Avery glances at her new roommate before mirroring her smile. The good genes must run rampant in their family, as she is a spitting image of Melanie, except that her hair is a golden blonde where Melanie's was black. Nikki is alarmingly attractive.

"Hi, Nikki, it's great to meet you."

"I am so excited to have you here. At first I thought it was Melanie and Max moving in, but then she told me all about you and I knew we would be a good fit."

"She told you about me?" Avery asks hesitantly, not quite ready to start answering any intrusive questions.

"She did, but I am certain you don't want to talk about it, so we'll just skip ahead and agree to be lifelong friends, ok?"

Chuckling at her bubbly personality, Avery says, "Sure," with relief. "Do you want to head inside and give me the low down on how we'll work this out?"

"Yep, follow me. Lucky for us, all of our neighbors are amazing. Mrs. Jacobson lives in the apartment two doors down and brings me cookies every Sunday. She is just going to love you." Opening the door to their apartment, she tosses her bag on the small table in the foyer before continuing on, "I left three cabinets available for you to use and feel free to use whatever cookware I have. No need to buy more, right? I also left a shelf free in the fridge for things you don't want to share. Otherwise, the top shelf is a free-for-all. If you get this job, we'll be working the same schedule so we can switch back and forth for dinners if that works for you. And I prefer reading to television so I only have limited cable channels."

Avery nods in understanding and responds, "I'm the same way."

"Great. We each have our own bath, so no worries there. And as far as guests go, I don't really care as long as we give each other a heads up. I don't want that sort of surprise," Barely pausing for breath, she gestures towards the mess in the living room and continues, "So, I'm a bit of a slob, but I'll try to keep that in check since you're here. If you notice it getting out of hand, please let me know. It won't hurt my feelings. Mel said you were a bit anal about that stuff."

"I just like things organized, that's all. Thank you again for this, Nikki. And please let me know if I'm getting in your way; I don't want to be a burden. I can always make other arrangements."

Grabbing the check from her bag, Avery hands Nikki the slip of paper and explains that she has a full year's worth of rent paid. Nikki tucks the paper into the back of her jeans and looks at Avery in a concerned manner before tilting her head and asking if she'll need any help unpacking. Luckily, Melanie helped Avery tackle that task right away, so she is free to relax for the night.

"Actually, I just need to get some groceries and a large picture frame. Can you tell me where to go for those?"

"I'll take you. I need to pick up a couple friends named Ben & Jerry anyway."

Avery smiles at her and laughs as she says, "More mutual friends that we have in common."

Avery asks Nikki about the town as they drive to the small shopping center. In her typical bubbly manner, Nikki explains that Carson, North Carolina has a population of a few hundred people, most of whom work at the new plant built in the next town over and live in their new apartment complex. Carson is the biggest town in the county and it's where most people find themselves, especially since Asheville is about a two-hour drive.

Strolling down the grocery aisles, they grab the items needed for a weekly menu that Avery created, thinking it would help keep things a bit more organized.

As Nikki tosses a pack of cookies into the cart she says, "So this practice is pretty big, five doctors that service this town and about twelve other surrounding counties. We don't really have a local hospital. If it's something major, most patients have to be transported out by helicopter or ambulance. Anyway, we have three older physicians: Dr. Fields, Dr. Mayner and Dr. Lunar; they were the original owners of the practice. As the town grew, they needed to expand and, lucky for us, brought on two new grads; Dr. Chamberlin and Dr. Burnette. And let me tell you that *both* of those men are sexy with a capital S. Dr. Chamberlin and I have been circling around each other for months and we had a date last night."

Interrupting her, Avery exclaims, "I am so sorry I barged in on your date!"

Hand in the air, Nikki waves her comment away with a 'shush', "It wasn't working out anyway. No biggie. I think we just both liked the idea of each other, not the actual follow-through. Where was I?" she ponders, finger tapping on her chin as she looks up at the ceiling. "Oh yes, so we're hiring medical assistants for each of the physicians, we already have a nurse on hand, but she's running pretty ragged. When I tell you that business has picked up, I meant that as an understatement. We've seen quadruple the amount of patients in the past three months."

"Really? Why do you think that is?"

"That big production plant opened up a town over and a lot of the locals took jobs there, giving them access to insurance that they didn't have previously."

"I see."

"Yep. So, everyone but Dr. Fields has hired their new MAs and they are holding interviews tomorrow and the next day. You will really like him. He is such a great person. All in all, that makes up the practice. Oh! And I'm the receptionist and office manager. I love my job." She beams, choosing a carton of Ben and Jerry's Chocolate Therapy ice cream.

"Well it sounds great." Avery replies, "My interview is on Thursday, so I'm hoping I will make a good impression. This is all I've ever wanted to do."

"Dr. Fields will love you, and from what Melanie says, you'll be a shoe-in."

RENEE HARLESS

Chapter Two

RRIVING AT HIS SMALL home after leaving Nikki's place, Logan can't seem to shake the vision of that dark cascading hair from his mind. All he can think about is running his fingers through the silky mass, those thoughts triggering unwanted desire through one of his lower extremities.

"Shit," Logan mumbles out loud.

Needing to get a handle on his brain and his dick, Logan walks into his kitchen and grabs a glass, filling it with some whiskey. Tossing back the warm liquid, he lets its smoky flavor penetrate his taste buds, focusing his attention solely on its husky taste. Swallowing slowly, Logan places his glass in the sink, making a mental note to wash it in the morning, and moves from the kitchen to his bedroom.

Turning on the light, Logan is pleased to find everything clean and organized, with stacks of clean laundry waiting on his bed. Once a week, a husband and wife team, the Stantons, come to his home to clean, complete the laundry, and landscape the outdoors. With his chaotic schedule, Logan finds it extremely difficult to devote any extra time to those things. Plus, growing up he was never taught how to do any of it.

Logan's mom left when he was born, discharging herself from the hospital after the delivery, so he never met her, but apparently to his dad, Logan is a spitting image of her. This revelation did nothing to endear him, but rather caused his father to hate him. Why his mother ever thought that leaving an infant with that no good, piece of shit was a smart decision, Logan will never know. He's surprised that he didn't die of starvation or illness because God knows that when he was growing up, food was hard to come by. But beer? Beer could always be found. And chores were not something handed out lightly. It was more of washing clothes in the sink when he needed something to wear. On the plus side, Logan became really good at making his own meals when there was food to be had.

Placing his clothes in their designated spot in his dresser, Logan shucks off his clothing and slides into bed, turning on the television resting atop the dresser on his way. This is Logan's favorite time of day: the time where he can sit in bed and not think about anything or anyone. Logan turns off his "doctor-mode" and loses himself in mindless drivel.

An hour later, Logan finds himself turning off the television, sliding farther down the bed, and closing his eyes as he rests his head against his firm pillow. It takes only a second, but the moment Logan finds himself drifting off to sleep, he pictures wave after wave of dark glossy hair. His dream comes farther into focus and he pictures this dark-haired goddess resting on all fours on his bed while Logan pounds into her from behind.

Jesus Christ!

Even in his dream, he can feel the buildup of release from deep within his spine. His visionary persona thrusts once, twice, three more times before coming inside the wet heat of his mate. Startled by the explosion, Logan sits up in bed and finds that he came all over himself like a fucking fifteen year-old kid. Disgusted, he quickly changes his sheets and tosses them in the trash. No need to explain that mess to Mrs. Stanton.

Lying back in bed after changing his sheets, Logan stares up at the ceiling, knowing he needs to do something to get his mind off this chick that he has yet to even see. He takes it upon himself to picture her face as an atrocity made for monster films. Chuckling out loud at his imagination, Logan continues to stare up at the ceiling, hoping that his mind will finally tire and rest.

The fatigued and grouchy mood Logan found himself in the following morning only intensifies as he notices that the waiting area in his practice is packed full of locals looking more than miserable.

"What's going on?" he asks Nikki as he strolls behind the counter to check his patient list for the day.

"Seems like a food poisoning outbreak from a retirement party for librarian Myrtle. Right now, Dr. Fields has them all scheduled for thirty minutes of IV fluids to treat the dehydration. Unfortunately, we just have the two interviews today. I think they'll run in the other direction if they see the office this way."

Nodding at her assessment, Logan walks back to his office before calling patient after patient to be hooked up to an IV.

Fifteen patients later, Logan sits at his desk, head cradled in his hands. He has been vomited on twice and had to help an elderly patient make it to the rest room before it was too late. It was just too much on top of his already irritable mood.

A knock on his door is quickly followed by Dr. Fields standing in Logan's doorway, reminding him of one of the two interviews they have scheduled today. Logan's already contacted Mary Bell about joining his team, so he's joining the remaining interviews just so he can get to know their potential employees.

Following the other physicians into the conference room, they sit around discussing the mayhem going on in their practice while they wait for their candidate, Avery Poindexter. Logan sits and checks his phone for any messages from Austin about meeting up after work tonight, since he knows he's going to need a beer or five. After calculating that ten minutes have passed, Logan angrily glances around the room, searching for any sign of the interviewee.

"This is ridiculous," he says to the room. "We've already waited ten minutes. Regardless of his resume or how knowledgeable he is, he is wasting our time and I have patients to see."

Logan storms out of the room and heads back to his office before calling the next patient back to a room. As he moves to the waiting area, he notices that Nikki has left and their nurse, Sandra, is manning the desk. Unable to waste time asking of Nikki's whereabouts, Logan instead hurries his patient back to the exam room and begins hooking her up to an IV.

The second interview arrives and doesn't go as well as Logan had hoped. The applicant had just found out his girlfriend is expecting, so he didn't think the hour commute each way to the town would work. It was unfortunate, given that the guy had a killer resume and Dr. Fields still hadn't chosen a candidate.

I wonder what happened to Melanie and Max? I'll have to ask Nikki later.

Offering that they share Mary Bell when she starts on Monday, Logan proposes he sit in on a few more interviews with Dr. Fields, but the doctor turns him down, inferring that he was just going to look through the candidates they had already seen.

Checking his phone one last time before leaving, Logan still has no messages from Austin. Not particularly in the mood to head to the bar alone, Logan quickly changes his clothes in his office before closing up for the night.

Passing by one of the large windows in the hallway, he takes notice of the angry storm clouds outside pouring sheets of rain onto the ground. Logan sprints back to his office to grab his umbrella, not looking forward to driving in the nasty weather.

After locking the two sets of doors, he turns and walks directly into a small, solid black mass. Looking more clearly at the figure, Logan finds that it's a girl hidden behind an overly large rain jacket. Not much more is visible behind the hood but the tip of her nose.

"Are you Dr. Fields?" she asks him with a voice that is shaking from the rain and chilled weather.

"Nope, you just missed him. Can I help you?"

"No, I was supposed to meet him earlier today about a job."

Realizing that this is the interviewee that wasted all of their time today, Logan finds it impossible to hold back the lashing words as they escape from his mouth.

"Well, Avery, was it? I'm not sure you'd be a good fit for us since you couldn't even make it to your interview. You wasted my time, and Dr. Fields', when we could have been helping our patients."

"I'm sorry, I didn't mean to waste your time." she says through a quivering voice, trying unsuccessfully to hold back a sob. "It really wasn't my fault," she murmurs, obviously cowed by the roll of his eyes. "My car died and I was on the bus, but there was an accident. They wanted to take us all to the hospital, but I knew I needed to be here. They wouldn't let me leave until I was checked out by a paramedic, which took hours. I walked here after taking a rain jacket that the man who sat beside me on the bus offered me."

Listening to her story, Logan glances down her body and his eyes land on her feet. Small black flats that have been torn up, clearly from miles of walking, give way to soaking wet pants.

"Look," she continues, "I'm sorry. I should have called, but I don't have a phone, and," stifling another sob, she finishes "It's been a rough year – hell, a rough life - and I really need this job."

The agony in her voice literally makes Logan's chest hurt - the pain radiating outwards to all the tips of his limbs.

"Ok, please stop crying. Come in tomorrow at nine and I'll get you a meeting with Dr. Fields. And I'm sorry I snapped at you after the day you've had."

Sorry? When the hell have I ever been sorry about something I've said or done? I live my life with no regrets. No second thoughts. Austin calls me blunt, but I say the truth and I won't sugar coat. But seriously? This girl has me apologizing?

"Thank you," she replies, turning to look back out into the heavy downpour.

Logan surprises himself again when he says, "Come on, let me take you home," and takes a hold of her elbow.

She hesitates at first, but then she must have decided to trust him because she easily follows his direction.

Under his umbrella, Logan steers her towards his black BMW M3 and holds the door open for her to slide onto his leather seats. At her reluctance to sit, Logan assures her that she won't ruin the interior.

Jumping into the driver's seat, he tosses his folded umbrella onto the floorboard behind his seat. Settled, he takes a deep breath and is immediately assaulted by Avery's sweet smell. Even through the rain and a stranger's coat, she has a fragrance of spring flowers and a hint of something else – something uniquely her.

Logan turns to look at her, but the hood remains upright on her head, blocking his view of her profile. Taking that as his cue, he turns on the car and asks which way he needs to go. She points to the right and Logan moves the car onto the street, following her directions as she points.

As they approach Nikki's complex, Logan feels a strange combination of curiosity and nerves at the same time. He hadn't considered that she might be the same girl he saw through Nikki's window last night. Logan's hands tighten on the wheel, turning his knuckles white, as he controls the urge to pull back her hood, see her face and delve his hands into her silky hair.

Pulling into the parking lot, he finds a spot close to the entrance and follows Avery up the stairwell and into the apartment while holding the umbrella over both of their heads.

"Oh my god," Nikki screeches as she rushes forward to pull Avery into a tight embrace, knocking the offending hood from Avery's head. "I have been looking everywhere for you! I heard about the bus. Are you okay?"

Standing alone in the doorway, Logan strains to hear a reply, but he is met with hushed tones as she whispers softly and then turns to walk down the hall.

Nikki's all-knowing eyes turn towards him as she tilts her head to look at him more closely. Logan quickly explains what happened outside the office to put her at ease, but he can tell that Nikki thinks Avery is someone special and wants to take care of her. Nikki has that look in her eyes that she gets when she sees sick patients.

She beckons him to follow her farther into the apartment, which thankfully, has been tidied up since he was here last. Situating himself on one of the bar stools, she moves into the kitchen, resting on the side of the counter opposite of him.

"She's delicate, Logan," she whispers in a condescending tone.

Startled at her assessment of the situation, Logan looks at her blankly and replies, "I have no idea what you're talking about."

Just as she is about to expound on her previous statement, Avery comes walking into the kitchen and heads straight for the fridge. She grabs a bottle of water before turning around and staring in his direction, eyes as wide as saucers.

Damn, she's fucking beautiful.

The dark brown hair that captured his attention last night is pulled up high upon her head, showcasing a smooth and long neck. But her face… her face renders him temporarily speechless. Her ivory skin is a blank canvas that showcases eyes the color of the Caribbean Sea. Her cheeks begin to turn a soft shade of pink and she licks her full, rosy lips before bringing the water bottle to her mouth and taking a sip, breaking Logan free of his trance.

She walks softly in his direction and extends her hand forward.

"Thanks for the ride…," she trails off, prompting him for his name.

Logan glances at her hand, then stares into her eyes as he places her delicate extremities into his larger grasp.

"Logan," he grits out, trying to ignore the sensation of sparks igniting through his hand as her skin brushes against his own.

She looks intently at their joined hands before raising her gaze to meet his.

Slightly bewildered, she responds with a shaky voice, "Uh, yes… Logan. Um, thanks for the ride," and removes her hand from his clutch.

"You said that already," he replies sarcastically, missing the feel of her touch against his palm.

A hint of pink darkens her already tinged cheeks.

"Yes, well…"she trails off, looking towards Nikki for help.

Chiming in for the rescue, Nikki asks, "Logan, do you want to stay for dinner?" whilst running her hand down his arm.

This is a familiar gesture from her that normally wouldn't bother him, but Logan has to stop himself from twisting away at her uncomfortable touch.

"No thanks. I'm going to head home. I'll see you both in the morning."

Feeling the need to leave as quickly as possible, Logan turns towards the front of the apartment, but nearly topples over Avery. She slivers past him in the hall, but he hears her gasp as her soft breasts brush against his other arm.

After exiting the apartment, Logan takes the steps two at a time and rushes down to his car, in dire need to return to his home and end the day.

*O*NCE LOGAN STEPS INTO the building the next morning, he quickly locates Dr. Fields and explains the situation with Avery. The elderly physician nods his head in understanding and gently pats him on the shoulder.

"You did well, Logan. Sometimes we all have bad days. It seems like you came to her rescue."

"I didn't do anything but offer to take her home and to set up another interview."

With a shrug of his shoulders, Logan brushes off Dr. Fields' endearing gaze. Logan's familiar with being the asshole, not the nice guy someone can turn to.

As the two doctors head down the hall, Logan is stunned silent when he finds Avery standing at the desk. Her back is turned to him and she has cased her hips and legs in a knee-length pencil skirt, a dark-burgundy silken shirt draping effortlessly over her chest and shoulders. Her dark hair has been meticulously twisted into a coil on the back of her head. At last his gaze drops to the black sandals strapped to her feet, the heels surprisingly taller than Logan would have expected.

Beside him Dr. Fields coughs, breaking him of his gawking, and Logan closes his mouth quickly. Avery manages to effortlessly combine both sex kitten and girl next door – a combination that only amplifies his lust for her.

"I'll go greet Ms. Poindexter and bring everyone into the conference room."

"I think I'll sit out this interview," Logan says, shaking his head. "I have an appointment right now."

Brushing past Avery quickly, Logan grabs a patient file and calls the young man back to a room, all the while feeling Avery's gaze on him, searing a hole through his skin.

*W*ALKING INTO THE MEDICAL practice behind Nikki, Avery tries hard to keep a blank yet cheery look on her face to hide her nervousness. After the catastrophe that was yesterday, she's feeling even more apprehensive than she did before.

Nikki leans in over her desk and whispers, "You look like you're going to throw up."

"I'm so nervous, Nikki," Avery says, trying to speak as quietly as possible, yet failing miserably when she squeaks her roommate's name.

"Don't be nervous, Dr. Fields is great. Oh, look, he's coming now."

Avery doesn't have to turn around to know that Logan is with Dr. Fields. She can feel his eyes burning a hole in her skin from behind. The feeling he ignites in her is once again realized as he passes by her to grab a folder, brushing his chest against her arm. A gasp of air permeates through her lips in a whooshing sound as the feel of him against her pebbles her skin.

There is an intensity between them when they're in close quarters. She felt the same force yesterday in his car and again in the apartment. Avery brushed off the sensation and attributed it to the cataclysm of the day, but now she realizes that his proximity was only fuel to the fire. His touch ignites a firestorm on her skin.

Avery stares at his retreating back as he ushers a patient into a room and continue watching long past a moment of appropriateness. A touch on her shoulder bounces her back to reality and she startles at the contact.

"Sorry," Nikki says with a questioning look in her eye, "I wanted to introduce you to Dr. Fields."

As Avery raises her hand for a polite shake, she looks at Dr. Fields and offers her name, immediately apologizing for her absence yesterday.

"I understand, Avery. Life happens and I'm glad you were able to make it in today. I haven't had much luck finding anyone that I'd like to work with, but I think we'll be a good fit. If you'd follow me, some of our team has assembled to conduct the interview. It's very informal, so don't be nervous."

Already feeling at ease with Dr. Fields, Avery follows him into a small conference room where she meets three of the other physicians.

"Dr. Chamberlin is in with a patient right now. As he won't be joining us, we can go ahead and begin," Dr. Fields says loudly, addressing the group.

Her nervousness dissipates knowing that Dr. Chamberlin - or Logan - won't be in the room. She barely has time to relax, however, before the group starts firing off questions related to her experience, schooling, and re-location. Avery does her best to keep her personal life out of the answers and, luckily, no one pries further when she explains that her re-location was only due to the need for a change.

After the interview, Avery follows Dr. Fields back to his office where he takes a seat behind his desk and prompts her to take the seat across from him.

"I think that went very well, Avery, and I'd like to offer you the position if you're still interested."

Avery lets out a deep exhale as relief washes over her.

"Yes, I am still very interested, Dr. Fields. Thank you so much."

"Please, call me Al. I do have some paperwork for you to fill out, but I'd like to ask you one more question."

Wringing her hands in her lap, she nervously nods for him to continue.

"We complete background checks on all of our employees and because we're in healthcare, you understand that they have to be very extensive. I'm the only one that has seen yours, Avery, but answer me this; why do you need this job? It seems to me you have enough wealth to own a small country."

Avery is embarrassed, but understands his concern. He wants to know if she received that money from shady transactions.

"I can assure you, Dr. Fields - I mean, Al - that I want this job for all the right reasons. That money was given to me after someone I loved passed away, and I plan on using it to better this small town of Carson."

He notices the tears beginning to shimmer in her eyes and moves from behind his desk. He stands by his door with the paperwork in hand, effectively ushering Avery out.

"I don't plan on sharing this with anyone, Avery, and I can assure you that your worth is measured not by those dollar signs, but by what you do with them. Here is the paperwork: feel free to take it home and finish it up. You can bring it with you when you start tomorrow."

"Thank you, Al. I'm really looking forward to joining your team."

By the time Avery exits the office and makes her way to the front desk, her nerves are shot. Earlier this morning, Nikki had offered to bring her back to the apartment during her lunch break. Avery had planned to take a cab from the apartment to go see about purchasing a car of her own, considering her bucket of rust refuses to move from its current parking spot.

As she searches for Nikki, she finds her tied up with a group of patients and a ringing phone. Knowing she is swamped, Avery indicates that she is going to wait on the bus by holding up her pass. Nikki nods in her direction in understanding.

Walking absentmindedly through the sliding glass doors, Avery suddenly whacks into a large and stiff object. Glancing up, she realizes she's run into the back of Logan as he was chatting with a patient outside.

"I am so sorry. I wasn't paying attention," Avery says, embarrassed, as she nervously bites her lip and tucks a stray hair behind her ear.

"Don't worry about it. Wait there for a second?"

"Um...sure?"

As he finishes speaking with the elderly woman, Avery can't help but let her gaze travel over his body. He is remarkably handsome, model worthy even. He stands tall, about six feet-four. His light gray button-down shirt is pulled taught against his arms and chest, showcasing his well-developed muscles. She can tell he spends quite some time at the gym. He has changed out of his black slacks from earlier and replaced them with well-worn, dark denim jeans that fit snugly against his legs and behind. Avery returns her eyes to his face and realizes his attention is back on her, and that he has caught her ogling his body.

"See something you like?" he asks, a smirk flitting across his face and a small dimple forming on his left cheek.

Words don't begin to infiltrate her mind. All Avery can think about is how she wants to gaze into his comforting hazel eyes, run her hands through his short, slightly wavy dark hair, and divulge all her deepest secrets.

Realizing he is casually waiting for her response, Avery quickly stutters, "No. I was just staring off into space. I do that sometimes."

Avery mentally chastises herself.

Great. He's going to think I'm a loon and who wants a loon working at a medical practice?

He cocks his gorgeous head to the side, looking at her intently before coming to his own conclusion.

"So, Avery," he pauses. A breath, then he continues, "did you pass the test?"

"I did. I start tomorrow and I'm really looking forward to it."

"Congratulations. Welcome to the team. I'm heading out for some lunch; would you like to join me? I can give you a ride home."

Avery hesitates when he offers lunch. She's sure he means it as a simple, innocent invitation, but she can't ignore her heart pounding in her chest.

"I don't think that's a good idea."

"Sure, it is. Come on. Nikki's tied up and I know you want to celebrate. There's a great place right up the road." Holding out his hands in mock-surrender, he continues, "Completely harmless, I swear."

The adorable pleading look he gives her is her down fall. Avery doesn't think anyone could say no to that face.

"Alright. I'll go with you."

"Awesome," he says as he moves toward the parking lot. Avery following closely behind like a lost puppy.

He stops at a beautiful bike and she excitedly looks around, hoping that he isn't yanking her chain.

"Is this yours?" she asks gleefully.

"Yep, I ride her whenever we have nice days like today. I only have the one helmet so I'll let you wear it."

Avery claps her hands excitedly as she walks around the parameter of the Ducati Multistrada 1200 S. It is white with black and chrome accents, beautiful in every way. And boy does the bike fit the man. As he straddles the bike, igniting the engine, Avery gazes at him in awe. Logan puts all those bad boys in romance novels to shame.

It's quite tragic, really, that she can't act on her attraction to him.

I am my own grim reaper. Taking the lives of those I love, she repeats in her head.

Avery takes the proffered helmet from Logan's hand and climbs onto the back of his bike. Her form fitted pencil skirt slides towards her waist, revealing most of her thighs as she wedges herself onto the seat. She gently reaches around Logan's body, trying not to awkwardly molest him, but he takes his hands and tightens her arms around his waist. Avery can feel his deep inhale as she presses herself closer to him.

"Ready?" he asks as he revs the engine.

Avery nods, uttering a breathless, "Yep," and clings tighter as they take off.

RENEE HARLESS

Chapter Three

AVING AVERY'S THIGHS PRESSED against his own and her body tightly resting along his back is one of the best feelings in the world. When she wrapped her arms around his waist, he couldn't help but hitch his breath on his intake of air. She was either going to be his worst undoing... or his life's antidote. Logan could already tell she was going to be important. He had this pull toward her that he couldn't explain, and couldn't help acting on - even though he knows he shouldn't. He was no good for her. And from the empty look in her eyes – a look of someone that has been through hell - Logan knew that she was going to be a complication. And he doesn't need any complications.

But for now, in this moment, he can enjoy her. Hell, any man would enjoy a beautiful woman pressed against him.

Logan takes the road slowly, more cautiously than normal since he isn't wearing a helmet, and revels in the feel of her body and the rumble of the engine. The bike comes to a stop outside a fifty's era diner, located just off the main road. He dismounts and his hands have a mind of their own, because soon he's grabbing Avery by the waist and lifting her off the bike. It takes all of his strength not to tug her skirt higher on her thighs, exposing more of the soft, pale skin.

They stroll casually into the diner and he waves at Ethel, who's manning the register behind the counter. After they take their seats, Ethel makes her way over to them and places the laminated menus on the table.

"Hiya, Dr. Chamberlin. How goes it?"

"Fine, Ethel. This is our new medical assistant, Avery. I'm sure you'll be seeing her around."

Avery and Ethel exchange greetings before both turn to glance at him.

"I'll take a water and your loaded big-bubba burger."

"That sounds great. I'll have the same," Avery says.

"How old are you?" Logan asks abruptly, as Ethel turns to walk away.

She is startled from a brief reverie and says, "I'm sorry, what?"

"Just a simple question. I'm trying to get to know our new employee."

"Oh, I'm twenty-four. You?"

"Twenty-nine. Favorite color?"

"Green."

"Me too." He grins, "I know you're from the same town as Melanie, did you grow up there?"

She simply shakes her head before taking a sip of water from the cup Ethel placed on the table.

"Outside Atlanta."

"Any boyfriend, girlfriend, husband?" Logan inquires, trying to get to the nitty-gritty.

A hushed, "No," escapes between her lips as she continues to stare down into her drink.

"So, what brings you to our small town then?"

At his simple question, she completely shuts down. He can see all signs of life completely drain from her eyes and face... in a word, she looks numb.

"I don't want to talk about it. And really, can we just finish our burgers then head to the apartment?"

Faking a yawn, she feigns exhaustion as an explanation for her attitude.

Whatever. I don't need to deal with some girl's problems anyway. Even if said girl makes me feel things I hadn't felt in years.

Ethel drops the burger-filled plates on the table and the two eat in an uncomfortable silence. Every so often, Logan lifts his eyes to meet hers. She offers a small smile, trying to patch the heavy feeling they've let settle over them.

Finishing his lunch, he leans back in the seat and patiently waits for Avery to finish eating. She really is stunning. Even after her outburst, Logan would still be willing to slide himself right into her smart mouth. He shakes his head at the vision he has created in his head. Logan can tell through her morose appearance that home is a touchy subject with her. He figures for the sake of his working environment, he need to make things right.

"Avery?" Logan starts and she looks up at him, large blue eyes questioning. "I'm sorry I upset you. I'd like for us to get along, friends even, since we'll be working together."

The most beautiful smile in the world glides across her succulent lips and Logan can feel his heartbeat quicken. All is right with the world.

Yep, I'll deal with all of her problems if she'll smile at me like this every day.

"Thank you, I'd really like that. To be friends, I mean."

His mouth has become significantly drier after watching her speak and he has to lick his lips before he continues, but as his tongue settles back inside his mouth. Logan sees Avery's eyes dilate and her cheeks redden.

Interesting.

"Friends it is. Are you ready to go home?"

"Yea, I guess so," she says wistfully, hesitantly moving out of the booth to stand next to him at the head of the table.

Placing his hand on her elbow, Logan tries to ignore the sizzle of awareness as he guides her out of the diner's door.

The ride back to her apartment is much quicker than he had hoped. Her body pressed against his sends delightful sparks racing through his nerves.

As she hands him back his helmet, Logan can't help staring at her as she glides her hands through her hair, unweaving it from its elegant up-do. Her head is tilted to the side as she fixes her wayward strands, eyes closed, lips pursed, and the sun beaming behind her. She looks like an angel. Logan finds that he has to adjust himself on the seat in the hopes she won't notice the effect she's having on him.

"Thanks for the ride," she says, her attention back on him, eyes scanning his face.

"You're welcome. Do you want me to leave you my number in case you need another ride?"

Shuffling her feet timidly, she tucks some loose strands of hair behind her ear before gazing at him behind her long lashes.

"I don't have a phone, but I was going to go purchase a new car this afternoon."

No phone? Who doesn't have a phone?

"Ok well, if you need me, just use Nikki's phone I guess."

Strapping the helmet back onto his head, Logan instantly regrets the deep breath he takes. His helmet is engulfed in her sweet floral scent. It must be from her shampoo.

"Well, see you later, Avery," Logan hollers as he turns the engine.

"Bye," she says, her mouth moving as if she wanted to say more but stopped herself.

Back at the office, Logan finds himself distracted by thoughts of Avery while he's busy seeing the remainder of his patients.

Logan's past is the reason why he doesn't trust women - or really anyone for that matter - but she wants him to be her friend… and all he wants to do is sink deep inside her. Sex with Avery would be explosive; their chemistry is volatile just when they're in the same room together.

But friends?

That's just something he hasn't done with a woman. They throw themselves at him and he willingly accepts, none of this mental foreplay that a friendship seems to require.

Logan releases a sigh as he opens the folder and views the symptoms for his next patient. All he can think about is her smile. Not her rocking body, not her lush tits and ass, no. Her smile, and that just infuriates him more.

Friends?

Yeah, for her, he'll take whatever he can get. Something about Avery makes him feel more than he has felt in years. She seeps into his bones, filling the empty crevices of his heart.

Logan's phone vibrates in his jacket as he exits the room where he was treating a little boy with a sinus infection. Fishing it out of his pocket, he peeks at the caller ID and sees Austin is on the line.

"Hey, man."

"Hey, Logan. Do you want to go bowling tonight?" he asks hopefully.

"Bowling?"

"Yea, this chick I met said she'll be there with some friends tonight."

Logan chuckles into the phone, having already figured there had to be a good reason why Austin wanted to go bowling. To Austin – chicks are a good reason.

"Sure that sounds good. What time?"

"Seven, I think."

"Alright, meet you there."

Glancing at the clock, he realizes he has about an hour and a half before he needs to meet Austin. Logan hastily grabs his helmet and rushes out the office doors, charging his way home.

Walking into the bungalow he rents from Al, Logan chucks his keys into the small bowl on the hallway table and moseys down the hall to his bedroom. The house is bigger than what he needs, but it was available and Al gave him a heck of a deal in return for some handiwork on the place. It's a four bedroom, two and a half bath, 1940's craftsman, desperately in need of a complete overhaul. It's been a long process as he has slowly worked to finish his projects, but at last all that remains are the full guest bathroom and the hardwood floors both upstairs and down. Logan had planned on simply refinishing them, but there was too much water damage after a previous tenant let the washing machine overflow. He makes a mental note to finish laying the hardwoods this weekend.

Stripping off his work clothes, he twists his shower knobs hoping to wash away his thoughts of Avery as Logan focuses on the group of girls he and Austin are going to meet. The water cools too quickly and he's forced to shorten his cleansing.

Tugging on a pair of jeans and a short sleeve Henley-style shirt, Logan slides on some shoes before grabbing his keys and a bottle of water and heading out the door. He slides into the BMW, anxious to meet a potential bed-warmer, and heads speedily towards his destination.

The bowling alley is fairly full when he arrives and he searches the lanes for his friend. Austin's Viking stature is usually a dead giveaway, but he is nowhere to be found, at least from Logan's view. As Logan turns on his heels to head to the food counter, he sees Austin duck out of the door leading to the men's bathroom.

"Hey, man," Austin shouts from a distance.

Logan meets him halfway and shakes his hand in a friendly gesture.

"Hey, Austin. Did you see the girl that dragged you and me here?"

"Yea, she's over in lane ten," he adds sheepishly.

Logan's gaze scans the room until he land on lane ten and he immediately bursts in obnoxious laughter.

"I know, I know," Austin adds shamefacedly, looking down at the ground.

"Dude, she's like barely eighteen and here with her family."

"Well, I didn't know that when I overheard her."

"Obviously."

"Do you still want to play?"

"I'm here, might as well. I could go for beer and some pizza, and maybe some nachos, too."

They exchange their shoes, order a few pitchers of beer and head to their designated lane. Neither of them has played since they were younger, so they're definitely rusty at first, but a couple rounds and a few beers in, they get the hang of it.

It's Austin's turn at the lane, and while he waits, Logan occupies himself watching a rowdy group of cowboys farther down the room enjoying themselves with their ladies. That's when he feels it - that inexplicable pull, that prickling that travels down his neck and out through his toes, causing the baby fine hairs on his body to stand on end.

Thinking that the air conditioning in the building has clicked onto full blast, he glances up, but quickly realize that the AC isn't the reason for the chill as sweat drips off of his brow and Austin's. Logan scans the room, beginning with the cowboys, and works his way towards the entrance. He shakes his head to clear himself of the sensation, but it does little good. Logan had just begun thinking that he's imagining the feeling, but then suddenly he sees her. She is standing at the front desk, exchanging worn black Chuck Taylors for ill-fitted bowling shoes. Her soft, satiny hair flows in glorious waves down her back, stopping right above the waist of her perfectly-fitted jeans. Enraptured, he can't help but continue to stare in her direction as her petite blonde friend, whom he realizes is Nikki, says something to make her chuckle. The movement causing the waves in her hair to bounce against her back, like a ripple in motion.

"Your turn," Austin announces, slapping him on the shoulder to garner his attention.

"Huh? Oh, yeah. My turn," Logan replies, but makes little effort to move from his seat, completely captivated by the new arrival.

"I see what has your attention. Damn."

"Back off," he growls as he stands up and marches over to where Avery stands, struggling to tie her shoes.

"Want me to get those?" Logan asks, his voice a bit huskier than he had planned.

At his question, she turns her head towards his voice and sets her mesmerizing eyes on him, a growing smile gracing her face when she finds him and not a stranger.

"No thanks, I'm almost done. Broken three shoe strings already," she chuckles as she commences her tying.

When her task is complete, she stands quickly and allows her gaze to travel his body, the penetration scalding his skin.

"Hi, Logan. What are you doing here?" she asks, returning her eyes to his.

"Hey, Avery. My friend Austin and I have a lane over there," he says, pointing in the general direction, "If you and Nikki want to join us."

"You sure?"

"Yep," he replies, tucking her hair behind her right ear. "Friends can bowl together, right?"

The question is posed as Logan looks into her eyes, watching the small black pupils dilate, the response causing his heart to pound.

Not waiting for an answer, he takes her hand and calls over his shoulder, "Hey, Nikki, you and Avery are going to play with us."

Logan can't help but secretly rejoice when Avery doesn't remove her hand from his grasp. If anything, she squeezes his hand a bit tighter as they walk toward the lane. Logan gazes down at her and smiles when she peeks up at him.

When they arrive at the lane he and Austin claimed as their own, Austin looks at him questioningly, his gaze bouncing between Avery and their intertwined hands.

"Austin, this is Avery. She just moved here and is working as a medical assistant at my practice."

Nikki joins them moments later and as Logan makes the introductions between her and Austin, he can see the spark of interest between the two. He isn't sure how they haven't met prior to this point, especially since they were all together the other night. But now that he thinks about it, they would make a great match; his calmness complimenting her quirkiness.

As Logan resets the game to include their two new players, Avery comes to stand beside him.

"I've never bowled before," she whispers in his ear, her sweet breath floating across his nose.

It takes all his strength to maintain his position at the kiosk and not cart her off to the bathroom to take his fill.

"You'll be fine. It's an easy game and I can help you, if you want."

"That'd be great. I don't want to make a fool of myself."

Looking at her, listening to her shaky voice, Logan murmurs, "You couldn't be a fool, even if you tried. Come on, you're up first."

Logan begins by showing Avery how to hold the ball, then line up her wrist with the arrows on the lane when she releases. She mimics the walk he demonstrated a few times before trying to release the ball on her first round.

On her first try, she gets a strike.

She jumps into his arms, completely exhilarated, while the rest of them stand stock-still, mouths agape in shock.

It takes him a few breathless seconds, but Logan quickly wraps her in his arms as her excitement seeps into him.

"You did great, Avery. Are you sure you haven't played before?" he asks as she slides away from his arms.

"No, never. I can't believe I got them all. I never expected that to happen."

"Well, you're a natural then. Congratulations on your first strike. Now we get to celebrate!"

Austin hands around cups of beer to celebrate Avery's score and they drink them in gusto before resuming the game.

They all acquire a few spares and strikes, the girls sharing another pitcher of beer to celebrate while he and Austin switch to water.

After the fourth game, Nikki and Austin can't seem to keep their hands off of each other.

"Looks like they're having a good time," Logan jokes to Avery, waggling his brows.

She laughs and smacks him lightly on the arm. He grabs her hand at its removal and he places it gently between his two significantly larger ones.

"I don't think your ride is going back with you tonight. You want me to take you?"

She glances in Nikki's direction, finds her in a close embrace with Austin, and nods her head.

"Sure, that would be great, thanks. I'm having fun. More fun than I've had in a while and I'm not ready for the night to end."

"Well, I'm your guy. I'm not ready for it to end either," Logan says as he stands, tugging her by the hand he still has in his grasp. "Come on. I'll take you home."

 OLLOWING CLOSELY BEHIND LOGAN, Avery hopes to catch another hint of his masculine scent. A heady mix of cologne, pine, and something else that is uniquely his own.

They exchange out their shoes and pay for their games, Logan picking up the tab for her and Nikki too, even after a bit of failed protesting.

Taking hold of her hand once again, Logan escorts her to his car. Avery slides past him where he stands holding the door, obviously offering her the chance to brush against him. It takes all her strength to avoid doing so. Avery takes a moment after he closes the door to pull herself together. She needs to remain unaffected; being close to him makes her want things she shouldn't, because she is far too familiar with the outcome - it's the same every time. Friendship; that's all Avery can offer, for his sake.

Logan enters the car and turns on his phone so that an Avenged Sevenfold song blasts through the speakers. A bit unexpected, but it instantly thrills her that they have a similar interest in music.

"I love this band!" Avery shouts exuberantly.

"Really? I've seen them live twice. Great show."

"I am so jealous," she says dreamily.

Avery looks over at Logan as he pulls out of the parking lot, heading towards her apartment.

"I had a really fun time tonight. I haven't laughed so much in…. well, ever."

"I had a great time, too. We need to get together like this more often," he says before glancing in her direction and seeing the shock on her face.

She can feel her eyebrows reaching towards her hairline and her jaw continuing to drop.

"By together," he adds, "I meant as friends, and as a group, if you want."

Logan turns back to the road, obviously nervous that he has overstepped their friendly boundary.

"It's ok, Logan. I know what you meant. I'm just not used to having friends to hang out with, that's all. You took me by surprise."

"Well don't be surprised, you're a lot of fun. And I guess if Nikki and Austin don't make things awkward, we'll be seeing more of each other."

"I didn't get to speak to him much, but what does Austin do?"

"He's in construction. Does pretty well for himself, especially since we've had the recent population boom."

Huh, construction? I'll have to keep that in mind.

The apartment complex comes into view and Avery feels dismay at the thought of their night ending. She feels a strong connection to Logan, like they are kindred spirits.

Wanting to continue conversing with him, Avery decides to take a leap.

He knows we're just friends. He knows I have boundaries.

"Would you like to come up? I can make us something to snack on and we can watch a movie or play a game, or whatever," she says nervously, wringing her hands in her lap. "Never mind," she whispers, shaking her head, "I was just being dumb."

"Avery," he says in a low voice, placing his hand on top of her own. "Avery," he says again, this time more forceful, garnering her attention. "I'd love to join you. I'm having a good time, too."

And then he smiles. Even in the dark, Avery can make out his perfect, pearly white teeth. His smile disarms her. She would do just about anything to see that smirk every day.

They walk upstairs to the third floor apartment and she can't help but rub her hand against her chest, right where her heart used to beat. A sudden pain shoots from the spot she's rubbing, down through her extremities - the pain so sharp and severe that it steals her breath. Logan glances back when he notices her movements have stopped and asks if she's ok. Assuring him that she's fine, they continue to walk up the stairs. The moment he grasps her hand in his own again, the pain evaporates - it completely fades into oblivion.

The landing falls beneath their feet and Avery searches through her bag for the key Nikki handed to her at the bowling alley. Finding the molded piece of metal, she tries to insert it into the lock.

Why is my hand shaking?

After a few fumbling attempts, she finally unlocks the door and leads Logan into the apartment.

"Do you..." she begins with a high-pitched shriek. Avery coughs lightly to clear her throat and attempt again, "Do you want something to drink?"

"Sure, water would be great. Thanks," he says, peering around the apartment.

The apartment looks vastly different from the way it did when he was here last. Avery has clearly spent some time rearranging the furniture and cleaning. He notices a few pictures dangling upon the wall: mostly Aria's drawings.

"These are amazing," he points out; captivated by the small collage Avery designed for Aria's creations.

"Thanks. My, um..." She clears her throat, "My sister drew them. She was really talented."

"Was?" he asks, looking at her with sympathy swimming in his eyes.

Not ready to talk about it, Avery simply nods her head and changes the subject quickly by asking if he wants to play one of the old-school board games she brought with her. They decide on a game of *Guess Who* and play a few rounds before switching to a game of *Uno*.

"You should know that I'm extremely competitive."

"That's alright, Logan. You may be competitive, but you'll still lose," Avery chuckles.

"Want to make a wager on that?"

Cheekily she replies, "Maybe," as a blush creeps up her neck.

"Ok, how about whoever loses has to do whatever the winner wants all day tomorrow."

Looking into his eyes, Avery can see the desire swarming behind them, ready to burst free. The spot beneath her breast begins to thunder again and she instantly places her hand against her chest.

He continues to stare at her before raising his hand for a shake, "Deal?"

Avery looks at his outstretched hand and then returns his gaze.

"Absolutely," she says, shaking his hand and trying to hide a shiver that races down her spine when their hands connect.

After playing the best two out of three, Avery wins. Logan was angry that she hoarded her "collect" and "skip-a-turn" cards, but she merely insisted that she never claimed she wouldn't play dirty.

Turning her attention to the clock on the wall and realizing that it's still fairly early, they decide to make some popcorn and settle in to watch television.

When Avery returns from the kitchen, she notices two things instantly. First, Logan has tattoos on his biceps that just show past the arm of his shirt. Second, his interest is set on the angel picture of Aria's that she had found when she moved.

She coughs quietly to alert him of her presence and he follows her to the couch.

"I haven't seen anything like that drawing before. The perspective is incredible."

"Mmhmm," she murmurs in agreement.

"Do you want to talk about it?"

"Nope," she says, throwing a handful of their snack into her mouth, "Popcorn?" she asks, holding out the bowl.

"You know if we're going to be real friends, Avery, you'll probably need to tell me more about you."

A heartbeat, and then,

"Ok, but not now," Avery whispers, ashamed of her inability to open up.

Bringing her legs up onto the couch under her hips, she fiddles with the hem of her pants nervously.

Logan takes a handful of popcorn and shoves it into his mouth before grabbing the remote and flicking through the channels before landing on a showing of the movie *Scream*.

Even the way he shovels food into his mouth is sexy, she thinks before she can stop herself. *Sexy? Where did that come from?*

They sit in companionable silence as the film rolls, but the tension continues to grow in the room. Whether that tension is awkward or sexual, Avery can't pinpoint because she's feeling both.

"You know," Logan says as he maintains his attention on the television, "I grew up poor. Dirt poor. And my dad used to beat me so bad I would need to skip school so that the teachers wouldn't notice the bruising."

Avery jerks her head in his direction at his sudden and unanticipated confession: a confession he gives so nonchalantly.

"My mom left us when I was a kid. Then my high school girlfriend left me when my dad caught us going at it, though I already lacked most respect for women at that point. I didn't really have the best examples in the trailer park."

He doesn't wait for Avery's response - not that she could have given one, judging by her widened eyes and slack jaw. She can hear the hurt in his voice, even though it's clear he's trying not to convey it. Hearing his pain sends a quiver to her throat for the little boy that was beaten and that missed out on so much.

"I prayed every day to get out of that hell hole. I worked my ass off in school and went to both undergrad and medical school on full scholarships. In college, I met Shannon and I thought she was my game changer and that we'd be together forever. I was so in love with her that I didn't notice any of the signs that she was cheating until it was too late…" He pauses briefly, staring at nothing, then resumes, "And boy was she cheating. I found her in her dominatrix getup on top of her plaything in our apartment, the day I had planned on proposing."

A gasp escapes the barrier of Avery's mouth at his heartbreaking revelation. She brings her hands to her mouth to cover her reaction.

"At that point I didn't want to consider another relationship and would sleep with any woman that threw herself at me. One of the girls in my residency program would come over occasionally and we would go at it. Man, she would do things I didn't even think were possible."

The thought of Logan having sex with another female causes Avery to cringe and that feeling alone makes her shake her head.

"I had thought we were exclusively screwing each other, apparently she didn't, because she told me she had been fucking other guys in the program too. Of course, that is after she told me she was pregnant and had aborted what she thought was my baby."

"Oh my god," Avery murmurs just loud enough for Logan to hear.

He turns his saddened eyes in her direction and places his hand on her cheek, wiping away tears she hadn't known seeped from her eyes.

"Women have done shitty things to me and I don't trust them. I haven't considered a relationship in a long time, Avery. But for some reason I trust you and I want a relationship with you, even if it is just a friendship," he says as his thumb brushes against her bottom lip. "You don't have to tell me anything now, but I hope that you'll be able to share with me one day."

"You don't even know me," Avery sighs as she closes her eyes relishing the feel of his hand against her face.

"Don't need to. I can feel it," he replies gruffly.

Seconds later she feels his hand slide into her hair and tilt her head upward. His lips softly brush against hers in the gentlest kiss she's ever felt. Before she realize what she's doing Avery matches the movements of his mouth as her hand comes to rest on his wrist.

The kiss is beautiful. It's a first kiss girls dream about and movies try to recreate. If there was a chorus of angels singing hallelujah, now would be the moment they would crescendo.

They continue to kiss, Logan testing her boundaries, as he tastes her lips with his tongue, but before she is able to respond in return a high-pitched screech coming from the movie startles them and they jump apart.

Chests are heaving as they both work to catch their breath and Avery sends a mental thank you to Wes Craven for his perfectly timed distraction that kept her from continuing down a path she knows she would regret.

"I'm sorry, Avery. I got carried away, you just had this otherworldly look about you with your eyes closed and I couldn't help myself."

"That's ok. It won't happen again. I mean, friends don't kiss like that, right?"

Logan looks at her closely, analyzing the situation.

"Right. Austin and I don't kiss quite like that anyway," he says, adding a smirk for effect.

Avery giggles at him and playfully swats at his arm, but when her hand connects with his arm he takes her wrist in the grasp of his other hand and tugs her closer. His arm snakes around her shoulders and he stokes his fingers through her hair.

She looks up at his handsome profile and asks, "What are you doing, Logan?"

He responds in a very valley-girl accent, "I'm, like, playing with your hair. That's, like, what we do at slumber parties. And then we're going to have, like, a naked pillow fight."

Laughter explodes from Avery's chest and she has a hard time catching her breath. She is grateful for his attempt to lighten the mood.

Once she finally calms down, Avery replies through bits of lingering chuckles, "Yes, to the playing with my hair, but no to the pillow fight."

"Damn," he says before tugging her head back onto his shoulder and commencing the hair stroking.

The feel of his fingers sliding through her hair settles her into an atmosphere of contention. They slowly slide into a lying position on the couch, Logan's chest to her back, as they continue to watch the *Scream* marathon.

At some point they both drift off into companionable slumber with Logan's arm wrapped around her and her head pressed to his shoulder.

7 HAT'S EXACTLY HOW NIKKI finds them the next morning.

Avery hears Nikki's shriek of surprise before she has a moment to collect her thoughts. Opening her eyes, she finds Nikki looking down on her with a sated smile adorning her face. Avery returns her smile and Nikki gives her a thumbs-up before turning towards her room.

Knowing she'll need to diffuse her thoughts about this situation later, she struggles to find a way to pry herself out of Logan's grasp. Before Avery has the chance, he turns her in his arms, smiling at her adorningly, and she can't help but return the gesture.

"Good morning," he whispers as he strokes his free hand through her hair again.

"Morning. Sorry we fell asleep on the couch," Avery says, closing her eyes against the decadent feel of his hands in her hair.

"I'm going to kiss you again if you keep closing your eyes like that," he adds, and she pops her eyes open at his admission, "And don't be sorry, I slept great."

They sit up on the couch, Logan stretching his arms above his head and causing his shirt to ride up, revealing a firm set of abs.

Catching the direction of her gaze, he laughs and asks, "Like what you see?" before standing and pulling his shirt higher. "Please get your fill, I work hard on these."

Damn!

He's beautiful, perfect even. His dark hair is an unruly mess that anyone else would have spent hours trying to recreate. His hazel eyes are bright and glowing above his straight nose and wide smile. Logan has a lot of muscles, more than she's ever seen in person, but they don't make him intimidating. The way they stretch beneath his shirt and pull the material taut makes you fantasize about his arms wrapping around your body.

Friends, Avery. You can only be friends.

The smile on her face dissipates and he releases the shirt.

"You okay?"

"Yea," she replies sullenly.

"What did you want to do today, Mistress Avery?"

"What?"

"You won *Uno*. It's your day."

"Oh, um...I think I heard there is a fair in town. I'd like to do that."

"The fair? You're sure?"

Tucking her chin to her chest, Avery replies shyly, "I've never been to one."

He smiles knowingly at her and offers to spend the day at the fair after he heads back to his home to shower and change. They agree to meet at noon at the fairgrounds.

Logan leaves after placing a soothing kiss on her forehead and Nikki comes out to join her in the living room.

The next hour is spent as Avery listens to Nikki divulging about her night with Austin. She seems to really like him and she says they did a lot of talking between the many bouts of sex.

Sex.

That's something Avery hasn't done in a very long time. Once Declan started showing signs of his illness, he had become too weak and they were afraid he would end up hurt.

Thinking of Declan causes the emptiness in her chest to radiate into aches that seep through her bones. The hurt is so drastic that Avery lets out a squeal of pain, startling Nikki in mid-sentence.

"You ok?" she asks, concern etched across her face.

She rubs Avery's shoulder gently, hoping to calm her.

"Yea, I'm fine," Avery replies, schooling her features in agreement with the lie.

"You're not fine. I'm here going on and on about my night of debauchery and it's making you miss Nick and Declan,"

A look of shock expels from her eyes.

"Don't be mad. Melanie told me only so I could look out for you; to be there if you needed me to be."

"I'm not mad, just…surprised that's all."

Avery continues to rub the sting in her chest.

"You're a terrible liar. But regardless, you know they'd want you to be happy, right? To move on and live a fulfilled life?"

The tears begin building in Avery's eyes. She has to work to hold back the walls of water from escaping past the lids.

"How can I move on when I did this to them? Why should I get to be happy when I'm the reason they're gone?"

Surprisingly angry, Nikki moves from the couch and stands before her.

"You can't seriously believe that, can you? There is no way in the entire world that you could be responsible for their death. Yea, I admit, bad things have happened to the people closest to you, but you can't let that fear rule your life. No one would want that for you."

My grandmother would.

Changing her stance, Nikki crouches in front of Avery and takes her hands.

"Look, Logan's great. If you're not ready for anything, that's fine. But if you are, then you should go for it! Nick and Declan would want you to be happy and I will do anything I can to help you see that. I'm a great friend that way," she says with a signature saucy grin. Continuing, she commands, "But either way, we have a fair to get to so go take a shower and wear something cute."

With a heavy heart, Avery makes her way to her bedroom and readies herself for the afternoon. Her joyful mood from this morning has been subdued by this angst-filled emotion she has become far too familiar with.

Maybe Nikki is right, she thinks, pawing listlessly through her closet. Maybe she should be happy and just live her life. Figuring out how will be the challenge.

RENEE HARLESS

L OGAN PULLS INTO THE driveway that leads to his home, excitement coursing through him, and finds Austin patiently sitting in his truck, awaiting his arrival.

"Hey man, what's up?" Logan asks as they both exit their vehicles and make their way to the front door.

"Heard we're all going to the fair today."

Damn. Guess there won't be any alone time with Avery.

"Yep, it's what Avery wants to do today."

"Avery?" he questions, tossing his keys onto the counter.

"Yep. She beat me in a card game last night so I'm her bitch-of-sorts for a day."

An explosion of laughter escapes from Austin's mouth and Logan can't help but chuckle along.

"Well, if I was to be a bitch to anyone, she would definitely be it. Smoking, man. She is smoking hot."

"Yea, Yea."

Turning to head down the hall towards his bedroom, Logan leaves Austin to rummage around in his kitchen for something to grub on.

"You hit that last night?"

Of course Austin would ask. Austin's never met a girl he didn't bed that same night. Avery is currently the exception.

"Uh, no. We're just friends, man."

"Huh," he replies, except it isn't so much a *huh* of "I can't hear you," but more like he had never heard of this concept before.

"Yea, you should try it sometime."

Moving towards his bathroom, Logan turns on the water and steps beneath the hot spray. His thoughts immediately move to the woman in question and he can't help but remember the way her body felt pressed against his on the couch. Or the way her kiss started as hesitant, but quickly morphed to match his movements. Her kiss was so sweet, yet aggressive. Just thinking about the night is enough to get his dick standing at attention. Boy, did he want Avery. She unleashed something inside him that he thought had long ago been buried beneath the piles of rubble that made his heart. And Logan didn't just want her for her body, though perfection was on the tip of his tongue in describing her anatomy, and he had only seen her fully clothed. No, he wanted her for more. Logan hadn't ever been able to hold a conversation with someone, without any effort, the way he had with her. They just clicked - it was effortless.

She is an enigma to say the least. Logan couldn't figure out what it was that made her tick. Why she was so withdrawn from life. He could tell that she worked extremely hard to stay in the shadows; to keep from forming connections. It was the way she talked, the way she moved, the way she masked her emotions. She is reserved, and he is determined to breathe life into her.

And if that brings her to his bed, then Logan wouldn't complain. Man, did he want to fuck her. Pound her hard into the mattress. Smack her ass from behind as he shoves his cock into her pussy.

UGH!

His dick starts throbbing and the hot water spurting from the shower head feels like pin-pricks across the shaft. Closing his eyes, Logan pictures Avery's face and body as she writhes in ecstasy, an orgasm sneaking up on as his tongue works frantically between her legs. His hand rubs his dick back and forth, mesmerized in his vision, until he ferociously erupts against the shower wall.

Disappointed in himself, Logan knows he needs to get himself together. She only wants a friendship and he wants to keep her in his life so that's what they'll be.

But if she ever comes around, he'll be waiting.

Arriving at the fair before the girls, Austin and Logan head to a food vendor to grab a drink while they wait.

Women eyeball them, sending them come hither looks as they stroll past, some even with men by their side. Austin and Logan can't do much more than shake their heads and smirk to themselves. This happens pretty much wherever they go, especially if they're together. Logan can understand the reaction. They're both good-looking – over six feet tall, muscular with broad shoulders, and they have the tall and handsome thing woman go for.

Austin sends a wink to a couple of the women; playboy that he is, he eats up the attention, while Logan prefers to ignore the advances.

Finally, Logan sees Nikki approaching with Avery trailing behind her, tugging at a short denim skirt wrapped around her thighs. He feels himself choking on his tongue. Literally, he can't swallow and he has to cough a couple of times just to catch his breath.

Avery is a walking vision of sex. Glancing down, he notices she has on a pair of worn cowboy boots, showcasing her toned legs, the short denim skirt of every man's dreams that just barely covers her to mid-thigh. A dark blue flannel shirt with the tails tied loosely at her waist hints at just a bit of skin above her skirt; the blue flannel enhancing the exotic color of her eyes.

As she walks up to him, Logan reaches forward and runs his hand through the silky waves of her hair, which hangs loosely around her shoulders.

"Do I look ok? Nikki made me change six times," she huffs quietly as she peers coquettishly into his eyes.

"You're beautiful, Avery," Logan replies, mesmerized by her. "You could wear a potato sack and still be beautiful."

Redness arises like waves across her skin and she bites her lip as she considers Logan's response.

"Thank you. I haven't dressed like this…well…ever. Nikki is so much shorter than me that I think my bottom is hanging out of this skirt."

Taking his chances, Logan twists to take a peek at her behind and, though remarkably perfect, it is completely hidden by the light denim.

Trying to loosen up her mood he assures, "You're good. Nothing is hanging out, but I can keep my hands there if you want, just in case." He holds up his hands in question.

She giggles momentarily and the sound is the most exquisite noise he's ever heard. Like the melodic song of an angel. She must have noticed his entrapment by her laugh because she quickly hardens her expression and sinks back into herself.

"Hm...," she says, glancing in the direction of Austin and Nikki, "do you think they'll come up for air anytime soon?"

Turning his head into their direction, Logan has to bite back a laugh. If he doesn't break them apart from their interlude, they may very well need a bedroom.

"Hey guys, want to get some lunch first or ride a few rides?"

"Lunch," Austin replies as he pulls back from Nikki, but continues to eat her up with his eyes. "I'm hungry," he follows up with a growl.

Hoping that they'll follow - instead of making every effort to get themselves kicked out of the fair - Logan takes Avery's hand, tightening his hold, knowing that at any second she'll try to pull away, and makes his way over to the food booth.

Everyone orders a turkey leg, Logan and Austin both laughing when they see the looks of surprise on Avery and Nikki's faces as they realize that the turkey legs are as big as their heads.

Logan may have snapped a picture or two with his phone at their flabbergasted expressions.

After finishing their lunch, during which Austin and Logan took the liberty of finishing the rest of the girls', they direct themselves to the games in hopes of letting the food settle before moving onto the rides.

Avery manages to kick their asses. He doesn't know how anyone can be so skilled at every game she touches, but when he ask her about it she simply shrugs her shoulders and hands him a giant teddy bear that she's won.

Holding onto the ridiculously large teddy bear, which in turn keeps him from holding Avery's hand, Logan follows alongside her as they head towards the rides. He notices out of the corner of his eye that Avery continues to glance back toward the picnic tables, eyeing the little girl they passed when they walked in.

They proceed to get in line for the Ferris wheel, but Logan can tell that Avery is distracted. She keeps biting her lip and wringing her hands; her eyes darting around the queue line. Suddenly she jerks, and before he has a chance to react, she yanks the bear from his grasp, jumps over the queue chains and makes a mad dash away from the ride.

"Avery! Wait up! Where are you going!?!" Logan shouts as he tries to escape the throngs of people in the line; his large frame not nearly as agile as Avery.

Continuing to run after her, people politely move out of his way as Logan mutters a few expletives.

He finally finds Avery crouched in front of the table where the little girl continues to sit, her parents now flanking her sides. Logan stays back and watches their interaction. The little girl beams up at Avery, hanging onto her every word. She must be telling her a story. And then

Avery gives the girl her bear, which is at least twice the child's size, and she illuminates.

Avery turns around and walks away, stealing a single glance behind her and sending another wave before heading out of the picnic area.

Astounded, Logan is so moved by her sweet gesture that he can't stop himself from grabbing her arm as she walks by and dragging her behind the gaming booths. She doesn't even have the chance to question his intentions before he has her pressed up against the wooden planks, his hands cupping her face, kissing her mercilessly.

Something in him snapped and he could no longer control his need for her.

Her hands gently rest on his waist, searing the skin beneath his shirt. Logan removes one of his hands from her face and reaches down to stroke the skin on the outside of her thigh, just below her skirt. A low moan breezes past her lips and he takes that as a cue that she wants more; he should have known better. As he skates his fingertips across to her inner thigh, inching up her skirt as he goes, her hands quickly move to his chest and forcibly push him back. He has to actually catch himself from stumbling.

"Please, stop," she urges. "I can't," she sighs, her breaths coming in fast little gasps, "I can't do this. I'm sorry."

The look of utter despair in her eyes is enough to bring any man down to his knees and Logan is no exception.

Hands up in an act of surrender, Logan closes the distance between the two of them.

"I'm sorry, Avery. Something came over me and I lost control. It won't happen again, I swear," he pleads as a vice grip tightens around the pieces of his heart.

He knew that he had overstepped the boundary she placed, but he feels so drawn to her, like a magnetic pull that has him questioning everything he ever thought of women.

She continues to look down at her feet, twisting her leg back and forth on the tip of her boot. Using his index finger, Logan tilts her head up by her chin and bites back a curse when he sees the tears swimming in her eyes. He quickly pulls her into a hug, wrapping her tightly in his grasp, as he whispers how sorry he is over and over again.

When he feels like she has calmed down, Logan pulls her back from where she rested against him and smiles.

"Why don't we go have some fun, ok? We still need to get a few rides under our belts."

She replies softly, lacking any assurance of excitement, "Ok."

He refrains from grasping her hand when they return to the line for the Ferris wheel, instead opting to tuck his hands deep inside the front pockets of his jeans.

They patiently wait in line, neither of them broaching conversation. He can't help but think about how he screwed up. His dick took over his thinking skills and messed up any hope he had of being with Avery. Right now she can barely look at him, finding the tip of her boot more interesting than her companion.

Their turn to load the car comes and he move to step up the ramp, but he notices Avery doesn't budge.

"Hey," Logan says, nudging her shoulder, "you ready to ride?"

She nods her head and apologizes before stepping in the car.

The ride jolts as it starts and causes the cars to rock back and forth; the commotion causing Avery to grasp his forearm.

"Sorry," she expresses as she pulls her hand back, looking at the palm of her hand tentatively as she does so.

And Logan knows she felt it - that spark; that fire; that electricity that surges between their touch.

She looks at him, her blue eyes wide in question, and he can do no more than shrug in explanation. There is no justification to the feeling. It's not something he has ever read in medical textbooks. It's something only ever mentioned in movies and novels; Logan never thought the sensation was real.

"You ok, Avery?"

"Yea," she mutters as she turns her gaze away from him. "Oh wow, would you look at that? It's beautiful."

Turning his attention to where she has her gaze pinned, Logan had to admit the view is remarkable. The sun shines brightly on the mountainous tree tops and between the valleys sits the county's lake. It really is a picturesque town and he's glad that he gets to share this moment with Avery.

"Gorgeous."

Taking a chance, Logan snakes his fingers through hers as they rest on her lap and, to his surprise, she leans to the side and rests her head on his shoulder. They sit like this as the car continues to rise to the top and then descends to the bottom five more times.

As they exit the Ferris wheel, they find Nikki and Austin waiting for them.

"Let's get some grub and then we can head over to the dance," Austin directs as Nikki snuggles into his side, Austin casting an affectionate look in her direction.

Logan notices this quick exchange, but opts not to mention it. He wouldn't have thought of them pursuing something serious together, but seeing them like this changes his mind.

"Dance?" Avery asks as she cocks an eyebrow in his direction.

And Logan's dick throbs as her come hither stare.

Adjusting himself subtly, he simply nods his head yes and lets her know that she'll have fun. Not that he plans on dancing; line dancing isn't really his forte.

Nikki steps away from Austin and takes Avery by the arm, escorting her to the giant corndogs. Austin and Logan stay planted to the ground as they watch the girl's hips swaying as they walk away. Apparently they've garnered the attention of a few onlookers as well, because a handful of wolf-whistles and cat-calls echo above the crowd. The girls don't even notice, too busy talking amongst themselves.

"I want her," Austin mutters to himself.

"I know the feeling," Logan murmurs in reply.

Boy, do I know the feeling.

The men trail behind the girls like lost souls, entranced by their siren song.

Nikki tugs Avery onto the dance floor the moment they cross the barrier and they immediately fall into step for a song Austin says is called the *Electric Slide*. Logan doesn't feel the need to question how or why he knows this.

Once the song switches, the girls are swooped up by some of the older men and shown how to "two-step," Austin once again informs Logan.

"How do you know so much about country dancing?"

"Uh, because I was born and raised here?" he replies, as if Logan had asked a ridiculous question.

Noticing how the man who is dancing with Nikki trails his hand a little low for Austin's liking, he stalks onto the dance floor and effortlessly pulls her into step with him. Avery stifles a giggle at Austin's caveman antics and sends a look of challenge in Logan's direction.

Good luck little lady. That ain't going to happen.

Swaying back and forth with a chick's ass pressed up against him is more Logan's style. But suddenly a slow song begins to blare from the speakers and Logan finds himself inching towards Avery.

"May I cut in?" he asks, gesturing with a full bow and hand extension.

He hears her laugh and sees her look up as she steps away from "Carl" and takes Logan's hand.

Continuing to laugh she divulges, "About time you joined me."

"Mmhmm, maybe you like them older," he says jokingly as he pulls her closer to him, not an inch between them.

"Maybe," she grins saucily. "Guess we'll never know."

Smiling back at her, Logan does his best to pull her even closer. She wraps one arm tighter around his neck, the other resting on his chest holding his hand, and leans her head on his shoulder. Logan inhales her sweet scent – spring and vanilla.

They continue to sway, even as the song changes to another fast-tempo beat. Lost in their own little world, they both jump apart when Austin and Nikki rock into them. A dark flush covers Avery's petite face and Logan has to work to hold back his laughter.

They all exit the dance hall and head back towards their vehicles, where it takes an immense amount of Logan's willpower to not walk Avery back to Nikki's car and kiss her goodbye. Instead, he opts for holding her hand and offering a quick, but tight, hug as they all move in different directions. He could have held her in his arms all night.

And that thought alone, as much as it should, doesn't terrify him.

*T*AKING A DEEP BREATH as she slides into Nikki's car, Avery can't help but feel a bit overwhelmed. Her response to Logan isn't something she has ever felt before. He ignites something in her - literally kick-starting her heart. The pounding in her chest only intensifies when he brushes up against her or holds her close. She can't even describe the feeling of his lips against hers, it's – otherworldly.

Avery can feel Nikki's smug look burning into her from the driver's seat. She doesn't think she has seen a face so haughty since she watched *How the Grinch stole Christmas* when she was ten.

"What?" Avery inquires innocently.

Nikki arches one of her perfect eyebrows at her, as if Avery should know why she is staring at her in that manner.

"Seriously, why are you looking at me like that?"

In a perfect sing-songy voice she replies, "You like Logan. You like Logan."

What? Are we in second grade?

"Stop, Nikki."

"Nope, you haven't stopped smiling since we got here."

That much is true, except for her moment in line at the Ferris wheel, but Nikki wasn't there to witness that course of events.

Intent on not sharing her feelings, Avery turns away from Nikki and stares out the window while saying, "You don't know what you're talking about."

Put out, Nikki huffs and starts the car before heading back home towards the apartment.

They both enter the residence, lost in their own thoughts, as they make their way to their prospective bedrooms.

The next morning Avery wakes early after a fitful night of sleep. Dreams of Logan plagued her throughout the night and she couldn't fight off the nightmares. Sitting up in bed Avery thinks back to the visions. They would start off the same; Logan and she would be in bed, him kissing and caressing every inch of her body, leaving no spot untouched. Then the moment before she would reach her pinnacle, the dream would shade to darkness and switch to another vision, one that just thinking about while awake sends shivers down her spine. Logan was lying on the medical building's floors, clutching at a knife wedged deep in his chest, but every time he would touch the cold steel, the knife sank further into his skin.

So messed up!

Avery shakes her head, trying to rid herself of the gruesome and somber thoughts. Before bed she had considered giving things a go with Logan, but now she was seriously considering removing him from her life completely. Not after remembering the things that happen to the people she loves. She can't risk his life like that.

Making her way to the kitchen in some serious need of coffee, Avery practically drops her mug when an urgent knock on the door distracts her. She checks the clock on the wall first, 6:00am, and notices Nikki's door is still shut.

She checks the peephole first and flings the door open-wide when she finds a frantic Logan waiting on the other side.

"Logan, what are you…" she begins to say, but is silenced as his lips press earnestly against her own.

He pulls away once, and releases one word after another between kisses, "I…Needed…To…See…You."

Loving the feel of his kiss, she indulges him momentarily, not caring in the slightest that she has on old boxer shorts and a t-shirt, her hair rumpled from sleep, and is certain she has a terrible case of morning breath. No, his kiss works better than any coffee she could have ever concocted.

Knowing she needs to slow things down she steps back from Logan, but keeps her hands resting on his chest.

"Logan, what's going on?" she inquires, her eyes darting back and forth, looking into his.

He takes one of his hands from her hips and runs his fingers through his unruly dark hair. As he struggles to streamline his breathing, Avery takes in his appearance. He looks gorgeous, as always, in dark denim and a burgundy long-sleeved fitted shirt, but his face looks tired, and his eyes look poignant, almost frightened. He walks past her and leans against their kitchen counter, eyes cast to the floor.

"I don't mean to barge in on you like this. I just…," he says as he runs his hands through his hair one more time, shaking his head in disbelief, then looks in her direction, "You're going to think I'm crazy. I had a dream about you last night. It started off really hot. Like, wow, kind of hot. And then it just switched, like that," he snaps his fingers to emphasize his point, but dread already fills Avery's tired bones.

"Then I just see flashes of images – me lying in a pool of blood on the office floor with a knife in my chest, you saving me by pulling the knife out, and then you stabbing yourself with the knife; fucking Romeo and Juliet shit. I tried to wake up then, I'm sure I was fucking screaming, but I couldn't open my eyes. The last thing I saw was a bird on fire - a phoenix, I think. I'm so messed up about this, Avery. I don't ever dream when I sleep, at least not to the point where I actually remember them."

Turning to face her, his alarm rises when he takes in her expression.

"Hey, why did you get so pale? Are you alright?"

He walks over to where she stands, perched on the back of the couch, and places his strong hands on both of her cheeks, running his thumbs along her cheek bones.

Avery swallows hard before allowing the words to trail past her lips. "I had the same dream," she whispers. "That's crazy, right? I mean I only had the vision of you, none of the others, but it's freaking weird. You think it's weird, right?"

"I do, but right now I just want to hold you, please? I know you don't want more, but I need to feel you in my arms."

She doesn't respond, instead wraps her arms tightly around his waist and holds on tight.

No place else I would rather be. Except...

"Do you want to try to get some sleep? I didn't sleep well either," Avery says, fighting unsuccessfully to hold back a yawn, unable to process the words escaping her mouth until it's too late. "Um, what I mean is..,"

"Avery, I would love to lay with you. I could use a few more hours."

Nodding her head, she steps away from his warm embrace and guides him to her bedroom. As she pulls back the covers from her freshly made bed, he works at removing his socks and shoes. When she turns to move to her normal side of the bed she catches herself staring at his muscular chest, abs, and arms.

Holy cow.

Logan has the body of a god. I mean, I knew he was muscular, but my goodness, I was severely underestimating him. And what is that a six, no, make that an eight pack? I didn't even know those existed.

She drops her gaze quickly and skirts around the bed, hoping to all that is Holy he doesn't notice the blood rushing to her cheeks or that she has to raise her hand to her chin to wipe away any drool.

As Avery tucks herself under the covers and settles into place, Logan looks at her and nods to the button of his jeans, his fingers placed on either side of the metal, silently asking permission to remove the article of clothing. She nods quickly and finds herself blushing again, so she buries herself deep into the soft sheets and down comforter.

Logan's jeans glide down his legs and pool at his feet, revealing a pair of black boxer briefs and toned, muscular legs. He bends down to grab his pants and places them on the chair with his shirt and then struts his way over to the empty side of the bed.

Slinking into the sheets, Logan pulls the sheets up around him and turns his head to look at her. Avery continues to look at the ceiling, silently willing him to turn away from her.

"You ok?"

"No, I'm not," she breathes, struggling to hold back frightened tears.

"Look, let's get a couple hours of sleep and then we can search the internet on dream meanings, ok? Even though it freaked me out too, I know that what you dream about is just a metaphor for something else; it's not a prediction of the future."

Angrily, Avery swipes at the few tears that managed to break away.

"You don't know that, Logan! I can't do it again."

"Do what, Avery? I know you're scared. I was scared too, but it was just a dream."

The waterfall of tears continues to cascade down her cheeks unchecked; the feeling of loss so utterly powerful that she can't control her reaction.

"Come here, baby," Logan whispers, tugging her into his arms and resting her head on his shoulder.

He murmurs words of assurance into her ear, with the hope to calm her down and it works. Her breaths turn shallow and she relaxes into Logan's warm hold.

They wake three hours later, to the sound of front door slamming. When she opens her eyes, Avery is met with a beautiful pair of hazel irises. Reaching up with her hand, before she has the chance for her mind to take over, she runs her fingers softly along Logan's jaw of scruff. She had assumed it would have felt bristly, but is pleasantly surprised by its softness.

A moan rumbles low in her throat when Logan's fingers run through her hair and Avery can feel a certain part of him, an already large part, begin to grow against her thigh.

Goodness, he's big.

"If you keep making noises like that and looking at me that way I won't be able to control myself."

Quickly moving her hand from his chin, Avery placed it back on his chest, hoping it is a safer territory. It's not. When her fingertips brush across his pectorals, a muffled growl grows from deep in his chest and she finds herself suddenly resting on her back with Logan hovering above her, his now generous member pressing against her stomach.

A look crosses his face, a look she hasn't seen before, but it instantly heats her from the inside.

"Avery, I'm going to kiss you now and then you're going to tell me why I'm not supposed to do it again, got it?"

Not offering a chance for her to reply, Logan pursues her mouth as if it's his last meal. At his insistence, Avery opens her mouth to his explorative tongue and meets his every movement. But true to his word they only kiss, even though Logan could overpower her easily and take what he wanted without much fight. His kiss turns her on more than anything she has ever experienced.

When Logan pulls away, Avery has a hard time deciphering the time, it feels like they had been kissing for ages by the bruising she could feel forming on her lips, but at the same time, it feels like time had halted, that there was no one else but them.

"Avery, I need to know why we can't be more than friends."

"Why?" Avery asks irritably. "That's all I can offer you right now or maybe ever."

"Is it me? You just don't want to date me?" he demands, rising from the bed and moving to the chair to pull on his clothes.

Well this morning has definitely taken a turn.

Sitting up in bed, Avery says to him in annoyance, "No, it's not you. It's not anyone. It's me. I'm not ready. I may never be."

Tugging on his shoes, he comes to stand beside the bed, resting his hands beside her, bringing his face close to hers.

"Then tell me why, Avery. I know you feel this between us. I'm not even romantic and I know that we have something special. Fuck, Avery, I knew you were special when I saw you through the window the night you arrived.

I mean, I'm going against everything I ever said about woman because I want this with you. So please, tell me why. Tell me what I have to do."

"I'm not ready, Logan," Avery chokes, a muffled sob escaping, "It hurts. It hurts too much to talk about."

Standing up from the bed, Logan moves to her bedroom door, but turns one more time and asks, "Will you ever be ready, Avery?"

Choking on another howl of despair, Avery replies lightly, "I don't know."

Logan hastily nods his head once, a look of confusion and rejection crossing his face, before opening her bedroom door to exit.

He must have run into Nikki in the hallway, because Avery hears him say that she may need her.

As the front door closes, Nikki rushes into Avery's bedroom and holds her close as she continues weeping helplessly.

"It hurts," Avery cries between hiccups. "It hurts so much."

"That's because you guys have something special. I told you that from the get-go. Anyone around you could see it. Don't worry, Avery. It'll all work out. I promise."

Nikki leaves briefly to grab some tissues from the bathroom and wipes Avery's eyes; she listens to Avery's dream and offers some insight from a psychology class she had taken in High School.

"Knife dreams - stabbings in particular - can symbolize, guilt, conflict, resistance. Your dream could mean that you feel guilty for wanting to pursue something with Logan and that you're angry about having to upend your life."

"So… it's not so cut and dry?"

"No, dreams never are."

Nikki tucks a piece of hair behind her ear and sighs, then divulges a secret of her own, "Austin told me he doesn't want to be exclusive."

"Why?" Avery gasps, momentarily distracted from the ache in her chest.

"He just said he wasn't ready. Whatever," Nikki said, rolling his eyes, "He's almost thirty. I think he's scared."

"I'm so sorry, Nikki. Logan said he acted differently with you."

"Oh, I know. I'm pretty observant. Austin doesn't realize that I know how he usually is and he wasn't like that with me. So I decided I'm going to have a broken heart day. Want to join me?"

Wiping her nose, Avery nods her head in agreement. "Yes, please."

Helping her from the bed, Nikki mumbles seemingly to herself as she helps her make the bed.

"You need to tell him, Avery. He deserves to know."

Avery doesn't respond. Instead, she follows Nikki to the living room and plants herself on the couch for the next five hours, indulging herself in chocolate cake and chick flicks.

7 WO WEEKS PASS AND Avery tries to find a moment at work to speak to Logan, though, in all honesty, she hasn't tried very hard. She can tell he has been avoiding her, seemingly buried under work when she would be just about to ask for a minute of his time… but she knew better. She would have avoided her too, she

supposes, especially with the way she led him on and then ended things.

As she stands in the hall, contemplating her next move and making notations in a patient record, Dr. Fields pulls her aside and asks her how she thinks the job is going. Avery discloses to him that she's happy, but she knows he is afraid she may up and go at any moment. It's not like she doesn't have the income to do so if she wanted. But what he doesn't realize is that she doesn't want the money, though she has had a few ideas regarding how to use it. Trying to ease Dr. Fields' apprehension, Avery brings forth her thoughts.

"Dr. Fields, is there a reason no one has pursued opening a pediatric clinic in the town? I mean, with the way it's growing, it seems like a good solution for your influx of patients."

"We've looked into it, but the startup money is a bit more than we can invest right now. We even have a building in mind that is due to be torn down soon - an old school about two blocks down on Main Street - but it would need extensive work." He sighs. "We really could use the help though. We are seeing more and more kids these days, and pediatrics isn't any of our specialties."

"Please keep this private, but what if I was looking to invest in a pediatric facility. Would you be able to help me navigate through all of it?"

"Absolutely, Avery. If it's really something you think you want to do, I can have the contractor we've been speaking with give you a call."

"Yes, please. This is definitely something I would like to spend that trust on."

"Well, I'll keep it to myself until you let me know otherwise. Now, do you need a ride home today?"

"No, sir. I picked up my new car yesterday evening. An Audi SUV. It's so pretty."

"I saw it out in the lot when I arrived this morning; suits you. We'll I'm off, don't stay too long."

"I won't. Have a good night, Al."

Dr. Fields waves as he walks out the office and luckily, after ten minutes, Avery is leaving behind him.

She spots Logan in the parking lot and she waves in his direction, the look on his face is one of irritation so she knows now isn't the time to speak with him.

"Nice car," he shouts across the lot.

"Thanks."

He quickly slides into his vehicle, halting any further conversation. Following his lead, Avery piles herself into the driver seat of her new vehicle and drives back to her apartment, downtrodden. She had been hoping to have rectified her situation with Logan at this point, but nothing seems to be working in her favor.

When Avery arrives at the apartment complex, she finds that Nikki hasn't arrived yet, so she stops and picks up the mail. Opening the front door, Avery slips on an envelope that had been slid under their door, almost tumbling to the ground as she reaches for the wall. Retrieving the ill-fated item from the floor, Avery glides her finger under the flap to open the package and takes out a large, stapled pile of papers. Amongst the legal-looking paper work is a letter - in her grandmother's perfect cursive handwriting.

Avery,

I hope this letter finds you well, and if it has, that means that I have passed. My attorney suggested that I write this to you as I finalized my will, so here it is.

Seeing her grandmother ramble on in letterform, or any form really, is not something Avery had ever expected.

I need to apologize for a lot, or really, for everything. You never deserved to have me treat you the way that I had when you were growing up. I let my shame rule our household and I took my daughter's mistakes out on you. Words can't express how completely sorry I am for that.

A little late for that grandmother.

We did love you, your grandfather and me. I'm sure you'll never believe that and I understand if you don't. I've kept an eye on you when you left with Aria and Mila. I hope you're enjoying Carson.

I was at both Mila and Aria's funerals. I never wanted you to see, so I hid. Losing Aria was a heartbreaking day and I knew at that moment that I needed to make amends somehow.

Now seems a bit late, I know.

You were always the brave one and I have no doubt that you will continue to be so. I'm not asking for your forgiveness, I know I don't deserve it after the way I treated you and your sister.

All I ask is that you live your life. I didn't, and I regret every moment of it.

I'm sorry for all the things you've had to endure, more than most, but you're strong, Avery, and you deserve the moon and the stars.

Don't think of me. Don't think of your mother. Think of you. Think of Mila and Aria. Think of Nick and Declan (yes, I know about them, too.). They would want you to have everything you wanted.

Make yourself happy. We all love you,

Your Grandmother Poindexter

P.S. Inside my will, which you need to take to a lawyer, is your father's name and address. I kept up with him too. It's nice to have a private investigator in the family. From what I know he never knew about you, so please don't be angry at him. He has a wonderful family that can give you all the love we never provided. It's up to you.

An onslaught of emotions races through Avery, scattering her thoughts every which way, as she rushes across the apartment. She tosses the letter and the will onto her bed before fleeing back outside to her car.

Racing away from the complex, Avery plugs the address she had stolen from work a week ago into her GPS, heading for the one place where she knows she will feel safe.

Chapter Five

*L*OGAN STOPPED BY AUSTIN'S parents' house on his way home. When he first moved to Carson, Austin's parents immediately embraced him and treated him as if he were one of their own. It was a nice sensation, feeling wanted and loved. Austin comes from a big family, six kids all together, and his parents show love and affection equally. It's a great environment to be a part of.

Today had been another rough one. Seeing Avery in the parking lot brought another pang to his chest, identical to the aches he's experienced for the last two weeks. He had no choice but to ignore her at work, because every time he looked at her, the urge to wrap her in his arms and never let go was almost irresistible.

While eating dinner with Joseph and Amy, Austin's parents, Amy instantly questions him, carefully trying to determine what was wrong. He didn't tell her anything more than that he wished he had grown up with her as a mother – though the thought only depresses him more.

Austin's family had invited him to hang around for a bit after the meal, but an overwhelming urge to head home was burned into the back of his brain. So after saying his goodbyes, he slid into his car and made his way back to the old Craftsman rental home.

Turning into his driveway, Logan is surprised to find Avery's SUV sitting sedentary in front of the garage. More shocking is that he finds her sitting on his steps, hunched over, head resting on her knees.

Now Logan understands that nagging sensation he had felt at dinner: she must have been upset and waiting for him. Their connection is so strong, so solid, that he can sense her emotions from miles away.

She doesn't budge as he pulls into the drive or as he steps out of the vehicle. At first, he suspected she had fallen asleep waiting for him, but as he hesitantly approaches her, Logan can hear the soul-crushing sobs wracking her body.

He wastes no time with questions, instead, he scoops her up into his arms and gently carries her into his home. Resting her on the couch, Logan leaves her momentarily to heat up some water for some tea. It's what Amy always does for her girls when they're upset.

The ceramic of the cup clanks against the wood as it is placed on the coffee table, alerting Avery of her surroundings.

"I'm sorry," she says between sniffles, wiping her nose with the back of her hand. "I didn't know where else to go."

Even though her face is blotched and red, wetness is dripping freely from her eyes and nose and her hair a knotted mess, Logan still feels his heart lurch. She's easily one of the most beautiful creatures he's ever laid eyes on.

"Take a few breaths and tell me what's wrong."

Situating himself in the corner of his sectional couch, he pulls her to rest against his side, offering her comfort. He waits patiently as Avery takes deep breaths, hoping to calm herself down.

"You're not going to like what I have to tell you."

"I doubt that's true, but we won't know until you tell me."

"Right."

She takes a few more deeps breaths - in through her nose, out through her mouth - and then she rests her head on his chest, pulling his arm tighter around her lithe body: using him as a shield from her demons.

"My grandmother passed away last week."

Logan looks down at her during her admission, but she offers no moment of silence for his commiserations.

"I hated her. With every fiber of my being, I hated her."

And then she launches into the story of her childhood, and of her sister, Aria. Logan is in complete awe at how strong this woman is - *his* woman. Because now, after listening to only a portion of her story, he can't help but feel an even deeper need to protect her.

"I was eighteen when I took Aria away from that hell. It's also when I met Nick. He was the sweetest guy I never knew I could have. And when he proposed I never thought twice about my answer."

Spurts of jealousy detonate beneath his skin, but Logan quickly squashes the emotion. He already knows the nature of this tale won't be a good one.

"I blame myself; one-hundred percent blame myself. Aria had a dentist appointment and I didn't think to reschedule my meeting to take her, so Nick offered. I hated having to depend on him to do it. But instead of coming up with another way, I thanked him and went on my way. And it was the weirdest thing; when we were all saying goodbye that morning, it was like we all knew something bad was going to happen. Nick and Aria were crushed at an intersection when a tractor-trailer overturned, taking a right-handed turn too tight. He was carrying some big highway concrete material. Nick's little car didn't stand a chance."

"Oh, Avery. I'm so sorry, sweetheart."

Avery doesn't even acknowledge his sympathy. She shrugs her shoulders and continues.

"I don't remember grieving, per se, I simply lived day-to-day to finish school and get a job. It's what Mila had worked so hard for and I refused to disappoint her. I got a job working with Nikki's cousin, Melanie, and her now-husband, Max. Of course, I worked with them prior to their elopement." For a moment, she chuckles quietly, a whisper of a smile crossing her lips,
"Ha, I didn't even know they were interested in each other. That's how much I paid attention to the goings on around me.

"Anyway, we were all working one day, when this guy Declan is at the main desk talking to Max. I hadn't met anyone like him before and he really wasn't what I would have thought I'd ever be attracted to, but I was. He was totally cocky and didn't even give me a chance to turn down a date. He pulled me out of the fog I had been in and I thought that finally my life was going to turn around.

"We talked about marriage about six months after we started dating. We were both really excited." She stares into the distance, unblinking. "Then he got sick - really sick. He had an inoperable brain tumor that continued to grow, crushing everything in its path. As you can imagine, he didn't last much longer after the diagnosis. I lasted two more years after he passed away before Melanie gave me the chance to move here and start over.

"I kill the people I love Logan and I refuse to let something happen to you. I don't even know if I have anything left to give you, but I know I don't have any more strength to watch you die."

Logan sits there in silence as she wipes the tears from under her eyes. He can't say it doesn't hurt to hear that she had been claimed before, that if not for these horrific accidents in her life, they never would have crossed paths.

"I'm sorry, Avery. No one should ever have to go through what you've been through, heck, not even a smidgen of what you've been through. I wish I would have had the chance to meet Aria, Nick, and Declan, especially seeing how much you loved them."

"You probably didn't want to hear about other men, but I needed you to understand."

"Understand what?"

She looks up at him, a shocked and confused expression on her face.

"Understand why I can't be more than friends with you."

"Avery," Logan says, reaching up and bringing her face closer to his, "We're already more than friends."

And then he seals his lips over hers to prove his point. And just as he expected, her body responds immediately. She makes no move to touch him, but her kiss says everything she refuses to verbalize.

Pulling herself away, she keeps her face a few inches from his.

"I don't want anything to happen to you. I wouldn't be able to handle it. I don't know when or how, but you already mean more than anyone else has, ever."

"Don't think that way. We'll take it slow and go one day at a time, ok?"

"Hmm," she hesitantly replies. She brushes her fingers along his chest, nervously biting her lip before she continues, "That's not all though. In my grandmother's will she left me my father's name and address. She said he didn't even know about me. I don't know if I should try to seek him out."

"Well, it's not like you have a time limit. Just think about it for a while, and when you make your decision, I can go with you if you'd like."

"You'd do that for me?"

"Haven't you realized yet that I'd do about anything for you? I've been miserable staying away from you, Avery."

"Me too," she murmurs quietly. "I'm sorry I have been so stubborn, but I'm so scared, Logan. It's going to take me a long time to let go of the fear."

"Have you eaten?" he asks suddenly, tenderly stroking the side of her face.

She ducks her head and shakes it in response.

"Well, let me make something for you real quick and then I'll run you a bath, ok?"

"You don't have to go through all that trouble," she replies, beginning to rise from the couch.

Finger on her chin, he tips her head towards him and simply states, "Avery, I'm more than happy to," then leans forward and kisses her again.

Damn, she tastes good.

Adjusting himself on the way to the kitchen, he opens up a bottle of red wine that Austin's sister Cassidy had given him for his birthday. Logan brings the glass to Avery where she remains unmoved on his sofa, but she manages to squeak out a thank you.

Back in the kitchen, Logan decides to whip up a quick chicken and pasta alfredo. As he stirs the sauce with a wooden spoon, all the information Avery disclosed churns helplessly through his mind.

My god, has she been through some shit.

Her mother was non-existent; her grandmother abused her and her sister, and worse of all, she had to endure the deaths of her guardian, her sister, and not one, but *two* fiancés. Even though Logan doesn't want to dwell on the fact that she has been engaged twice, he can't imagine losing two different people that you had once planned on spending your life with. His chest physically aches when he thinks about losing her. His reaction to the dream he had about two weeks ago only cements his feelings for Avery. Logan would be devastated, utterly and completely devastated, if she was no longer in his life.

Lost in his own reveries, Logan doesn't notice when Avery walks into his kitchen and rests against the counter beside the stove. He startles when he hears her sorrowful sigh and he looks into her eyes, seeing the exhaustion written there; not just from today, but from the years of mourning.

"Smells good."

"Thanks, it'll be ready in about twenty. Why don't you go ahead and take that bath and I'll get you when it's ready?"

She smiles, but the creases don't reach her eyes, more like she's acting complacent.

"Great, let me get it ready for you."

Heading into his master bathroom, he fills the claw-foot tub he had Austin install when they renovated the place. It was his understanding that women love these kinds of tubs, and Logan aimed to please. Now he is even more satisfied with his choice knowing that Avery will feel comfortable.

He pours in some vanilla and lavender oils to the water, courtesy of Austin's mom, Amy. When the water reaches a good level, he dims the overheads and lights a few candles. This should definitely help her relax.

Preparing to exit the bathroom, Logan turns to find Avery standing at the entrance; she must have followed.

She murmurs timidly, "You didn't have to go to all this trouble."

Logan walks closer to her and weaves his fingers in her hair; he knows she loves when he does this.

"I am happy to do this for you, Avery."

Leaning forward, she cautiously presses her lips against his in thanks, but as his body is so tightly wound, Logan reciprocates ten-fold. His fingers tighten in her hair, urging her closer. Her hands slip past his shirt and rub against his lower back, eliciting feelings that he knows shouldn't exist right now. He steps back from her embrace and she drops her hands in rejection, but as Logan looks in her eyes he doesn't find anything. No desire, no lust, just emptiness. She's hollow.

"Soon, sweetheart, but not now, not tonight."

Pressing a quick peck to her forehead, he exits the bathroom before he loses anymore self-control. The press of her lips against his drives him crazy.

Back in his bedroom, Logan removes a pair of boxers and a t-shirt from his dresser for her to wear when she finishes her bath.

Heading back to the kitchen he grabs her glass from the living room and refills it, placing it on the table for later.

As Logan waits for Avery to make her appearance, he is answering a few work emails when suddenly a text from Austin pops up.

> **Austin: Hey man, are you out? Have you seen Nikki?**
>
> **Me: Naw man I have Avery here so I don't know where Nikki is.**
>
> **Austin: Let me know if you or Avery hears anything. I think I screwed up big time.**
>
> **Me: I hope you find her. And I'll let you know if we hear anything.**
>
> **Austin: Thanks. Oh and get laid!**
>
> **Me: Eat a dick.**
>
> **Austin: Fuck you! Later bro.**

Me: Later

As Logan finishes his conversation, Avery stumbles into his kitchen, looking like a vision. Her cheeks redden as he gazes at her appreciatively. Never has Logan seen boxers and a t-shirt look so seductive – so entrancing.

"Dinners ready," he squeaks out, sounding like a pre-pubescent boy.

But I'll talk like that the remainder of the night if I receive the true and honest smile that currently graces her face.

"This looks great. Thank you. And your bath is a dream."

Holding the chair out for her, Logan slides her under the table once she plants herself on the seat.

"Well I'm glad I made a good investment; you're the first person to use it."

"Really? Why do you have it then if you don't take baths?"

"Do you really want the answer to that?" Logan says, chuckling under his breath. "In all seriousness, Al planned on flipping the house and reselling it to a family, but it sort of grew on me. Plus, Al lets me rent this thing for pennies."

"It's adorable; what I've seen of it anyway. Do you still flip homes?

"I try to fit it in when I can. Austin finds a property and when I have time, I help or I invest. We've made a pretty penny with all the newcomers that have flocked to our town. His entire family helps out, really."

"That's so neat. And to have the whole family involved."

"They're a great group. I'd love to introduce you sometime. Austin's parents are like the parents I never had."

She nods her head as she finishes off her plate of alfredo.

"This was great, Logan. Thank you."

"You're welcome, I was happy to do it. What do you want to do now? Watch some television? A movie?"

A look crosses Avery's face. One Logan can't decipher, so he holds his breath, waiting for her response.

"Logan, can you..." She fumbles for words for a moment, "Would you just hold me? Please?"

"I would be happy to, sweetheart. Let's go. I'll clean this up in the morning."

Taking her hand in his own, he directs her to his bedroom and tugs back the sheets so that she can climb into his large, four poster bed.

Logan turns his back to her as he removes his pants and shirt, then startles slightly when he hears her strong intake of air.

"What's the matter?"

"Your tattoo. It's incredible. I don't know how I missed it last time."

Smiling at her, he continues to remove his clothes before strolling over to the other side of the bed. Lying on his stomach, he leaves his back exposed for viewing and Avery wastes no time in exploring. Logan doesn't mention to her that the fingertip trails she weaves, back and forth over the feathers, is complete torture.

"They're wings," she whispers to herself.

Spanning the majority of his back and wrapping around his biceps are intricately detailed feathers, wings. The pain staking process took eight sessions of design and shading, but it was worth every second of agony. His friend Cliff did an amazing job.

"They represent my flight. My voyage to get away from the trash I grew up in and make something of myself."

Her breath coming heavier now, she says, "They're angel wings, Logan." Continuing to trace the feathers, she speaks to herself, "They seem so familiar."

Yanking her down from where she hovers beside him, Logan rests her back against his chest.

"Thank you for telling me everything." Logan says, placing kisses along her shoulder and neck.

"Thank you for listening and being open-minded."

Responding with a moan as his hand brushes across her breast, he feels her nipple harden under his touch, her gasp alerting him to her enjoyment.

"You need to stop, Logan," she says in a husky breath that insinuates the complete opposite, but he knows the moment isn't right, so he pulls his hand back and rests it against her waist.

"Sorry, darling. I'll control myself better."

And with a final kiss on her shoulder, Logan falls into the most peaceful sleep he's had in years. All thanks to this beautiful woman that trusts him to save her.

7 HE FEEL OF SAFETY and warmth envelopes Avery as she lies wrapped in Logan's arms, but duty calls and she slinks away from his

embrace to head to his restroom. Disclosing her tragic past with him yesterday evening removed this incredible weight that had so long been bearing down on her. She feels lighter, freer, as if she can breathe for the first time ever.

Opening the bathroom door slowly, as to not wake Logan, she find herself stopping mid-stride as she witnesses the beauty resting under crumpled sheets. Logan lies on his stomach, head turned to the direction she slept, the sun streaming in through the windows to the right. In this moment, with his tattoo in full view, he looks like an angel - halo and all.

Needing a way to capture this moment, Avery grabs her new phone from her purse, which is resting on the chair in the corner, and snaps a picture.

Finished with her business, she quietly closes the bedroom door. Avery strolls to the kitchen while checking her phone and listens to a voicemail that Nikki left late last night. Apparently, she had another fight with Austin and had gone to Savannah to stay with Melanie and Max for a few days.

Lifting her head from the phone's screen, Avery gasps as she notices the mess left in the kitchen and makes quick work of cleaning the dishes and storing them away. Once the last plate is put away, her stomach grumbles loudly. Checking his fridge, Avery grabs a pan, scrambles some eggs and fries up some bacon that she found.

She finishes plating her concoction and is pouring some orange juice when Logan walks into the kitchen, looking like a sex dream come to life. He's tugged on a pair of sweats that sit low on his waist, but the rest of him is bare. When she looks up at him, he runs a hand through his bed head and Avery can't help but find herself staring at his masculine beauty.

Apparently she must have stared too long because Logan says, "You alright? I don't think the cup can handle anymore juice."

Jerked out of her ogling, she straightens the juice container.

"I am so sorry!" Avery cries as she rushes to place the container back on the counter and grab some towels to clean up the mess. Tears begin to stream down her cheeks in both embarrassment and a long-engrained fear of disciplinary action – just one of the many take-aways from life with her grandmother. She wipes at the juice that has spilt from the cup, onto the table and floor, frantically trying to erase signs of her mistake.

"Avery, calm down. It's ok. Mistakes happen."

"I'm so sorry. I made a huge mess."

"Avery," he says as she continues to dab at the mess in haste. "Avery, stop!"

Taking a hold of her hand to stop her movements, he finally garners her attention.

"It's fine, sweetheart. Let me help you."

Grabbing a few more paper towels from the dispenser, they make easy work of cleaning up the juice. As they stand to toss the towels in the trash, Logan wipes his hand on the dishtowel that hangs over the edge of the sink, then places his hands gently on her sodden cheeks. Logan's thumbs gently brush away the wetness while he aptly gazes in her eyes.

"I missed you waking in my bed this morning."

"I'm sorry…for the mess I mean."

"It's ok. Breakfast looks great, but you're my guest, you didn't need to cook."

"I wanted to. I needed to thank you for last night."

"Sweetheart, you don't have to thank me for anything. I'll be here whenever you need me."

Avery nods her head in understanding and then stands back, moving her head from between Logan's grasp. Turning around, Logan pours half of the over-filled cup gracefully into the empty cup and gestures for her to sit down for breakfast.

Shoveling the food into his mouth, he barely ushers out a thank you.

"This is so good. Thank you. I usually don't get more than a protein shake in the mornings."

"You're welcome."

An awkward silence rests over the room and Avery keeps her eyes trained on her full plate – her appetite diminishing by the minute.

"Do you want to talk about last night?"

"Um...not really, no."

"Ok, I understand. Did you want to do anything today?"

"I didn't have anything in mind. I just want to forget everything going on in my life right now."

Logan looks at her longingly and with a bit of disappointment.

"Everything?" he asks.

And then understanding dawns on Avery; he's hurt.

She reaches out to touch the hand that rests on the table.

"Well, not you. I like being with you... though, I am still completely terrified."

"We're all terrified of something, Avery. Your reason is just more valid than most."

They continue to sit at the table, her picking at her food, Logan watching her do so.

"I know what we can do today," he says confidently.

Avery looks up at him hesitantly; a little worried about his enthusiasm.

"There are a few great wineries around this area. We could go to one for the afternoon."

"That sounds fun. I'll need to go back to my apartment to shower and change first."

He nods in agreement before offering to take her himself, but she declines, needing to wrap her head around everything that occurred last night. If memory serves her, she is now in a relationship with Logan.

Throwing on her outfit from yesterday, Avery searches through Logan's medicine cabinet for a spare toothbrush and she's both happy and jealous to find one. He watches her through the open doorway of the bathroom, causing her to fumble with the toothbrush in her mouth. Spittles of frothy paste dribble from her mouth, mortifying her. Avery rushes to wipe her mouth with the back of her hand and turns to glare at Logan, expecting to find humor in his gaze, but instead she's met with heated eyes.

"Come here," he whispers.

Avery steps towards him, weary of the butterflies floating in her stomach, a feeling that seems ever present in Logan's presence. He puts both of his hands on her cheeks, in a possessive manner that she has truly come to love in the past few weeks.

"We are going to prove each other wrong, Avery. Understand?"

She nods her head in agreement before his mouth swoops down for a melding of their lips.

His kiss unleashes a part of her she had long forgotten existed. The feeling of passion Avery had so long ago pushed aside comes barreling forth, and it takes all her strength to keep from pushing Logan towards the bed. Instead, she wraps her arms around his neck, bringing her body closer to his, and mingles her tongue against his. A growl releases deep in Logan's throat and she knows if they continue, their plans for the day will vanish into air.

Reluctantly pulling her lips from his, Avery works to level her breathing. Closing his eyes, Logan bends his head forward, resting his forehead against hers.

"You do something to me, Avery. I lose control of everything when you kiss me."

"I'm sorry," she whispers.

"Don't be sorry, baby. It's not a bad thing. It's a feeling I've never had before. We have something special, something incredible."

"You think so?"

Leaning back and cocking his eyebrow, he says, "You don't?"

"Oh, I do. I've never felt anything remotely close to how I feel when we're together; I'm just surprised you said something about it. I didn't get the impression that you were the type."

"Well get ready to be surprised, a lot."

A cocky smile spreads across his face and Avery feels herself swooning.

Damn that smile.

Logan walks her to her car and promises to pick her up in two hours, though mentioned after another heated kiss against her car.

Back at her apartment, she takes the letter and information left from her grandmother and places it on her desk. With shaking hands she opens the paper containing her father's name and address:

Joseph Connelly

1255 Blue Mountain Way

Carson, NC

OMG! He lives here! In this town? What are the chances that my escape would bring me closer to my father?

Exasperatedly running her hands through her hair, Avery can't seem to grasp the fact that her father lives here. She contemplates back and forth with herself as to whether or not she wants to look him up. Her initial reaction was to open a search on the internet, when she suddenly stands from her chair in complete disgust, closing the screen on the laptop.

If I'm going to do this, then I am going to do it in person. And I'm not even sure that face-to-face is something I can handle.

Growing up, she never took the time to ask many questions about her father. She asked her mother once why her father didn't live with them. Her mother's response was to snarl and slap her across the face before sending her back to work. From that moment on, she never asked another question about him.

Mila, on the other hand, gave her as much information as she could after overhearing a conversation between Avery's mother and grandmother. From what Mila had gathered, he was older than Avery's mother, much older. Growing up, she had been completely disgusted because her mother had gotten pregnant with her at fifteen. But knowing now what she did about her mother, Avery wasn't the least surprised. She'd seen pictures of her mother at fifteen: she had looked much closer to thirty in age. Mila had also learned that Avery's mother had met her father at a bar. From that conversation Avery learned two things: One, that her father would have had no idea that her mother was nowhere close to the age she claimed and two, she was the product of a one-night-stand.

Conversations about her father never continued, and as a child, Avery never thought to ask more. Eventually, any thought of her father left her consciousness and she never thought about him again - until this letter.

Needing to think about *anything* else, Avery strips and moves into the bathroom and turns on the water. Stepping into the scalding spray, she lets the rivulets wash away all of her unwanted thoughts. The tension slowly releases from her body and she can feel a sense of calm wash over her with the water. Avery fills her loofa with soap and runs the soft cushion over her heated skin. As she shampoos and conditions her hair, she luxuriates in the feel of her fingers massaging her scalp. Rinsing herself off completely, she steps from the shower into the steam-filled bathroom.

Avery wipes the mirror clean with her hand and gazes at her haunted reflection in the glass. She questions if she's ready to move forward with Logan – if she's willing to risk pummeling into a deep and dark hole of despair if she loses him, too. But Avery immediately knows her answer when she envisions Logan; in her mirrored reflection, there is lightness in her eyes. He sparks something in her that had so long ago been buried deep within.

Blow drying her hair quickly, not realizing how long she had spent in the shower, Avery braids it over her shoulder in a fish tail design to keep it out of her way. The fall weather is a bit cooler here than in Savannah, so she tugs on a pair of dark wash jeans and a burgundy sweater, the color bringing out the blue of her eyes, then pairs the ensemble with brown leather knee-high boots. Back in the bathroom Avery applies a little bit of make-up, something she hasn't done in ages, but she doesn't need to sit and wonder why that is. She knows it's because she wants to impress Logan.

Soon a knock sounds on the apartment door and Avery tries not to rush to answer, but she can barely contain herself. Looking through the peep-hole, a cautious measure, Avery swings open the door to gape at the handsome man waiting on the other side. Logan pairs a cream-colored, long-sleeve shirt with dark wash jeans and distressed brown boots. His hair is a disheveled mess, which she adores, and his hazel eyes glisten in amusement. Reaching forward, he uses his finger on her chin to close her mouth, and being bold, he uses the tip of his thumb to wipe away a collection of moisture that had congregated at the corner of her mouth.

"Oh my god, I am so embarrassed," Avery blurts out as she covers her cheeks with her hands, a blush hastily broadening across her skin, causing her cheeks to match her shirt.

"Don't be embarrassed," he says with a quick laugh. Removing her hand, he leans in closer, lips next to her ear and whispers, "You weren't drooling, yet."

And then he kisses her cheek as he chuckles.

"You're a big meanie!" Avery exclaims as she jokingly slaps his arm.

"Wow, I haven't been called that since elementary school. How old are you again?"

"Hardy har har. I am twenty-four and way more mature than you. I just need to grab my bag. You can come in if you want."

"Thanks."

Turning around, Avery walks towards the kitchen to grab her purse. He must have followed her into the kitchen because when Avery spins around, having grabbed her bag off the counter, she smacks into his muscular frame. Without hesitation, he wraps one strong hand around the end of her braid and yanks her closer.

A sincere and compassionate expression crosses his face.

"You look beautiful, Avery."

His voice sounds like velvet floating across her skin, the melody sending goose bumps in their wake.

Not waiting for a response, Logan tilts his muscular frame, bringing his lips closer to hers. Avery's breathing becomes erratic and she closes her eyes in anticipation of his kiss.

"Avery, kiss me," he growls, his hands clenching part of her sweater at her hips, as he waits for her to reciprocate.

Her eyes fly open and he stares into her - lust and desire penetrating her all the way to the core, but also something else, something she is far too weary to comprehend.

Dropping her bag, Avery's hands slither up his arms, slowly sliding across his shoulders, weaving into his hair. Waiting barely a second, Avery stands on her toes, bringing her closer to his mouth, and she seals her lips over his. Her tongue licks at his upper lip, begging for entrance, and he eagerly obliges.

Before long, Logan's strong arms completely wrap around her waist and lift her in the air as he straightens. Turning, he places her on the countertop next to them and tugs her to the edge, aligning their hips. Avery rocks against him twice before she hears a low groan echo around the room and she can't be sure if it came from him or herself. Suddenly Logan pulls away from her and gazes into her eyes. Avery can't help the disappointment that skitters across her face at his withdrawal.

Tucking a loose strand of hair behind her ear Logan assures, "If we don't stop now we won't at all and you deserve better than that."

That darn blush creeps up her chest and neck before residing on her cheeks.

"You're right."

He helps her off the counter and grabs the purse that Avery had haphazardly dropped onto the floor.

"Come on, pretty girl. Let's go have some fun."

Chapter Six

OGAN TRULY HAD TO refrain himself from tugging Avery's braid and hauling her away to her bedroom like he was some sort of caveman. For so many years, he forced away any feelings that were more than lust for a woman. He thought he knew that all women were conniving, sneaky, and untrustworthy. That was his gospel. But boy was he wrong; at least, he was hoping to be. Something about Avery was different; they were kindred spirits, both hurt in their pasts and in need of something more.

After helping Avery into his car, he headed east, further into the mountain range and towards the lake. There was a wine he had picked up at the store recently and saw it was local, so he was eager to check out the winery. After viewing their website this morning, it looked like a perfect place to relax with a bite to eat and a bottle of wine.

With the sunroof open and the windows down, Logan let the warmth of the sun wash over him. He release a contented sigh and glanced over to find Avery's head resting against the seat, her arm draped casually along her open window. As the sun beamed down on her porcelain face and rich chocolate hair, Logan can feel his heart lurch in his chest. He's never felt the need to fight so hard for something. To conquer an invisible enemy that lurked deep within her soul.

An urgent need to hold her overwhelms him and he removes a hand from the steering wheel and grasps her free hand tightly. She doesn't turn her head to acknowledge his action, but she twists her fingers so that they rest between his, and a small smile dances across her lips.

The winery slowly comes into view as they creep into the valley of the mountain range. A sigh expels from Avery's lips and he feels a sense of nervousness and excitement at bringing her here.

After parking, Logan offers Avery his hand as they walk up the steps to the large wooden and stone structure that houses the winery's tasting room. Sneaking a glance towards the side area facing the lake, Logan sees that the band is setting up. Perfect timing. They acquire their glasses for the tasting and join a party that's about to begin.

Avery and Logan relax into a conversation as they let the subtle taste and aroma of the wine loosen their nerves. He makes a point to bring home a few of the wines she took the most pleasure in, while also grabbing a bottle of white wine to enjoy on the terrace.

He ushers her out the side door and helps her find a table before making his way back inside to grab the tray of food he had ordered earlier. Thanking the server behind the bar for keeping the food chilled, Logan heads back out to the terrace.

Before taking his seat, Logan stands back for a moment, mesmerized by the site of Avery resting back in her chair enjoying the music and scenery. She looks the most relaxed he has seen her in the few weeks he's known her. He observes a few of the other male patrons taking notice of her effortless beauty, but Logan can't find himself to be angry or jealous. She commands the attention of the room without even trying.

Logan shakes his head and smiles as he makes his way over to where she sits and he leans down quickly, brushing his lips softly against hers. She startles at first and then relaxes against his touch.

"What do you have there?" she asks, her voice tainted with huskiness, as she peers as the tray Logan sits on the table.

"Just some snacks. It's a beautiful day. I thought we could hang out here for a little while."

"That sounds lovely. It's really pretty here."

Looking at her as she continues to watch the band he says, "It's remarkable."

Glancing at him from the corner of her eyes, Logan knows she catches his meaning when the sweet blush rushes up her cheeks. She licks her lips in a nervous gesture before turning her attention back to the band.

Watching her pink tongue barely escape past her lips causes the muscles in his groin to tighten. Needing to tap down his desire for her, Logan grabs a few pieces of cheese and crackers from the tray, stacks them, then takes a bite. Sipping the refreshing wine that Avery poured into his glass, Logan leans back in his chair, content to enjoy the atmosphere as well as his guest.

Unfortunately, his calmness doesn't last long when he notices a buxom blonde he had taken home from the bar one night, strut her way over to their table, leaving her date in the dust. She ignores the fact that Logan is here with another woman and plants herself directly on his lap - which truly is comical since his legs are crossed and extended forward, resting on the porch rail.

A voice which he's certain she thinks is attractive, but is truly a nasally pitch that makes his skin crawl and would keep dogs at bay, squeals from her mouth.

"Logan, what are you doing here? Why didn't you ever call me?"

He huffs and remains in his seat, moving his hands to her waist in an almost successful attempt to move her from my lap, only she takes it as an invitation to snuggle closer. Her perfume is nauseating and Logan can't help but question his judgment.

Must have been the alcohol and nice rack.

Logan is finally able to remove her from his legs and he pushes her as far away as he can without making a scene.

"I didn't call you because it was only a one-time thing. I told you this."

And he knows he did because he tells everyone it's a one-time thing.

"But I thought we had a good time," she says, pouting her lips in an attempt to be cute.

"Look, I'm here on a date and enjoying myself. Why don't you head back to your date and do the same."

She finally acknowledges Avery's presence and shoots venom from her eyes before storming off in the other direction, grabbing her date's arm along the way.

He brings his attention back to Avery and he finds her with her head down and a hand pressed against her mouth.

Nervously Logan says, "I'm sorry about that," while adjusting himself on his seat, bringing his feet to the floor, and running a hand through his hair.

And then by complete surprise, she starts laughing out loud; head tossed back in an explosion as laughter erupts from her body.

"Oh my goodness, I'm sorry, but that was too funny," she says through spurts of giggles. "Did she sound like a helium balloon when she had sex, too?"

Unable to control himself, he can't help but join in her laughter; glad he was too drunk to remember what she sounded like during sex.

Reaching across the table, Logan takes Avery's hand in his own as they let the laughter subside and enjoy the rest of our afternoon.

*A*S SUMMER CREEPS INTO FALL, Avery and Logan form a steady relationship. They have kept their status hidden from their work companions - Avery's doing, not his - but they come together almost every night for dinner. Her original hesitance at their joining seems to have dissipated and she seems more open and carefree than when they originally met.

Tonight though, Logan has a surprise planned in a neighboring town. He made reservations this morning at a nice restaurant and booked them a room at a hotel. In the few weeks they've been together, Avery and Logan haven't done more than most High-Schoolers and strangely enough he's ok with that, though it's probably the longest spell of no sex he's ever had. Logan didn't even reserve the hotel room with the notion of getting laid tonight, he just thought she'd like it and it would allow him to drink at dinner tonight.

Logan sits at his desk, finishing up his final patient file. He absent-mindedly makes notes as he sits, eagerly waiting for the clock to land on that magical number five so he can hightail it out of town with his favorite person. As he closes the folder, he's startled when he finds Avery sitting in the chair across from him, biting her mouth in nervousness.

"Hey, babe. You okay?"

She releases her bottom lip, the plumpness returning to its natural pink shade, and takes a deep breath.

"I think something is wrong with Nikki."

"What makes you say that?"

"I heard her tell Dr. Fields that she was quitting. And now I have this note from her," she says, holding up a ripped piece of notebook paper, her trembling hands shaking the flimsy parchment. "I'm scared to read it. Will you do it?"

"Sure."

Taking the folded paper from her fingers, Logan skims the neatly written lines.

"Seems she is going to stay with Melanie for a while, but she has paid a year's worth of rent on the apartment so you didn't need to sublet."

"Isn't that weird - that all of a sudden she is going to up and go without an explanation?"

"It's a bit strange, yeah," he says more to himself, but Avery's shoulders slump as he agrees to her assessment.

"I think her and Austin had a falling out. He hasn't come by in a week or so and I thought I heard her crying the other day. I questioned her about it, but she just brushed me off."

They sit and stare at each other for a few minutes, both waiting for the weirdness of the day to subside. When he notices the clock finally turn to five, Logan smiles warmly at Avery and stands behind his desk.

"Do you have your bag in your car? Did you want to change?"

"I have my bag in the break room. Can I use your office to change my clothes?"

"Definitely, I'll help Dr. Fields close up while you get ready."

Fifteen minutes later, Logan heads back to his office just as Avery steps from behind the door and he finds himself rooted to the floor. She looks breathtaking in a short black dress that hits her mid-thigh, showing off mile-long legs. Her hair is swept up onto her head, elongating her slender neck, which has become one of his favorite parts to kiss.

"Wow, Avery. You look…" Logan trails off, still mesmerized by her appearance.

She twists her hands in front of her body, nervously looking down at the floor.

"I look what?"

He steps forward and brings his hand forward to rest on her cheek.

"You look stunning. Absolutely stunning."

Leaning forward he presses his lips against hers.

Whispering against his lips, but making no move to pull away, she says, "Logan, someone will see us."

"Everyone's left. It's just you and me. Open up for me, baby."

Following his instructions, she opens her mouth against his kiss, letting his tongue dance against hers. She grips at his shirt, pulling it tight against his back in her need to pull him closer. Breaking off the kiss he pulls his head back, only inches, and sees clearly the desire swimming in her eyes.

Logan lunges forward, bringing his mouth to Avery's again, more forceful than before, and he pushes her against the door jamb where she stands. The heated exchange only fuels him further and he removes his hand from her face and trails it up her thigh, inching closer to her center as he moves higher. When his fingers meet the wet silkiness of her panties, she lets out a ragged cry of pleasure. Before he's able to slide his digits through her heat, the alarm on his phone goes off, letting him know that they need to head out for their reservations.

They pull away from each other and he finds himself drawn to the heaving of her chest beneath her scoop neck top. And then Avery giggles - one of his favorite sounds. Logan joins her with a chuckle and scoots past her to enter his office.

He makes quick work at changing out of his work clothes and replaces them with dark dress pants and a gray button down. When he's ready to go, he grabs Avery's overnight bag and ushers her out the building towards his car.

They arrive at the restaurant an hour and a half later, and the hostess seats them immediately. Logan makes a point to ignore the subtle touch on his arm from the hostess as she seats them, but it doesn't go unnoticed by Avery, who rolls her eyes at the gesture.

"Is it going to be like that every time we go out?" she asks in an unexpected surly tone.

"Uh, I don't know. I can't really control people."

She nods as if she understands, but he knows that it bothers her. It would bother him too if the roles were reversed.

"We can leave if you want, Avery."

She releases a short burst of air and sags her shoulders.

"No, I know it's not your fault. And this place is really lovely. I'd like to stay."

They continue to browse their menu and order a bottle of wine from the server when he arrives at their table. When he returns with their beverage, Avery orders the roasted chicken and vegetables while Logan orders the prime rib and potatoes. They talk about the day at work and he asks her to talk a little more about her relationships with Nick and Declan. She tells him about the classes she and Nick had taken, then about the guitar lessons she sat through with Declan.

When she used to talk about her past, there was a darkness that encased her, but now she seems lighter as she relays those memories. Logan can only hope that being with him has caused the change. He hopes that she's allowing herself to love again.

Love?

Glancing at her across the table, eyes open and excited, hands gesturing wildly as she delivers her story, Logan can't help but smile. Yes, this foreign emotion can't be described as anything else but love. Mid-sentence, he grabs her hand from its ascension into the air and grasps it within his own. As she continues on, he repeatedly draw circles on her wrist with his thumb and he can feel her heart rate increase with each stroke. They are seated closely to one another and he can't resist using his hand that is closest to her and placing it on her thigh, right below the hem of her dress. At the gentle touch of his fingertips on her skin, her pulse jumps wildly and she shoots a nervous look in his direction before glancing around the restaurant.

"Continue your story, baby. No one can see."

She continues to stare at him, lust overtaking her features, as he slides his fingers under the tight fabric that encases her body. Her breath hitches as Logan gets closer to the spot that craves his touch. Unknowingly she spreads her legs, her body automatically responding to his touch, hoping that he heeds her invitation. As Logan continues to slide his fingers up and down her smooth leg, shifting closer to her womanhood at every path, she reaches for her glass of wine. With a shaking hand, she takes a sip of the cool liquid and grips the stem of the glass when he lets his finger trail across her soaked panties.

When the waiter returns to the table Logan frees his hand from Avery's grasp and pays the check as he continue to slide a finger softly across the wet silk. Logan circles his digits around the area containing her swollen bud of nerves and Avery releases a throaty moan which she quickly covers up with a cough. He has to work to combat his chuckle.

Removing his hand from the warmth of her thighs, he asks, "Are you ready to go?" as he examines her reddened cheeks and slight glare.

Remaining silent, she bites her lower lip, only nodding to acknowledge that she's ready.

Logan stands from the table and moves behind Avery's chair, sliding it out for her to exit.

Pressing his chest against her back, he grips her hips in his hands and whisper in her ear, "I can't wait to make you come with my dick buried inside you. All your muscles clamping down on me like a vice; your pussy won't want me to leave."

She quickly turns in his arms and at first he's alarmed that she didn't like the dirty talk, but as usual, this beautiful girl does something completely unexpected. She leans forward, placing her hands on his chest, stands on her toes and takes the lobe of his ear between her teeth, biting down gently.

She releases the pierced skin and whispers, "I can't wait," then she turns around and saunters out of their alcove, leaving every man in the room panting after her.

Logan adjusts himself before he hurriedly catches up to her at the front of the restaurant where they wait for the valet. Turning her attention back to him, she coyly licks her lips before sitting down in the passenger seat.

Good Lord, I hope I can make it to the hotel.

7 HEY WALK INTO THE expansive lobby of the hotel and hurriedly make their way to the reservation desk. Avery doesn't listen to Logan

speaking with the receptionist, her attention is locked on the grip that he has on her hand and the throbbing between her legs. All she can think about is those large fingers sliding in and out of her, spreading her juices around her folds.

Logan beckons her by calling her name and she startles at his signal.

"Sorry. I was in my own world."

He leans forward slightly and whispers, "I know where your mind is. I can't wait to get you out of that dress."

He winks at her as they turn and swiftly make their way to their reserved room.

Opening the door, Logan tugs her into the area and she presses herself against the wall, anticipating his next move. Avery imagines Logan charging towards her and ripping her dress from her body, but he surprises her instead. He walks towards her, stopping a few inches from her body, and slides two of his fingers from her collarbone to her hip, grazing her breast along the way.

"You look so fucking beautiful tonight, Avery. It's taking everything I have not to fuck you against this wall."

A moan releases from deep within her at his words. Her core clenching tight in anticipation.

"But you don't need that. I'm going to love you slow and sweet for our first time."

His fingers start to inch up the hem of her dress, the tips of his fingers trailing along the outside of her thighs. He leans closer, pressing his thickening erection against her stomach, and caresses his lips against her own. As he swipes his mouth back and forth across the plumpness in a gentle brush, Avery deftly unbuttons his shirt, removing it from his body. As she places her hands on his chest, her nails lightly scraping against the skin, Logan releases a hiss between his teeth.

The lower half of her dress rests bunched around her hips, exposing her thong to his gaze.

"God, I want you so bad," he growls, skimming his fingers across the silken waistband before tearing it away from her body – the fabric disintegrating into nothing.

"I want you too, Logan. Please."

Avery's eyes close tightly as his finger strokes the folds of her sex, and she knocks her head backwards against the wall in ecstasy. Logan increases his pace and places the heel of his hand against her swollen numb, rubbing small circles across the nerves. She grips his shoulders, overcome by the sensation that is ever-tightening, lower in her belly. Moving her hands quickly, she works the button of his pants loose, sliding them down his hips as he continues to love her with his hand.

As her pleasure continues to mount, she can't hold back the groan that reverberates from deep within. The sounds mix with the heavy breaths emanating from their bodies and echo in the sparse room. When her orgasm emerges something within her snaps - as she crests, wave after wave, she finds herself pulling Logan's face to hers and unleashing an unknown forcefulness as she explores his mouth with her tongue. Logan grabs her hair in his free hand in an attempt to bring her closer while continuing to prolong her release. He toes his shoes and socks off and kicks his pants free from his muscular legs.

As he steps free from his belongings, he unzips her dress and yanks it over her head, only breaking their kiss for a second. Avery's bra slides down her arm, freed from its front clasps by Logan's agile fingers. Her nipples rub against his large muscles and she has to suppress a gasp at the sensation.

Between the steamy kisses and crushing orgasm, Avery finds herself whispering against Logan's mouth, "Fuck me hard, Logan."

"You sure?" he asks, pulling back from her face, but reaching down to stroke her hardened nipple. They pebble under his fingertips.

"God, yes. I need to feel you inside me," she replies as she licks and bites softly at the point where his neck meets his shoulder.

"Then hold on, baby."

Without hesitation, Logan takes a hold of her thighs and wraps them around his waist, gripping her behind in his strong hands. She wraps her arms around his neck, continuing to press her mouth against his.

He teasingly slides his erection through her folds, coating his manhood in her wetness, and triggering mini spasms within her as he directly connects with her clit. Thoroughly encased in her liquid heat, he thrusts hard and deep into her center. The feeling of fullness overwhelms her and she finds herself pulling back from Logan and groaning loudly into the empty room.

He takes a moment to let her accommodate to his size and asks, "Are you okay?"

"Yes," Avery whispers. "Move, please. I need you to move."

Logan doesn't hold back. Relying on their hips and legs to hold her up, he takes her hands from his shoulders and places them above her head, one of his large hands holding both of her wrists. His other hand moves down her chest to caress her breast, rolling the pert nipple between his fingers.

As his thrusts increase the pressure begins to build deep within her center, the feel of her muscles tightening spur him into a fevered pace.

Their expenses of air collide into each other, enveloping them in a damp heat, the sweat dripping and meshing between their bodies.

"I need you to come again, Avery. Fuck, you're so hot and tight."

He reaches down with his free hand and places it where their bodies are joined, gliding his fingers in a circle around her swollen nub. Avery closes her eyes, allowing her body to give into the explosion.

"Come on, babe. I can feel you squeezing me."

Avery didn't think it was possible, but Logan thrusts harder and deeper, prolonging her orgasm and helping him reach his own. Moments later he grunts and his seed spills into her, the pulsing of his penis rubbing against her sensitive spot.

Logan doesn't say anything; he simply carries her over to the bed and gently places them on top of the soft down comforter. He eases out of her and steps to the bathroom. Logan startles her when she feels a warm cloth cleaning their essence from her body.

Returning to the bed, Logan rests beside her and rolls to his side, resting his head on his hand. Reaching across, he tucks some stray hairs behind her ear and brushes his fingers across her cheek. As Avery's erotic high wears off she stares at the ceiling, uncomfortable with the thoughts and feelings floating through her head.

"You okay?"

She nods in response, unsure how to voice her conflicting feelings.

"I'm sorry if I was too rough, Avery. I hope I didn't hurt you. I just sort of...lost control."

Looking at him, absorbing his sincerity and despair, wetness floods her eyes.

"Did I do something wrong?"

The tears flee from their gates behind her eyelids as she turns her body towards him. Reaching forward, she rests her hand against the overgrown scruff on his cheek and jaw.

"You were perfect, Logan. It was more than I ever imagined."

"Then what's wrong, sweetheart?"

Reaching up, she swipes at her moist cheeks, removing the wetness that settled there.

"I swear it's not you, Logan. I just...haven't done this...in a really long time and it's bringing back too many memories I'm not ready to deal with."

"What do you mean?"

Huffing she replies, "I don't want to think about Nick or Declan when I'm doing this with you, but I can't help it. I'm not comparing, Logan, but I am so freaking scared. All I can think about is 'Why wasn't it ever like this with them? Was I wrong all along?' and then I wonder if I ever really loved them. God, Logan, I don't want to feel like this."

"Babe, calm down," he says as he sits up, bringing her with him, resting her face between his hands. "I know that you loved them. And I know that you loved them completely differently than you love me." As shock envelops her face, Logan continues, "Yea, I love you; we'll talk about that in a minute. But what we have is intense, and fierce, and so overwhelmingly passionate that we couldn't control it if we tried. Avery, we have something people search their entire lives for, but that doesn't mean you loved them any less. We just have something different, something that waited until this very moment to encompass us. I wish you never had to go through the things you did, but watching you survive and thrive makes me love you even more. It's ok to think about them. I'm ok with it. It only proves how compassionate you are. Okay? No more tears?"

Avery can only nod in response. His words soak deep within her soul and cleanse her heart. He's right, Avery did love them differently. With Nick everything was new, with Declan everything was whimsical; now, with Logan, everything is passionate. It's this wistfully, all-encompassing combination of lust and love. And just letting that notion roam across her mind confirms that she loves Logan, too. She doesn't know how or when it happened, but it snuck up on her and wrapped her heart in its warmth, forcing it to pulse with affection.

Blinking away the remaining tears, she gazes into Logan's beautiful hazel eyes and says, "You're right and I love you, too."

"You do? Really?"

"I do. I don't know how it happened and I'm so afraid something will happen to you, but I can't fight it anymore."

"I love you, Avery. I'll do everything I can to make you happy."

Leaning closer to him, Avery presses her lips lightly against Logan's then says, "Just stay with me," then forces her lips harder against his.

Logan pulls her closer to his body and she instinctively wraps one of her legs over his hips, allowing his hardening bulge to rub against her still slick mound. Avery pushes Logan onto his back and she slides down his legs, bringing her face within inches of his ever growing cock. Tentatively she wraps her small hand around the solid base, testing its weight. Licking her lips in anticipation, Avery brings her mouth towards the darkening tip and then allows her tongue to venture forward to taste the dripping of moisture. A growing need to feel him in her mouth has Avery dipping her head closer, tossing her wild hair over one shoulder, and encasing Logan's erection between her lips. The mixed flavors of both of their need combine within her mouth as she glides the slick erection in and out of her mouth.

Too soon Logan grips her from under her arms and brings her to his hips. She straddles his waist, rocking back and forth slowly against his erection, stimulating against her sensitive nerves.

"You make me so hot, Avery. I need you again."

"I can tell," Avery says saucily, sliding her hands across his pectorals, teasing his cock by gliding the tip in and out of her entrance.

Before she has the chance to react, Logan returns her to her back and begins fully sliding his member in and out of her slowly.

"This one won't be quick. I want to feel all of you this time."

Logan's mouth moves down her neck, leaving heated bite marks in his wake as he slides down to take her breast in his large hand and her nipple in his mouth,

"You're beautiful, Avery. When you come it's like viewing a masterpiece."

"Logan," she moans as she feels the subtle waves of her orgasm springing forth.

He continues to roll her nipple around with his tongue, the feel sending sparks directly to her core, spurring on her release. Avery grips at his back as she feels herself reaching that point of ecstasy, her nails digging harshly into his skin leaving trails in their wake.

"Logan," she whispers huskily, "I'm going to come."

A scream violently escapes from her when her body pushes over the pinnacle. Her emotions so raw from her surrender, she can't contain the few escaped tears that leak from the corner of her eyes.

"Feels so good, baby. I could make you come all night."

Avery groans in response. The thought of him sliding in and out of her for unforeseen hours causing her muscles to clench and a surge of wetness to expel, coating his shaft in more of her juices.

"I need you to come again, Avery. I want you to fall apart with me."

Those words are her undoing and the symptoms come so fast that she barely has time to react.

"I can feel it. I'm going to come again, Logan."

Rocking her hips in rhythm with Logan's thrusts, she increases her pace, hoping to unleash his orgasm as well.

"Mmm, Avery. Feels so fucking good."

The headboard rocks underneath her clenched hands as she attempts to fend off her release.

"Shit," Logan growls, and she knows that the new angle of her pelvis frees any of the restraint he had been barricading within his body.

His thrusts become frantic, frenzied, and maniacal as he works to finish. Tilting her hips up a smidgen higher than before, she can feel the tip of his steel-like erection rubbing her sensitized inner area. After three passes over the pleasurable spot, she detonates around him, her muscles tightening and then retracting as he continues to thrust inside her.

"Yes, that's it. Fuck!" he shouts as he spills deep inside her, the powerful spray causing mini aftershocks to wreck through her core.

Spent, they lay on the soft bed, Logan resting beside her, one of his arms and one of his legs draped across Avery's body; their heavy breaths filling the silent space of the room. Without opening his eyes, he reaches up with the arm cloaked over her and tangles his fingers in her hair. With a bit of force he turns her head and pulls her towards him, pressing a soft kiss against her lips.

"That was incredible," he says contentedly, eyes still closed.

"Mmhmm," Avery replies in her own dreamy state, watching the small smile grow on his face.

Pressing her lips against his once more, becoming addicted to their soft feel, her body turns towards him, leaving only a few inches between their chests, but aligning their hips together and tangling their legs. She fits one palm between their sweaty skin and places it over his chest, where his heart beats erratically from the previous exertion. Logan's large hand leaves her scalp and trails back and forth along her spine, leaving the nerves shivering along his path.

"I could kiss you all day." Avery says in between moments where her tongue dances with his.

"By all means, you have my permission."

Unknowingly, her hand travels south on Logan's body, down the rippling muscles of his abdomen, and skating across the soft skin of his hip. As her finger grazes the deep V of his waist, she feels his manhood pulsate against her thigh.

"Ignore him. He doesn't understand that you're tired and sore."

The full mast projecting proudly from his body draws her attention and she pulls back from their kiss.

Holy shit he's big. How did that fit…anywhere?

The sound of chuckling brings her back to the moment and she looks at a bright-eyed Logan.

"Sorry, you just looked extremely surprised. I'm sorry if I hurt you. Let me go draw you a bath so you can relax your muscles.

"That's sweet, Logan. Thank you. But I'd prefer a shower if that's ok?"

"Alright, well, while you're in there I'll look for some pain medicine. I don't want you to be uncomfortable."

The concern etched on his face is enough to bring her to her knees. After hearing about all of his past exploits she can't imagine that this is the same man that turned away from anything serious and had steady one-night stands for the past few years.

"Thank you, Logan."

Sitting up, Avery crawls off the bed and makes her way to the enormous glass and tile enclosure. She turns on the shower and waits for the steam to fill the room before stepping into hot water, letting the moisture wash over her overly sensitive skin.

With the look of desire in Logan's eyes as she sauntered from the bedroom, she holds off washing her body, knowing that in a few short minutes he will undoubtedly join her.

And she's definitely not sore enough to keep herself from hoping he'll take her again.

Chapter Seven

7HE LOOK AVERY GIVES Logan as she crawled off the bed is enough to bring any man to his knees. Not to mention the view of her swollen pussy as she moved on all fours across the bed.

Logan releases a heavy sigh when he hears the door to the bathroom click shut. The sex with Avery was nothing short of amazing. And amazing is an understatement. She unleashed something deep within him that he didn't know existed; some primal need that could only be satiated by her. And fuck, if he doesn't feel like a complete ass for taking her so roughly the first time. She hadn't had sex in a while and Logan knew he needed to ease her into it, especially considering his size. But seeing her pressed against the wall panting his name - an exploding bomb couldn't have stopped him from taking her.

His protruding dick pulsates at his wayward thoughts and Logan chastises himself one more time before laughing at the vertical stance it refuses to relinquish. Needing to release some tension of his own, he finds himself opening the bathroom door and contemplating joining Avery.

Surprisingly, his decision is made for him when Avery says, "Took you long enough."

Stalking towards the glass enclosure, he opens the door, slinking in behind the beauty as she lets the streams of hot water cascade over her perfect body.

Wrapping an arm completely around her waist, he pulls her against him before leaning down and whispering in her ear, "Sorry, did you miss me?"

Her breath hitches and Logan continues to hold her tightly, but he lets his other hand skim down her shoulder, to her chest, and then slide between her legs.

Deep within his mind, he knows she is sore and that he really should try to hold back, but right now his cock has taken control of all of his brain synapses. All he can think about is taking her again and making her his.

Luckily, she isn't thinking with her brain, either.

"Logan, that feels so good."

"You like it when I touch you? When I let my fingers caress your soft skin before sinking deep inside you?"

She releases a moan from deep in her throat and he can feel a rush of wetness coat his hand.

So she does like it when I talk dirty.

Avery turns around in his arms and gazes up at him, desire infiltrating her features and Logan finds himself taken aback by the combination of lust and love mirroring his own feelings.

"God you're so hot, babe."

She leans into him, taking his nipple in her mouth and swirls her soft tongue around the skin before biting down softly.

Unable to contain the groan building in his throat, he follows suit and releases it as a low growl that echoes in the small space.

Logan moves them to the teak bench that rests in the corner of the large shower. Sitting down, he lifts Avery up with both hands so that she can straddle his body. Not waiting for her to slide down his shaft, Logan thrusts up into her hot center, her body fully encasing him.

"Oh god," she shouts, eyes closed and head thrown back in ecstasy.

"Ride me, baby. Take me how you want."

She doesn't hesitate, nor does she need instruction; she rides him like it's her dying wish and damn, if it isn't exactly what Logan wants.

Neither of them lasts long, rocking back and forth into each other before simultaneously exploding amidst shouts and profanities.

Avery relaxes into him and Logan rests against the cool tiled wall, both attempting to catch their breath.

"I don't know what came over me," Avery admits as she trails her hand through his hair.

"Passion, babe. And we have a hell of a lot of it."

Logan helps her stand from the bench and he works quickly to clean off her body with the provided soap. Her eyelids droop as he runs his hands over her skin and he knows that she is fighting a losing battle to stay awake. Logan runs the soap over himself quickly and then shuts off the water before draping the warm towel around Avery's body.

Leaning down, he picks up her small body and carries her into the bedroom where he sits her on the bed. He turns down the covers and helps her slide between the cool sheets.

"Night, babe."

"G'night."

With a kiss on her forehead Logan goes in search of his bag, hoping to find his toothbrush and cell phone charger. He stops in his tracks when he opens his bag to find his last packed item, an unopened pack of condoms. None of which they thought to use tonight.

He takes a deep breath, letting it fill his lungs, and runs his hands through his damp hair. He's definitely not ready to be a father, but fuck if it didn't feel good to claim Avery without any barriers.

Turning back towards her sleeping form Logan lets the tension expel through another sigh. Knowing he can't prolong this conversation, he walks over to her side of the bed and crouches down so that he's even with her beautiful face. He tucks some loose strands of her wet hair behind her ear and envisions her pregnant with their child and what their children would look like. Strangely enough, a smile crosses Logan's face at that notion – much less terrified than before.

"Avery, sweetheart. Can you wake up for a minute?"

"Hmm," she murmurs sleepily.

"Hey, um, I don't really know how to say this and I take full blame, but we, uh, forgot to use protection."

She doesn't respond, just opens her eyes a bit wider, as if that will allow her to make a more sound decision.

And then she grins. It's small, but it's there, and he smiles in return, glad she isn't upset with their careless decision.

"I'm clean too, babe. I just had a physical. I'm just sorry I wasn't more careful," he adds.

She shuts her eyes, the grin still poised on her lips, as if she is amused at the situation.

"It's okay, Logan. I can't get pregnant. Now come lay in bed with me."

"Okay," he replies as he stands from the bedside and moves to the other side, a bit disheartened to realize he won't see Avery pregnant with his child.

What the hell is wrong with me?

Logan lies in bed behind Avery, bringing her body close so that it rests against his and he closes his eyes, hoping to sleep quickly. Instead, sleep eludes him as he dreams of Avery with child, and then playing with a boy and a girl about the age of five, and then the dream switches to a vision of Avery and him, each holding a small infant, while they gaze at each other across his living room sofa.

Due to his dream-filled slumber, Logan wakes Avery twice during the night. Once, she wakes to find his face buried between her legs, lapping at her sweet honey, moments before she explodes onto his tongue. The next she wakes to his hand softly rubbing her breast and his dick sliding between her legs, coating himself in her wetness. When he hears her breathing increase, Logan slowly glides himself into her core, filling her completely. He whispers to her the things he wants to do and the things he feels while he's fucking her and she meets each of his demands.

Fuck if she isn't perfect for me.

In the morning they both fully rise later than normal, his erection still buried deep within her channel, and hard as a rock. She tilts her hips forward, making him believe that she is going to remove his body from hers, but Avery surprises him when she rocks back against his hips and groans in pleasure. He leans forward and kisses her shoulder, then sucks on the sensitive skin on her neck.

Avery reaches back and holds his head in place as she continues to pump herself against his cock. His hand slides down her smooth skin and he moves her leg over his hips, opening her up, exposing her center. Logan glides his fingers across the damp curls of her mound and swirl them around her clit, as it begs for his attention.

She cries out when she pushes over her threshold and Logan quickly turns her onto her stomach, lifting her hips in the air. Plunging back inside her warmth, in dire need of release, Logan unleashes steady lunges against her sex. Though spent, Avery pushes back against his thrusts, assisting him in his need to expel.

Soon the buildup surges deep in his spine, the crackling of his nerves alert him to his release. Logan thrusts harder, faster, holding Avery in place as he pummels into her body. When the explosion is about to overtake his senses, Logan lays a hand on Avery's backside before he winds back and smacks his hand against the soft skin.

"Fuck!" she screams as she comes against him once more.

Logan simultaneously yells, "Shit," as he spills himself deep inside her.

"Fucking hell, Avery. I think you're trying to kill me."

Avery lazily turns her head in his direction and smiles a drunkenly, satiated smile.

"I can't help it if you feel good," she whispers, her voice hoarse from her screams.

Beneath a chuckle he replies, "I think we woke up the entire hotel."

Logan would have assumed that she would be embarrassed by that notion, but Avery surprises him again when she says, "Oh well. Rise and shine."

Now that he's starting to come fully awake, he knows Avery and him need to talk more about the fact that they've had sex four times without condoms, but Logan opts to wait until she seems more alert. Right now, he wants nothing more than to soak with her in the giant tub.

"Come on, babe. Let's take a bath to soothe your muscles."

"You're going to join me right?" she questions lazily, her eyes scanning up and down his body.

"Of course, sweetness, but we're just going to relax, no sex."

She mocks a child's pout and then smiles.

"I don't know what came over me yesterday and this morning, but I'm good now. I won't jump you in the tub."

"Shame," Logan says, smacking her behind on his way to the bathroom, letting her giggles trail him along the way.

After their bath, during which they unsurprisingly found themselves making love once more after Avery claimed that she had years of pent up desire that Logan unknowingly unleashed, he heads across the street to a coffee shop to grab them a late breakfast and some caffeine.

When he returns to the room, he anticipates that he will find Avery in the same position she was in when he left, naked on the bed. Instead, Logan finds her curled up in the chair by the window. She doesn't respond when he enters the room - it's as if she's focused on something completely out of their realm.

He puts the muffins and coffees on the dresser and makes his way over to where she is perched, his chest aching at every step.

Crouching down, he rubs his hand down her arm while inquiring, "Everything okay?"

Looking at her, he can see the anguish in her eyes and Logan works to hold in his panic. Afraid that she is second guessing their night together and their relationship as a whole, Logan suppresses his breath, waiting to hear her response.

I just got her; I'm not ready to lose her.

"I'm fine, really," she says as she brings her hand forward to rest her palm against his cheek. "I was just thinking of something completely unrelated to us."

A heavy breath releases from his body and he places his hand atop hers.

"Sorry, I got a little worried. Is there something I can help you with? You look like you're lost in another world."

He takes her hand from his face and kisses the soft skin at her knuckles before encasing it between both of his significantly larger hands.

"I think I'm going to go see my father."

"Wow, really? Do you want me to go with you?"

"Um, no, I don't think so. It's not that I don't want you there, I just feel like I need to do this on my own."

"Okay. When do you think you'll set something up?"

"Tomorrow?" she says as she looks to him for affirmation. "I only have his address. I was thinking of just showing up."

"You're going to be okay if he isn't happy to see you?"

"Yes...no...I don't know. My letter said he didn't know about me so I'm sure he'll be shocked. I just....I figured I have nothing to lose."

Logan nods his head in understanding.

"You're absolutely right and I'm behind you one-hundred percent. Once he meets you he'll love you, Avery. Just like I do."

"I love you too, Logan."

"Can we have that discussion now...about the no condoms?"

"Oh, yea. I mean I trust you. It isn't a big deal. I had gone on the pill once I started college, but it threw my hormones for a loop, and my body never went back to normal. My doctor thinks my likeliness of getting pregnant is pretty slim."

"Oh. Does that upset you? That you may not be able to have a baby?"

"I don't know. I honestly hadn't ever thought it would be something I would want. But yea, I guess I'm a bit upset that my body doesn't work right. But there are other ways to have children if I ever want."

"That's true. Thank you for telling me."

Logan leans forward and presses his lips against hers in a chaste kiss before pulling her from the chair.

"Come on, we need to eat something. I bought muffins."

After breakfast, Avery and Logan check out of the hotel, anxious to head to the folk festival in Asheville that the receptionist mentioned on their way out.

Patrons line the streets, enjoying the nice weather and the vendors that border the sidewalk. Avery and Logan walk through the throngs of people, her arm around his waist and his arm across her shoulders, intimately joined. They steal a kiss or a smile every hundred feet, unable to keep their attraction hidden. A bakery comes into view and they duck inside the building, both inhaling the sweet scent of bread and cakes.

"Wow, this place is adorable," Avery cheers happily as she gazes around the 50's ice-cream parlor-ish design.

"You're adorable," he replies as he lays a gentle kiss on her lips.

She motions him over to a small display of cupcakes at the far end of the room and he stands beside her, admiring the shop's work.

"We should get some to take back to the office."

"We could do that."

"Do you think I should take some to my father's?" she asks, nervously twisting her fingers around and gazing up at him.

Logan tucks a hair behind her ear and says, "I think he'd like that."

The high school-age worker places Avery's selections into two boxes and they head to the register where an older woman greets them. She speaks momentarily with the other worker and comes back to the register to give them their total.

"That's thirty-five dollars for both boxes."

While Avery busies herself paying for the cupcakes, the woman inquires, "You two make a lovely couple. Are you from around here?"

"No ma'am. We live in Carson. Not too far from here."

"Oh I've been to Carson. Cute town."

"It is."

Out of nowhere she throws out a topic, tossing Logan for a spin when she speaks directly to him.

"You two will be together for a long time. I can tell. You can trust her."

"Excuse me?"

Avery notices his hackles rising and listens intently as an older man joins the woman.

"This is my wife; she has a 'sense' about people. She's been pretty spot-on since we met in elementary school. She told me in first grade that we'd get married and open up a bakery. I didn't believe her until we were twenty-four, closing on the location, and getting married the next week. She's 'sensed' things about... I'd say... eighty couples and has been right every single time," he says with a chuckle, casting an adoring look at his wife.

Avery and Logan glance at each other, confused by the strange situation.

The woman begins again, looking at Avery, "You've lost a lot in your life - more than most. You're a survivor." Avery gasps at the accurate depiction.

Then the woman turns back to him and says, "You've been lied to by everyone you've loved. But she won't lie to you. You can trust her, love her."

"Jesus Christ," Logan murmurs under his breath.

Continuing to speak to him, as if in a trance, she discloses, "You're the air she needs to breathe; you're what keeps her alive. She'll be the reason you live, and you're what brought her to life."

The elderly woman takes a deep breath and hands us our cupcakes while her husband looks on tenderly. Avery grabs the bag containing the boxes and glances at Logan nervously.

"Thank you," Logan says, a bit perplexed and a bit gleeful at her attestation.

When they reach the door, about to step out on to the street, the woman hollers out, "I can't wait to see you all in a few months. The wedding is going to be beautiful."

Avery waves to the couple as the door closes quickly behind them and they walk out onto the street, holding hands, but completely silent, busy absorbing the details from the woman's revelation.

They practically make it back to the car in complete reticence before Avery speaks up, "That was weird, right?"

Logan bursts out in laughter, unable to hold back his relief at Avery's words and their utter appropriateness. Avery joins in with a few giggles of her own.

"It was a bit weird, yes."

Avery slides into the passenger seat and looks over at him, a calmness exuding her.

"It's so strange how she knew those things. I mean that definitely wasn't a coincidence."

"Not speaking as a doctor; yes, it was pretty fucking eerie how spot on she was."

"Is it bad that it made me happy?"

He looks over at Avery's beautiful face and he can't help but think, *mine*. Logan grasps her hand and places his lips on the back in a soft kiss.

"I can't fucking wait to be married to you, too," Logan says as he gazes across the console mentally replaying every word the woman spoke.

You're the air she needs to breathe; you're what keeps her alive. She'll be the reason you live, and you're what brought her to life.

VERY TAPS HER FINGERS nervously on the steering wheel of her car. She's parked on the street, two houses down from her father's. She had hoped that he wouldn't be home, but the two cars in the driveway give the impression that luck is not on her side.

Trying to calm her nerves, she takes a few breaths, closes her eyes, and leans her head back against the headrest. She thinks back to her night with Logan.

When they arrived in Carson, Logan took her to his house after she agreed to stay with him for the night. They made stir-fry and stayed up watching a football game. They never left each other's side while they talked about random things, like what school was like when they were kids and what she thought of Carson.

After the game, Logan took her back to his bedroom where he feasted on her body as if he were a starving man and she was his favorite meal. His mouth touched every part of her skin and his tongue left wet paths that sizzled beneath the surface. He brought her to orgasm twice with his fingers and tongue before he penetrated her body with his erection.

God, he was marvelous.

The way he would speed up until he knew she was getting close, then he would slow down, prolonging their coming together. They couldn't get enough of each other. It was like being a part of this magnetic field that only felt complete when it met its other half. And she truly believed Logan was her other half. As much as she loved Nick and Declan, she never had this connection with them - this all-consuming need to be with them.

This morning they talked about the woman from the bakery and laughed at her pronouncement, but she couldn't stop secretly hoping what the woman said was true. Everything she surmised about their pasts was correct, so how could she be wrong about their future?

Logan made love to Avery one last time, on his kitchen counter, while she was making them breakfast. It was passionate, sultry, and steamy; a combination Avery couldn't get enough of, and apparently Logan couldn't either.

He brought her back to the clinic so that she could pick up her car, then Avery returned to her apartment after promising to head to Logan's after her visit with her father.

Avery opens her eyes and takes a deep breath, thinking back to the words Logan whispered to her before she left. The most calming statement he could have uttered.

"Avery, there is nothing about you not to love."

Putting the car back into drive, she steers the vehicle into the driveway and parks it behind a new red pickup truck. She grabs the cupcake box and exits the vehicle, shuffling her feet as she ascends the brick stairs.

Before ringing the doorbell she gazes up at the large two-story brick structure. The colonial style house is the largest in the neighborhood, taking the full plot on the cul-de-sac. But the size of the home isn't what alarms her. It's the fact that the home looks lived in, welcoming. There is a Duke flag hanging from the flagpole, a mix-match of flowers in the garden bed, worn paint on the front door, and six small handprints on a wooden board propped up against the house. Avery glances left and right taking in her fill of the large porch before pressing the button that could forever change her life.

Ringing the bell she waits patiently for someone to answer the door and after two minutes with no response she presses the doorbell once more. Her anxiety level has sky rocketed at this point and she feels herself nervously rocking back and forth, tapping her fingers along the cupcake box. Feeling her hands start to sweat, she sits the box on a chair next to the door and wipes her palms on her black pants.

Avery presses the bell once more, as a defeated presence overcomes her emotions. As she takes a step back, intending to head towards her car, Avery hears the doorknob turn and she holds her breath, frozen in place.

She turns her attention to the brick porch as a woman with beautiful blonde hair the color of straw, cut into a medium length bob, answers the door. She is dressed smartly in a pale pink cardigan set that Avery is certain is made of cashmere, and a pair of dark denim jeans with gold flats. The dark brown eyes nestled against her olive skin assess Avery kindly.

She smiles and asks, "I'm sorry we were out back and I didn't hear the bell. Can I help you with something?"

"I...um...is there a Joseph here?" Avery whispers, her gaze still fixed on the ground, though she tries to make eye contact and peeks up from behind her lashes, anxiety fueling her nervousness further.

"There is. Was he expecting you?" she inquires, her eyes narrowing slightly in question of Avery's intentions.

"He wasn't. I'm….um…." Avery begins, then reaches into her pocket to retrieve the note she wrote with Logan this morning. "Could you just give this to him? I didn't mean to barge into your day."

Avery steps forward to hand her the note, continuing to look down at the ground and the kind woman places her hand on Avery's wrist, capturing her attention.

When Avery glances at her, the woman gasps and tears well into her eyes.

"Oh my god," she whispers. "You're here, oh my god."

Before Avery has a chance to speak, the woman turns and runs off, yelling for Joseph.

Standing at the door awkwardly, not sure if she should stay or turn around and run home, Avery takes the note still gripped in her hand and turns to place it on top of the cupcake box.

A large thud onto the porch startles her and Avery turns around just before she's wrapped tightly into the arms of the man she assumes must be her father. Minutes pass before the man releases his hold and when he pulls away slightly, holding her at an arm's length, her assumptions are put to rest when Avery sees the wet blue eyes that mirror her own.

"We have been searching for you for twenty years. I...I can't believe you're here. Can you stay for a few minutes? Maybe we can head out back."

"Sure," Avery whispers, overtaken by the moment.

As she follows him through their house, not noticing any of the interior space, Avery's engulfed in another hug as she passes by the woman she met earlier.

They usher her to a seat on their brick lined patio, offering her a glass of water.

As she politely declines, she asks, "You said you'd been searching for me?"

Joseph continues to stare at her in disbelief, his eyes full of tears. His wife answers for him.

"We have. Twenty years ago, we received a letter from your mother that claimed she had a child with Joseph and that she had sent you away. She left no name or your whereabouts. We've contacted practically every child services office in the country and no one had any information on you. But we never gave up. We always held out hope that we'd find each other."

"I don't understand. My mother never gave me up for adoption, she practically banished me as a servant at my grandmother's and she ran off. She had me when she was fifteen and I shamed their family. So they treated me like I never existed," Avery confides through her tears.

"Fifteen?" Joseph asks, anger, disgust, and confusion lacing his voice. "She told me at the time that she was twenty-two. She was in a bar for god sakes. I'm not a pedophile, I swear to you!"

Avery attempts to calm him down, seeing how upset he is at her mother's lies.

"Joseph, you're not a pedophile. My mother was a sick human-being and I have no doubt she lied to you. I was told by a friend that she had been having sex since she was thirteen, not to mention she had already had two abortions with children – who were fathered by my grandfather's friends - before she had me. I was discovered too late apparently." The admission stings her heart. "I'm not upset with you. I just never knew that you knew about me. It all makes sense though. Why everyone was always so keen on keeping me hidden."

"What's your name, sweetheart?" the kind woman asks as she hands Avery a few tissues. "We've been searching for so long, and we don't even have your name yet."

"It's Avery. Avery Poindexter, and I live in Carson too, but I'm from just outside Atlanta, Georgia."

"I'm Amy, dear. And well, this is your father, Joseph. We want to hear all about you."

So Avery tells them. She divulges her entire past, holding nothing back: her entire life up until she moved to Carson. They are so welcome and open that Avery doesn't hesitate as she reveals her turbulent history. Their presence is so comforting that Avery felt every moment of her life spewing forward without hesitation. She tells them of the abuse, her sister, her fiancés... everything.

"I'm sorry for everything you've been through, Avery. My wife and I can't imagine what it must feel like to lose those close to you."

A question burns deep in her mind and she tries my hardest to stomp it down, but with her emotions running high, it spurts forth without hesitation.

"May I ask what happened? Why I even exist? You two look like you're really happy."

Joseph squeezes his wife's hand and takes the lead saying, "We are really happy and we were then too. We had just had our third child and I felt outnumbered, everyone needing something from me. Avery, don't get me wrong, I love my family and I loved them then. Amy knows this. But I was thirty and I felt lost and she began to resent me and the long hours I pulled at the office. We had a mutual separation - we needed time apart. Her sister came to help with the kids, and I took some time to get my life on track. We had been separated about a month and I was hurting. I wanted my family back, but I knew Amy was still angry at me. I would have been, too, after all the nights I had come home and locked myself away in my office. On a business trip I went out with a few coworkers and I met your mother. I was two sheets to the wind when I went home with her, and I never even got her name. I swore we had used protection, but those things aren't always fool-proof.

"The next day I felt like complete trash and came straight home to Amy. We talked and I told her everything that had happened. I explained how overwhelmed I felt with all of the changes in our life, but as always, Amy surprised the hell out of me, welcoming me home with open arms and she forgave me for every sin I committed.

"Until we received the letter four years later, we never thought twice about my indiscretion, but I always knew in the back of my mind that it would catch up to me. Amy was knowingly upset when she learned I had fathered another child and I feared every day that she would pack up the kids and leave me. But again she surprised me. I came home from work one day, just glad to see her car in the driveway and her standing on the porch waiting for me. To say I was petrified is an understatement, but when I looked at her... man, I remember like it was yesterday... she poured out her love for me. It was in her eyes, the way she smiled, the way she held me close as I wrapped her in my arms. And she told me...she said 'Here's a list of every adoption agency in the country. Let's find our little girl.'" Tears sparkle in the corner of his eyes, and he dabs them away quickly. "I cried. She took an ugly situation, turned it around and embraced it. We had absolutely nothing to go on but your birthday, which we know she could have changed when she turned you in. But we never suspected that she had lied, though in hindsight we should have."

"So, Amy, you forgave him? You just turned a blind eye?"

"I did. I had to, there was no other way. I love Joseph with all of my heart and we were separated, there is no question in my mind that had we not been, he wouldn't have strayed. He isn't wired that way. And I understood where he was coming from. Our kids are all two years apart and that's a lot to handle for a man that was hesitant to become a father to begin with. But he truly is the best father to our kids," she says, smiling at her husband with love pouring from her face.

"Wow, I'm just...I don't know what to say. How many kids do you have?"

Joseph replies excitedly, "We have six amazing kids. Everleigh is a few months older than you at twenty-five, Joseph Jr. is the oldest at twenty-nine, Cassidy is next at twenty-seven, then Sydney just turned twenty-three, and our twins Ryker and Jameson are the youngest at twenty-one. And now you, sweet-girl. Welcome to our family."

Avery's eyes well with more tears at their instant love and envelopment into their family.

Before she can even hug her newfound parents, her phone rings and she apologizes profusely before stepping away when she see Nikki's name flash across the screen.

"Hey, Nikki. How are things? Are you doing okay?" She asks, wiping away the wetness on her cheeks.

She hears a distinct sniffle across the line and Avery waits with baited breath for her response.

"Nikki?"

"I'm pregnant," she whispers.

"What? Oh my gosh, Nikki! Is that why you left?"

"I had a feeling, but I just went to the doctor and they confirmed. I'm eight weeks."

"Oh, Nikki. What can I do?"

"Just keep it to yourself, please? I don't want Austin to find out."

"I'll do whatever you ask, but don't you think you should talk with him? He should know if he's going to be a father."

"I know, and I will; I'm just not ready yet. I'm thinking of moving back here with Melanie. She offered to help me with the baby. Austin just doesn't seem like the kind of guy that would embrace fatherhood."

"I don't know him very well, but I think he may surprise you."

"I'll be back soon. I'm just really messed up right now. And the morning sickness is killing me."

"I wish there was something I could do for you, Nikki. And I hope you feel better soon. I'm here if you need me."

"Thank you, Avery. We'll talk soon. Bye."

"Bye, Nik."

Avery returns to the porch, having taken her call out onto their immaculate lawn.

"Everything okay?"

"Yes, everything is fine. My friend is having a rough time right now. She found out she's expecting, but she doesn't think the father will step up. I'm really hoping he proves her wrong."

"Me too, dear. Family is important," Amy reminds.

Joseph stands from the table and Amy follows suit.

"We have a meeting at the community center for the Christmas program, but I wish we could catch up some more."

"Oh I'm sorry, I didn't mean to intrude on your day."

"Please don't apologize! We are thrilled you found us and we can't wait to find out more about each other," Amy exclaims, pulling Avery close.

Joseph places his hands on Avery's shoulders and stares at her lovingly.

"Our family gets together every Sunday night for dinner, except for today since we had the meeting scheduled. No pressure, but we'd love for you to join us next Sunday. We planned to meet at Angie's around six. It would be a good opportunity to introduce you to your siblings. We won't tell them anything in case you decide against this. It's a lot to take in and we completely understand."

"I don't want to impose on your family."

"You're a part of this family now too, Avery."

"Do you think they'll like me? Will they think I'm lying?"

Amy looks at her and grins, "Darling, they only need to look at you. You look just like your father. Just like our other children."

"If you're sure…I'd love to meet everyone. Do you think I could bring my boyfriend?"

"Sure. We'd love to meet him."

Joseph pulls Avery close and hugs her tightly, like a father that openly expresses his love for his children.

"I love you, Avery. I can't express how incredibly grateful I am that you've found us."

"Me too."

She follows them out of their house and directs herself towards her vehicle, stopping to wave to them as Joseph helps Amy into their car.

Avery sits down in her vehicle and takes a few deep breaths. She feels more content than she has in a long time. She's astounded at how welcome and open they were to her arrival. It could have gone downhill if they weren't so deeply in love – a love that she hopes she shares with Logan.

After starting the car, Avery heads out of the neighborhood and towards Logan's home.

Maybe Logan and I will grow old together, loving each other more each day.

Wow, talk about a complete one-eighty. At first Avery couldn't handle more than friendship. Now all she can think of is introducing him to her father as the love of her life.

RENEE HARLESS

Chapter Eight

*L*OGAN WAITS PATIENTLY FOR Avery to arrive back at his home. She texted him when she left telling him that all had gone well, but he knows he'll be able to look in her eyes and see the truth. She's entitled to have a family that offers her all the love she deserves.

While Logan waits for her to pull into his driveway he answers a text from Austin.

Austin: Hey man. Have you heard from Nikki?

Me: Naw. What's up?

Austin: Let me know if you or Avery hear from her. I need to talk to her.

Me: Will do. You ok?

> **Austin: Yea, I just need to speak with her. I totally fucked things up.**
>
> **Me: Well I'll send her your way if I hear from her.**
>
> **Austin: Thanks.**

Logan's worries about him. Since Nikki left he's been acting a bit off kilter, definitely a far cry from the womanizing man he met three years ago. Nikki is a pretty strong woman so he must have done something major to piss her off. Guess they'll have to find a replacement for her at the office as well, Logan thinks in annoyance. He hadn't taken her seriously when she said she was quitting.

A sound in the driveway alerts Logan to Avery's arrival. He jumps from the couch and races outside. As she exits the car, he wraps her in his arms and holds her close.

"How did it go?"

"It was...it was incredible, Logan. They were so much more welcoming than I could have ever imagined. I...I have a family," she cried into his shoulder, the excitement of the day taking its toll.

"I'm so happy for you, Avery. You deserve this and so much more. I knew they'd welcome you."

"Thank you, Logan."

He scoops her into his arms and carries her inside his house, resting her on the corner of his couch.

"So, tell me everything. What happened?"

"Oh, Logan, they were perfect. They've been searching for me for twenty years! Apparently my mother sent them a letter when I was four, telling them she had put me up for adoption. Of course that wasn't true, but they've contacted every agency in the country looking for me. Can you imagine? Searching for a child you love with all your heart, but never met. And, Logan, there is so much love in that house." Tears stream freely down her cheeks, her eyes sparkling with joy. "And I have siblings! I am so excited I can't even think straight. Oh, they invited us to dinner next Sunday at Angie's so I can meet everyone. Would you come with me? I'm afraid I may chicken out if I don't have someone there."

Logan rests his hand on her thigh and smiles.

"I'd love to meet your family, Avery."

His phone rings from its place on the kitchen counter and he rushes over to answer, noticing it is the general hospital in Charlotte. Logan volunteers there if they are short staffed when an emergency arises and this ringtone signifies an emergency.

"Hello, this is Dr. Chamberlin."

"Yes, Doctor, would you be able to come in for the next week? We know you have your own practice, but we are out four emergency physicians that were part of a missionary trip, apparently the airport was targeted by a militia group and the U.S. won't be able to evacuate them for a few days."

"Jesus Christ, of course I'll help," Logan says before turning to look at Avery, worry etched on her face. "I need to call my office and rearrange some appointments, but I can be there tomorrow morning."

"Thank you so much. We have an emergency pediatrician coming in from Raleigh so you will only need to work in general medicine. We really appreciate your help."

"You're welcome. I'll see you tomorrow."

Logan ends the call and walks back over to the living room where Avery has curled up on the couch with a pillow squeezed in her lap.

"So it seems I'm going to be gone most of this week, probably until Saturday."

"I heard. It sounds like they definitely need help."

"Stay with me tonight?"

"You sure you don't need to rest? You're going to have a long week."

He yanks the pillow from her grasp and wraps his hands around her ankles, tugging her towards him on the couch. The quick movement causes her to recline her body along the cushions. Logan lays his body over her, using his arms to hover above her face.

"Rest is overrated," he whispers before he swoops in for a kiss.

It doesn't take long for Avery to respond and she quickly wraps her arms and legs around his body, anchoring him close to her.

Logan breaks away momentarily and questions, "Are you sore?"

She shakes her head and tilts her head forward to capture his lips again. Logan stands from the couch, placing his hands under her thighs and carries her to his bedroom, never giving her a chance to break their connection. He sets her on the bed and begins peeling away her clothes.

"Get ready, sweetheart. We have one night for me to get a week's fill of you."

While Logan packs the next morning, Avery lies across his bed wearing only his t-shirt. It's a vision so beautiful he instantly whips out his phone to take a picture.

"Logan!"

"Sorry, babe, but you looked all beautifully seductive lying like that. I needed to capture the moment. Plus, it gives me a visual for when I'm gone."

She feigns a frown and eye-roll when she says, "Great."

He finishes packing, zips up his duffle bag and joins her on his bed, bringing her into his embrace.

"So I was thinking….maybe you could stay here while I was away?"

Avery moves her head from the spot she had claimed on his chest and gazes down at him.

"Why?"

"Um...peace of mind?"

"That seems silly, Logan. I don't have any of my stuff over here."

"Well, maybe you should move in. Would you want to move in with me?"

She sits up and looks at him intently.

"That's a big step, Logan."

"I know, and it may seem a bit sudden, but I love you and I want to be with you all the time."

Her eyes narrow, absorbing his words and contemplating her decision. By the look on her face, he starts bracing himself for a certain disappointment.

"Okay, Logan."

"What? Really?" Logan inquires, shocked by her answer.

"I want to be with you all the time, too. I'll bring a few things over this week and you can help me with the big stuff when you get back."

Logan reaches forward, his hands framing her face and he kisses her senseless.

"I love you so much, Avery."

"I love you too, Logan."

*L*OGAN HAS SPENT FOUR straight days at the hospital working in the emergency department and he is beyond exhausted. He's also missing Avery like crazy. They finally have a lull in the crowd and when he sees the pediatric emergency physician, Brooks, he asks him if he wants to grab some lunch in the cafeteria.

"That sounds great, man. I feel like I haven't sat down in days. It's like the entire city of Charlotte was either sick or in an accident."

As they wait for the elevator, Logan replies, "Tell me about it. I miss my practice in my small town, with regular hours I might add. I forgot what the craziness can be like in the ER."

They step into the elevator car and rise to the fourth floor, where they exit and head to the cafeteria. They both grab sandwiches before they sit themselves by the window.

A gaggle of nurses sit at the table across from them and continuously wink and smile in their direction. Brooks eats it up; Logan just ignores them, familiar with the game.

"Hey, Logan, that's some fine pickin' over there. You sure you're not interested?"

"No way, man. Been there, done that. Plus, I have someone back home."

As if summoned subconsciously, Logan's phone starts to ring and he curses when he thinks it's a call from the emergency room, but his smile broadens when he sees Avery's name flash across the screen.

"Hey, babe," Logan says enthusiastically.

He's missed her these past four days and he keeps his fingers crossed that he'll be able to go home earlier than expected.

"Hi, Logan. I miss you."

"I miss you too. Everything going okay?"

"Yea, I made some room in your closet for my clothes. Was that okay?"

"Definitely, but you seem a little off. Work good?"

"Yea, I'm sorry, I just got off the phone with Nikki and she has me all out of sorts. She's told me some things that I'm supposed to keep private, but I need to talk them through with you when you get home."

"Okay, we can do that."

"Oh...and the office may have found out about us."

Logan sits back in his seat and gazes out the window. He's strangely relieved that the office knows. It means no more hiding their relationship.

"Are you mad, Logan? I'm sorry."

"It's fine, Avery. I'm not mad. How'd they find out?"

"I'm not really sure. I just think maybe we weren't as good at hiding it as we thought we were. Dr. Fields asked me at the meeting this morning if I had heard from you and I just sort of froze. They all smiled at me like they had a secret and kept on with the meeting, but when we were leaving Dr. Fields asked me in front of everyone when the wedding was taking place. I don't think I've ever been so embarrassed."

Logan chuckles, thinking about how Al must have put her on the spot.

"I'm sorry you had to deal with that. I can address it when I get back, but I won't lie, I'm glad they know now. I don't want to hide you."

"I love you. When do you think you'll be back? Soon?"

"I don't know, sweetheart," he murmurs devastatingly. "Hey, I've got to run but I'll call you tonight, okay?"

"I'll be waiting."

He ends the call and faces Brooks who has a cheesy "all-knowing" grin on his face.

"Man, you are such a goner. Is that the lovely girl from back home?"

"Yep," he replies, turning his phone around to show Brooks the picture Logan took of them at the fall festival last weekend.

"Jesus Christ! How the hell did you snag her? Are all the women in Carson as hot as that?"

"I won't lie, there are a few, mostly my best friend's sisters, but don't tell him I said that. And yeah, this one here is the love of my life, so back off."

Logan's angry tone ignites a chuckle from Brooks. Logan ignores him and stands to dump his tray and head back to the ER. Brooks follows suit, laughing the entire way.

When Logan arrives downstairs the ER director pulls him into her office and tells him that they only need him to pull a half shift tomorrow and then he could go home.

Hell yea!

Logan finishes seeing the triaged patients before tucking himself away into a spare room set aside for him to sleep. He changes out of his scrubs and calls Brooks to head across the street to grab something to eat.

They meet at a sports bar, intent on watching the football game, and order some beer and food. Logan tells Brooks all about Carson and when he asks about Logan's family, he gives him his back story. Logan doesn't know why he opened up to a stranger like this, but Brooks proves to be a good listener. He tells Logan that he intended on playing professional baseball in college, had even been scouted by the Braves, but he tore his shoulder and it ended his career. Logan can tell the shoulder bothers him still; he noticed Brooks wincing while lifting weights at the gym this morning.

As a younger group starts crowding in on the bar, Logan leaves Brooks to enjoy himself while he heads back to his room. Logan lies in his bed and boots up his laptop, hoping to catch Avery as she's getting ready for bed. He's been debating telling her that he's coming home early, but he has finally ruled that out and decided to surprise her instead.

Suddenly his black screen disappears and he's met with the gorgeous face of his angel. She looks stunning, standing there in a soft pink robe, makeup removed from her face, and her hair twisted back.

"Hello, beautiful."

"Hey, handsome. I was getting ready to take a shower, it was a rough day."

"I know how to make your day better," Logan responds with a wink.

Grinning, she replies, "Oh yeah, how's that?"

"Take off that robe, go lie on the bed, and spread your legs. I want to see you touch yourself."

She giggles and hesitates at first, then positions her laptop on the dresser. She does as Logan asks and arranges herself on the bed so that he can see her swollen folds and the pink tips of her breasts. His cock throbs against the fabric of his boxer briefs.

"Come on, babe. Slide your hands down your breasts and touch yourself. Pretend it's my fingers feeling you," Logan declares as he reaches down and grips himself, working his rough hand up and down his hardened shaft.

She follows his every command, writhing against her own hand as she calls out his name in release. Logan follows closely behind her, biting his lip as he comes all over his hip.

"Fuck, I wish I was there, baby."

"Me, too. Not much longer, right?" she asks, her voice still dripping with sex.

"No, not much longer."

It takes all he has to hide the fact that he's coming home the next day. Logan can't wait to see her look of surprise.

"Ok, well I need to clean up. I'll talk to you tomorrow, okay?"

"Sure thing. I miss you, Logan."

"I miss you too."

The next day Logan's relief arrives around three in the afternoon; just after he finishes setting a broken arm due to a car crash. Logan waves to Brooks on his way out and eagerly jumps in his car, thrilled to head back to Carson.

It's around six when he arrives home and since it is Thursday, he expects to find Avery just getting home from the office.

As Logan opens the door he doesn't think twice about the smell of spaghetti wafting through the air or the candles lit around the house. No, his attention is drawn to the man's jacket draped over his couch. A jacket he recognizes.

Rage builds quickly in his gut and he has to work hard not to explode: losing his temper would make him no better than the man that called himself his father. But as he walks around the corner into the kitchen his desire to tamp down his rage evaporates. The feelings of betrayal, hatred, and broken trust erupt from his chest. Images of Shannon run through his mind.

"What the fuck is going on here?" Logan shouts, his hands gripping the back of one barstool, turning his knuckles white.

Before him Avery stands beside the table, leaning over, bringing her chest at eye level to the man she's entertaining. At his outburst, Avery stands quickly, practically falling over herself as she turns around startled. Austin pushes back from the table and puts his hands up as if surrendering.

Too fucking late for that!

"Logan, you're home. I wasn't expec…"

Cutting her off, Logan bellows, "I can see that you weren't expecting me." Pacing from the kitchen, he runs his hands through his hair, completely tormented by the vision of Avery and Austin. "God, how long did you wait? You're all the fucking same - liars and cheats. I should have known all along."

Logan can see the tears building in Avery's eyes, but his anger is so overpowering that he can't stop himself from spewing hatred.

"Logan, I…" she exclaims as she cries out his name.

"Was I not enough for you? What more did you want from me?"

Austin goes to stand beside Avery, but smartly she steps away from him.

"Logan," he says loud enough to override Logan's temper, "it's not what you think."

"Sure it's not. You fuck everything with two legs anyway, so you needed to add my girlfriend to your list. Both of you get the hell out of my house."

Logan turns to walk away, ready to toss everything of Avery's out of his bedroom. As he closes the bedroom door he can hear Austin console Avery and his heart breaks even more. Logan loves her more than anything, far more than Shannon, and he was ready to marry her. No, Avery tore out his heart and disintegrated it in her palm.

He sits on the end of his bed, unable to touch a single thing of Avery's, petrified of how he'll feel if he removes her completely from his life. Instead, Logan sits and thinks.

Why would she do this to me? I thought we had something special, something remarkable, something people search their entire lives for. How was I so wrong? We're just one more statistic, one more break-up on a long list of break-ups.

Logan hears Avery's car exit the driveway and then the front door closing, followed by boot-laden footsteps on his hardwood floors. A knock on his bedroom door startles him, but he makes no move to answer.

"You completely fucked this up. That girl loves you more than anything and you completely threw her away."

Logan continues to sit in silence, hoping that Austin will take the hint and go home.

Instead he continues, "I know what you've been through, Logan, and I know what it looked like when you walked in, but don't be a fucking dick. When you're done pouting like a little sissy ass baby, come out here and I'll explain why I was here and hopefully that will give you enough time to fix this."

At the sound of Austin's footsteps retreating Logan continue to stew, wallowing in his own anger. Ten minutes later, after shedding a few tears of his own, Logan steps out of his bedroom and walks down the hall. He finds Austin relaxed on his sofa, beer in one hand, remote in the other. Austin makes no move to stand from the couch, only grunting at Logan's arrival.

"You can leave now," Logan growls, the hatred still burning deep inside.

"No thanks, I think I'll stay to see the good doctor realize he was wrong," he says. "You need to go see the dining table."

"Why?"

"Don't ask, just do it."

Logan mutters a few expletives under his breath as he walks to the table. Spread out before him is a blueprint of the old school and a rendering from Austin's construction company.

"What's this?" Logan asks finding Austin next to him.

"This, my friend, is why I was here." He looks at Logan and continues, "Did you know your girlfriend had money? Like a lot of money? Twenty million, I think she said, and the lawyer in town said her grandmother left her quite a bit as well, but she mentioned she didn't want any of it. Any who; she called me and asked about a pediatric hospital because she had spoken with the boss of her asshole boyfriend – aka, you - about extending their services in the growing town. Now, I can't begin to say that I understand why she would want to spend that much money and continue to work, but she seemed happy about it. I believe she had planned to unveil it at your staff meeting on Monday."

Logan looks down at the drawing, a three-story building of glass and stone meant to house a pediatric office on the first level, as well as the option to lease offices to others. He can feel his chest constrict, the pressure overwhelming him. He grips his hand in a fist and pounds his chest.

"So she wasn't cheating on me?" he murmurs, turning to face Austin's accusatory stare.

Instead, Austin pats his back and smiles, "No way, that chick is only hot for you, nor am I attracted to her. Go apologize, she'll forgive you. She knows what you've been through."

Rushing towards his kitchen, Logan grabs his car keys before shouting on his way out the door, "Thanks Austin... Now get the fuck out my house and stop drinking my beer."

He takes the path that leads him to Avery's apartment, not paying attention to much of the surroundings, but when he stops at an intersection, he's surprised to find her SUV parked on the road in front of an old school. Logan parks behind her, gets out and looks in her car window, but doesn't find her in the vehicle. There are a few restaurants close by, but he has an inkling deep in his heart and follows his instincts.

Following the overgrown sidewalk, Logan walks on the laid concrete and stops where it ends at the school playground. He finds Avery perched on one of the plastic swings that barely hang on the rusted chains. She rocks the swing back and forth with the toe of her boot, and his heart aches at the despair infiltrating the air, wrapping its coldness around him, squeezing his chest tight.

Logan can't believe for a moment that he didn't trust her. Avery is the most pure-hearted person he has ever met. And he loves her - a profound emotion twisting and turning through his veins, seeping through his bones to the marrow, pumping life through his heart. She barricaded herself in Logan's core, deep within his soul, and nothing will ever pull her free.

"How long are you going to stand there watching me?" she asks, never ceasing her movements.

"You looked so beautiful. I couldn't help myself."

She simply nods, but offers no more means of conversation. Logan walks over to the swing set and wearily sits on the plastic board next to hers, afraid the rusted chains won't hold his weight and also that she'll push him away. Anxiety and nervousness aren't two emotions he's very familiar with.

Logan doesn't rock his swing, he sits there contemplating the best way to explain himself, but he comes up short. Instead, he finds himself needing to wipe away the wetness forming in his eyes at the thought that this may be the end for him and Avery. The concept alone fills him with more sorrow than he could have ever anticipated.

And it's all my fault.

"I'm not mad or upset, Logan. I love you." He looks over at her and he sees the shine reflected in her eyes as well. "I'm just hurt, Logan. But I understand what you've been through and I know that you weren't expecting what you saw when you came home."

"I'm so sorry, Avery. I jumped to conclusions. I'll do whatever I can to make it up to you. I don't want to lose you."

She looks out towards the play yard in front of her and starts swinging again by the toe of her boot.

"When I left your house I couldn't catch my breath. It was like someone was squeezing my lungs from the inside. I could feel every capillary exploding in my chest; it was terrifying." She pauses as she struggles to take a deep gulp of air. "I knew when you found me because I could finally breathe again. The noose in my chest unraveled and I could feel the cool air fill my lungs. I knew then that I couldn't be mad at you for your reaction. I can honestly say I probably would have reacted the same way. I know you trust me. You couldn't love me if you didn't. Just don't push me away, please."

"I knew the minute I turned around that I made a mistake, but I was too prideful, I needed to calm down. Avery, I love you far too much. I was prepared to grovel for your forgiveness."

"No need for that," she says with a chuckle, bringing her attention back to him.

The love exuding from her eyes induces a smile on Logan's lips. He tugs the chain of her swing and brings her face close to his, sealing his mouth over hers. Fireworks, explosions, detonations, whatever they're called, Logan feels them. He feels the electricity race from the tips of his boot clad feet to the ends of his overgrown hair. This kiss is more powerful and potent – though no less lustful - than their first kiss.

"Can you feel that?" she whispers against his mouth, eyes still shut tight.

"Every burn," he replies, placing a kiss at the corner of her mouth, then repeats the motion on each eye as he says, "Every sizzle. Every spark." Pulling back slightly, cupping her soft face in his hands. "I feel everything with you so deep that it becomes a part of me. There is no part of me that exists without you."

"Who are you?" she giggles.

"I have no fucking clue. It's like I kiss you and my brain turns into a Hallmark card. Austin will tell you that normally I'm a complete dick."

"Well I like it. It'll be our secret."

She kisses him once more and then sits back on her seat.

"Did Austin tell you what we were working on?" she asks shyly, picking at a piece of torn denim on her pants.

"He did. Avery, it's an incredible thing to do for these children. We need a pediatric office badly and you couldn't have chosen a better location."

"I just...it isn't my money and I hate having it. It's a reminder of all I've lost. I work hard and I save, I don't need it. And using it for something like this is exactly what Declan and his family would have wanted. It feels like I can let his memory live on in that building." She takes a deep breath and looks at Logan expectantly as if she thinks her next words will change him. "Logan, there is twenty million dollars in my bank account that I don't want. It will most likely grow once I meet with a lawyer again about my grandmother's will."

"I don't care about that, Avery. I make decent money on my own. I think it's admirable what you're doing. You could also look to work with some charities and maybe instead of selling your grandmother's home you could donate it to the historical society. You said it's been in your family for generations."

"I hadn't thought of that. It's a great idea. So are we okay?"

"I think so. And I've missed you this week. I can't wait to sleep with you in my arms."

She smiles that glorious grin, showcasing her perfectly straight white teeth.

"I can't wait either. I love you, Logan."

"I love you too, babe."

LOGAN AND AVERY LEAVE the playground and return to their vehicles, agreeing to meet back at his house. Neither of them has had a chance to eat dinner, so she's hoping she can make-do with the spaghetti she had finished cooking before Logan surprised her.

This evening truly took her for a spin. Avery wasn't even upset at Logan's outburst, she knows what it looked like when he walked in - his girlfriend and the town playboy nestled close over the dining room table. Anyone would have jumped to the same conclusion. But no, Avery couldn't be upset with Logan for his reaction, she was more distressed that she caused the reaction in the first place; that he mentally placed her with the other liars and cheats in his life.

The pain Avery felt when he demanded she leave was indescribable. It had felt like her body was subjected to every ounce of pain it could tolerate and then increased a notch. When Aria had died, she believed then that she knew torture. The loss of her sister overshadowed the pain Avery had felt when Nick and Declan had passed. Aria was her flesh and blood, her companion. But the agony of believing Avery had lost Logan eclipsed any of the anguish she had previously felt. The heart he had worked so meticulously at piecing back together, bit-by-bit, squeezed tight as if being forced through a sieve.

As she drove from his home, she couldn't capture any air in her lungs, a full-on panic attack set to take place. Avery wanted to get away as quickly as possible, grab a few things and head somewhere new, somewhere she could pretend to not exist, but she needed to rid herself of the anxiety. Avery tried to take short steady breaths, but nothing worked. She stopped the car, fearing that she would black out from the lack of oxygen and hurt someone else on the road, and then noticed she was at the old school. Avery stumbled out of her car, tripping a few times as she made her way down the concrete path, using the old stone wall for support. As the first swing came into view, Avery sat down and rested her head against the rusted metal of the chain.

Sitting down caused a short jerky movement of the swing, which rocked her into an anxiety-fueled haze. The noises from the outside world surrounded her in a bubble, the pressure of Logan's declaration weighing down on her. Then she saw them. Mentally, Avery knew the lack of oxygen to her brain was causing her to hallucinate, but in that moment they seemed far more real to her than her own person did. Before her stood Aria, flanked on both sides by Nick and Declan, surrounded in a grayish white mist, not uncommon for a chilled fall night. At their presence, Avery's heart rate increased and she began gasping for air, the scratchiness of her throat evident as she took each shallow breath.

"Calm down, Avery," Aria said, her melodic voice floating around Avery, flitting around her ears and hair. The hallucination feeling far more real to Avery than they had in the past. "Take a deep breath; let the air fill your lungs. Let your body feel the coolness of the breath."

Avery followed her instructions, desperately gasping for air, not even accounting for the fact that her dead sister was in front of her.

"He's coming," Nick's apparition said, but Avery didn't need him to say it out loud, because she could already feel it.

The hairs on Avery's arms prickled upwards and the tiny flutters in her stomach that appeared whenever she's with Logan started their rapid vibrations.

Aria spoke again, this time more passionately than before, "Don't be scared, Avery. We've been watching you, worried that you wouldn't be able to handle all the loss in your life. But you're so strong. And now we can move on - he will take care of them, he will take care of you. We love you, Avery; we will always keep our eyes on you."

Avery continued to take deeper breaths, unable to acknowledge her sister's spirit as she drifted into the air. A cool breeze wrapped around her body and Avery distinctly recognized the smell of the strawberry shampoo her sister always used. Incapable of speaking, Avery let a single tear drift down her cheek.

"You're a beautiful person, Avery," Nick said, "and you have a beautiful heart. You have so much love to give, don't regret sharing it. You're going to have a wonderful life."

And he too followed Aria and melted into the mist. A coldness brushes against Avery's cheek and the tear faded, its wet path gone, as if it had never appeared in the first place.

Declan floated closer to Avery, much closer than the others.

"I don't have long, I guess we're sort of used to that," he joked, chuckling in that deep laugh Avery came to love. "Avery, neither of us was meant to be with you forever, it wasn't in the plan. But Nick and I are thankful that we got to spend some of our last days wrapped up in your love. You were always meant to end up here - to find your soul mate and to find your father. And he is your soul mate, he's your other half, you two were created for each other. I have to go now, but remember we're always looking out for you. You're about to have everything you ever wanted. He's coming for you now."

Declan vanished more abruptly than the rest. Avery blinked her eyes, trying to determine if what she saw was real or just a figment of her imagination. She struggled to fill her lungs with more air, the pressure closing in again. Then Avery felt a coolness brush across her mouth, the smell of Declan's cologne filtering through the air and caressing her nose. As quickly as she imagined it, the smell and touch disappeared, and Avery was again left alone and empty.

A car door slams and Logan finds her as she sat still perched on the swing, looking as though she's been lost in her own thoughts, the hallucinogenic visions idly slipping from her mind.

They reconciled and as she left the playground, Avery could faintly smell the strawberry scent lingering in the air, in the distance a smaller play set's swing rocking back and forth, as if pushed and tugged by the breeze. In her heart, Avery knew it was Aria continuing to watch over her.

At Logan's house, they find the spaghetti stored in a glass dish and placed in the oven for reheating, courtesy of Austin. They sit at Logan's table and Avery tells him about her plans for the pediatric clinic while dinner warms in the oven. As they serve the meal, they open a bottle of white wine she purchased at the store, planning to open it on Saturday when Logan was schedule to return home.

"I'm really glad you're home, Logan."

He looks up at Avery with his captivating hazel eyes, his hair a bit disheveled and hanging over his forehead, and a panty-wetting smirk etched on his face.

"I'm so happy to be home. And I really can't wait for the makeup sex. I've heard remarkable things about it," he says as Avery stands from the table to dispose of her dishes, his eyes hungrily perusing her body.

Warmth instantly spreads across her body, settling in her center.

Logan stands from his chair and removes the dishes from her hands, resting them back on the table.

Avery licks her lips as she gazes at the tent forming in his pants and she murmurs, "Remarkable things, huh?"

"Mmhmm," he replies, greedily feasting his eyes on her exposed cleavage due to the oversized V-neck shirt she's wearing.

Before Avery has a moment to realize, she's flung upside down, fireman style, on Logan's broad shoulder as he stalks towards his bedroom.

"I hope you're ready, baby. We have a lot of lost time to make up for."

In the bedroom, he flips her over and releases her onto his bed, settling on top of her, devouring her in open-mouthed kisses as he claims her body as his for the rest of the night.

Avery calls out of work on Friday, wanting to spend the day in bed with Logan, but he has other plans. He wants all her things moved into his house.

Austin lets them borrow one of his work pickup trucks and a large trailer, but Avery didn't come to Carson with many things, so they were able to make one trip.

In just two hours, her stuff is moved from one location to the other, leaving Logan and Avery the remainder of the weekend in bed with each other. Avery never would have guessed that she would have such an insatiable hunger for a man, or that he would have one for her. But she can't get enough of Logan and every time she thinks she's gotten her fill, he'll do something unremarkable, like opening a can, but the way his biceps tighten as he twists the lid sends her synapses into over-drive and she has to have him again.

This morning Logan came after her, claiming that the way she cooked scrambled eggs was sexy, her hips moving along with the movement of the spatula, and he took her against the counter. She had to send him out of the kitchen so she could make a second, more edible, batch.

Avery hasn't spoken much about her father and his family to Logan. And as she stands at the closet pulling out potential dresses for the evening, she wonders why that is. At first, Avery thought it was because she wasn't sure if she was going to follow through with the dinner to begin with, telling Logan would have been like asking a trainer to make sure she exercises. He would have held her accountable. But Avery believes, in actuality, she was scared that he would know them - Carson is a small town after all. She didn't want to learn anything bad about the only family she had; the family that had embraced her with open arms. Instead, Avery brushed off any questions and changed the subject. Luckily, Logan let it go.

She chooses a deep-red dress that hits her just above the knee and pairs it with a set of blank ankle boots. She leaves her hair down, letting it fall in soft natural waves down her back, the same hair that mimics her father's. Grabbing a small handbag and a black cardigan, she exits the bedroom and collides with Logan, who was posed to knock on the door.

"Wow, Avery, you look beautiful."

"Thanks," she replies shyly. "You look handsome, too." And he does. He is wearing a light gray button down shirt, which is stretched tightly over his arms and chest, showcasing the rippling muscles below. His dark gray slacks flow from his trim waist, wrapping around his tight behind and thighs. "I'm going to have to beat the ladies off of you."

He reaches forward and strokes his thumb along Avery's bottom lip and she closes her eyes at the sensation. She can feel the air change as he leans forward, his minty breath swirling across her face. His hand moves from her lip to her chin and he tilts her head up slightly.

"You're the only one I'll ever want, Avery. And remember, you're the one who gets to come home with me and let me make love to you."

Eyes still shut tight, Avery groans at his proclamation before he captures her lips with his, sliding the soft skin of his mouth against hers. He pulls away quickly, far sooner than she wants. Avery opens her eyes and harshly sets her gaze upon him.

"Don't look at me like that, sweetheart. I'd take you against the wall right now if I knew that we had the time. But we need to leave. We'll continue this tonight. I promise"

Avery pouts childishly, disappointed that he's right, but Logan growls when he sees her lower lip jutting forward.

"Fuck, you can't do that, baby."

He looks at his watch momentarily and then turns Avery, pressing her against the wall, securing a kiss against her lips. Using his knee he spreads her legs wide and he slides his hand up her dress. He groans when he touches her tender flesh, wet and dripping for him.

"No fucking panties?"

Avery shakes her head, dropping her bag and sweater as she reaches forward with her hands to grip the back of Logan's head and pull him in for another scorching kiss. Her body rocks against his hand as his fingers thrust in and out of her heated core, his palm rubbing circles around her tender bundle of nerves. It doesn't take long before she explodes from the movement of his digits and Logan lets her rest against the wall.

"Better?" he asks as he sucks his fingers into his mouth, inducing another wave of aftershocks in her body.

"Temporarily," Avery replies as she gazes at the hard-as-steel bulge preparing to burst from the waist of his pants. "It will hold me over until we get home."

Under his breath she hears him say, "Naughty girl," as he reaches for her bag and sweater, hands them to her, then takes her hand and escorts her from the house.

They arrive at the diner fifteen minutes later and stand at the host's desk, waiting to be seated. She directs them to a private room off the back hidden around a corner, but instead of entering Avery rests against the wall and takes a few deep breaths.

"Logan, what if they hate me?"

"They won't hate you sweetheart. They may be confused and upset, but none of this was your fault. And if they make you feel uncomfortable, we'll leave okay? You can still have a relationship with your father," he says as he gently tucks some loose hair behind her ear. "Come on, you can do this. I'm here with you."

Logan opens the door to the private room and steps in behind Avery. Conversation flows around the full table, but her attention is clutched by the two men at the end of the table.

"Mr. Connelly?" Logan asks, his vision focusing on the same men at the end of the table. Shaking his head in confusion and a hint of betrayal, he takes her hand, looks at her and then back to the man sitting beside Joseph. "Austin, I swear I didn't know."

"Didn't know what?" Austin inquires. "I didn't realize you were joining us."

Avery is rooted in her spot, unable to speak as seven pairs of eyes focus on her, narrowing in question.

Joseph stands from the table and walks over to the entrance of the room, wrapping his arm around her shoulder. Avery makes sure that her clammy hand never leaves Logan's grasp.

"I believe I can answer that for you, Austin. Everyone, this is your sister Avery."

"Sister? What the fuck, Dad?!?" Austin hollers, his voice bellowing across the room as he stands from his seat.

Avery glances nervously at Logan, biting her lower lip, letting her teeth sink deep into the tissue as the room fills with hushed chatter, the murmurs overtaking the small room. She works to keep the tears at bay.

Thankfully, Amy speaks up, instantly taking charge of the situation.

"Sit down, Austin. Yes, she is your sister - your half-sister. And if you all would stay put, your father and I will explain everything to you. Let's help Avery feel welcome; we've been searching for her for a long time," she clarifies, "Let's not scare her off."

Avery continues to stand frozen, but when she feels a tug on her hand she glances up at Logan and he smiles down at her.

"Where would you like to sit?"

She looks around the table at the random spattering of open seats unsure if she's willing to sit apart from Logan. Luckily, one of the females at the table removes her bag from the chair next to her, opening two seats next to one another.

"You two can sit here," she says quietly.

Moving in that direction, Avery sits down beside her, taking notice at how similar she looks to her mother. Long straw colored hair, chocolate brown eyes, pale skin, and cute tortoise shell frames perched on her nose. She's cloaked in a black turtleneck and a long brown wool skirt. She looks a bit dowdy for someone with such striking features.

"Thank you," Avery murmurs as she sits down.

Settling into the chair next to Avery's, Logan says, "It's, uh...nice to see everyone," before interlacing their fingers together.

The woman across from Avery, who also has the same brown eyes and blonde hair as her mother, only with her blonde locks in a short wavy bob, gazes at her in astonishment as she mutters, "Christ, she looks just like Jameson."

Realizing she spoke the words out loud, she shakes her head and turns her attention to the head of the table, glaring at her father expectantly.

"Avery, would you like anything to drink?" Logan asks, leaning close to her ear, his concerned voice wrapping around her like a life raft.

She responds with a shake of her head, knowing that her trembling hands couldn't handle a glass of liquid at the moment.

"You all are probably not aware that there was a time your mother and I were separated." Gasps ensue and Avery can hear Austin begin to form a question, but Joseph stops him cold, "Please let me finish before you ask or say anything. This isn't easy for any of us. I love you all and I love your mother, don't ever question that."

Avery glances around the table and instead of seeing anger or confusion, she sees the faces of the children that love and respect their father. Willing to stand behind him and follow his lead.

"As I explained to Avery, while I was separated from your mother I had met a woman. It happened only once and that moment made me realize that all I needed was back at home waiting for me. I told your mother everything that happened and she forgave me. You have to understand that I hated myself for how weak I was, but I was so lost. I was only thirty, with three kids and a wife, and I lost sense of who I was. Your mother took me back and I thank my lucky stars every day that she has such a forgiving heart." He grabs her hand and kisses the back of it in a sweet gesture.

Amy blushes at the contact and love pours out of the shy smile she gives him.

Joseph turns his attention back to his children, the stress of the secret released from his stance.

"I want you to know that I'm sorry for what I've done, but I'm not sorry that I was given this wonderful gift. You all need to know that Avery didn't know anything about me. We were given a letter twenty years ago that said she had been given up for adoption and we've been searching for her ever since. Instead, she found us. I'm sure you're all feeling confused and upset, but know that Avery being here doesn't change the dynamic of this family. You're all more important to me than anything else in this world."

He sits back in his chair, Amy leaning close and kissing his cheek. Other than a few moments with Logan, Avery has never seen or heard a man speak so freely about his emotions. It is refreshing.

Seven faces turn in her direction, five of them gazing at her expectantly. Logan squeezes her hand in reassurance.

"Hi, I'm...um...Avery Poindexter. I'm from Atlanta and I moved to Carson about three months ago. I work as a medical assistant at the doctor's office where Logan works."

A question barks from the far end of the table and when Avery turns in that direction, she's startled at the similarities of their features. From what she noticed, he seems to be the only sibling that shares the same eye color as her and Joseph.

"Are you here because of the money?"

Avery gulps and squirms in her seat, uncomfortable with the accusation, but she's saved by Austin's deep voice.

"No she's not. She has more money than anyone at this table."

Everyone's eyes widen in surprise as Austin continues to speak, addressing her, "Sorry, Avery. I don't think anyone mentioned that we all have trust funds worth a couple million and we all do well in our respective jobs. No one here needs to worry about you using them." He leans forward and rests his arms on the table, looking at Avery as a grin grows along his lips. "And it makes sense that we're related. Why else would you turn me down right?"

And with that joke, Avery bursts out in laughter, thrilled for the ice-breaker. The rest of the family follows suit and she laughs even harder when she hears Logan mutter, "Fucking bastard," under his breath as he joins in with a snicker.

Now that the tension has dispersed and most of the awkwardness subsided, Amy takes the opportunity to introduce her children, Avery's brothers and sisters.

She starts with Austin, who is closest to her side of the table and works her way around.

"This here beside your father is Joseph Jr., or Austin as he likes to be called."

"That's why I never put two-and-two together; you only ever called him Joseph Jr."

"Yes, well, he was my first born and we wanted to pass down his father's name. He owns Connelly Construction and works as a contractor."

"Oh I know. We're working on a project together. He does great work. I'm hoping to turn the old school into a pediatric clinic and what he's come up with is remarkable."

Austin blushes under Avery's admission and his mother beams with pride.

"A pediatric clinic is exactly what this town needs, with the surge of families moving to the area and all. Sorry, I'm Everleigh, I'm a pharmacist at Nelson's Drug Store."

Her hair is a few shades darker than her sisters' and mother's, as if her chromosomes couldn't decide on a color and chose a combination of both her mother's and father's.

Amy nods to the woman sitting next to Avery, "This is Sydney; she's a baker and just revamped my old place. It's now called Wake and Bake."

Sydney chimes in next to Avery, "I bought the lot next door and I'm looking to add a coffee shop and grill."

"That sounds amazing."

"Next we have Jameson beside Logan. He just graduated with a degree in software programming. He also creates and sells apps for companies. His twin is Ryker, who couldn't be with us. He's busy touring with his band overseas."

"Ryker Connelly...why does that name sound familiar."

Logan leans in and says, "That's because he's the lead singer of the band Exoneration."

"Oh...wow."

"Finally, this is your sister Cassidy. She's runs the world-famous label under the same name."

"Oh my...there is so much talent in your family."

"You do wonderful things, Avery. The medical field is a tough one and you did it all by yourself. You should be proud of yourself, your father and I sure are," Amy replies.

The food arrives and Avery eats her meal quietly, listening to the chatter around her. Even Logan is feeling more at ease, speaking freely with his best friend and his family.

Suddenly Avery feels a nudge on her arm from Logan's elbow as he says, "Jameson asked you something."

"Oh, I'm sorry. What did you ask?"

"How was it for you growing up? Were you adopted? Did you live in foster care?"

"Oh...um...well..." she stutters, first looking at Joseph and then at Logan.

They both nod for her to share her story. Logan takes her hand under the table and holds it in his warm loving grasp.

Avery lets out a sigh and answers, "Honestly, I lived in hell. My mother left me with my grandmother, who was so ashamed that she pretended I didn't exist. I was born into an affluent family, but was brought up as if I was a servant in the home. It wasn't until my sister was born that I learned the truth about my family. I was taken care of by one of the servants. She treated me with more love and care than my own mother. My grandmother began abusing my sister, so when I turned eighteen I begged my grandmother to sign over her over to me. I promised to leave and I never looked back. My sister died in an accident four years ago and I miss her every day. The only good thing to come from my grandmother is the note she left in her will, giving me the address of the father that had never been mentioned in her home. She said that he had a family that would love and care for me. So here I am."

With her free hand, she reaches up and wipes away the tears that have escaped from her eyes.

She looks at Logan first and he whispers, "I love you," before she turns her attention to the rest of the group.

Tears streak down the faces of her sisters, Joseph, and Amy, though Jameson continues to show spurts of anger in his features, the questioning eyes and scowl evident on his face.

"Even the second time hearing it isn't any easier," Joseph says gruffly.

The family all seems shaken by her background, except Jameson who seems to be studying her closely.

"It's okay, please. Don't feel sorry for me. If I hadn't gone through all of that, then I wouldn't be here today with all of you and your wonderful family."

"You're our family, too," Sydney says as she envelopes Avery in her arms, the warmth of her embrace radiating through Avery's body.

They sit around the table a bit longer exchanging a few stories, but mostly Avery relaxes with Logan and takes in all that surrounds her. It's amazing how easily they were all able to bounce back from the news of their father having an affair and another child. But it's easy to see and feel all the love in the room. Avery glances at Logan and he smiles, but she knows he feels as out of place as she does. They both grew up in broken homes and have never felt the kind of compassion that currently zings through this room.

Until I met him.

She tightens her hold of his hand and leans into his body, tilting her head towards his ear as he exchanges a joke with Austin.

"I love you, Logan."

He turns in her direction and kisses her softly.

"I love you, too, sweetheart," he echoes.

Joseph and Amy rise from the table, bringing the family's attention to their stance.

"We're getting a bit tired so we wanted to say goodnight to everyone. But first I want to thank all of you for welcoming Avery with open arms, though I never expected anything less. Avery, you may already have plans, but we would love to have our entire family with us at Thanksgiving in a few weeks," Amy requests.

"I'd love to. I've never had a traditional Thanksgiving. Oh, I'm excited!" Avery peeks at Logan once more and finds notes of disappointment skimming in his eyes. "Amy, would you mind if Logan came too?"

"Oh no, Amy; I don't want to intrude on your family's day," Logan rushes, embarrassed by Avery's request.

"Nonsense of course you're coming. You're important to Avery and Austin and that makes you family. And no arguing."

"Yes, ma'am."

"Ok then. Boys you should head out, too. I believe you're all on duty tonight."

They all grumble at the table and Avery arches her brow towards Austin in question.

"We're all volunteer firefighters just like our dad. The town isn't large enough for its own firefighters, except for dad who runs the department."

"Oh, I had no idea. That's very admirable of you all."

He nods and as he scoots his chair from the table, the rest of the Connelly clan stands as well.

"So, how do you feel?" Jameson asks as they leave the restaurant.

Logan is walking ahead with Austin, most likely inquiring about the school rebuild and Avery walks behind the group.

Jameson's question takes her by surprise and her confusion is detectable when she nervously replies,

"What do you mean? Of course I'm happy to meet all of you; I've never had a real family like this before."

Wrapping his large hand around her arm, he halts her movement.

"No, Avery. Don't let them fool you. How does it feel to destroy a family just so you can have one?"

And then he stalks off, anger seeping from his body in his rigid stance.

"Don't listen to him, Avery. He's upset. Growing up he never liked surprises."

Avery turns towards the voice coming from the private room they just exited, that's when she notices Amy's petite figure shielded by the door.

"I'm sorry, Amy. I never considered how this would affect your family. I was too wrapped up in the notion of meeting my father and spending time with him."

Amy steps forward, out of the shadowed weight of the door.

"Avery, you're a special girl that deserves to be in the lives of her father and siblings. Don't forget that your father and I have searched for you since the day we knew you existed. There was never any question that we loved you and wanted you to be a part of our family. Jameson and the others are just struggling to understand how the father they grew up with could be this man, who in their eyes, cheated on their mother. But, sweetie, it was never like that and I'll speak with them to make sure they understand that, too."

"I just never expected for any of this to happen, you know?"

"I know. You're a smart girl with a kind heart, always putting others ahead of herself." She looks off down the hall, towards the exit and smiles. "I think you've met someone that understands you and wants you to have everything your heart desires. They way that man looks at you reminds me of how your father looks at me."

Avery follows her gaze and smiles when she sees Logan heading their way.

"I love him."

"He loves you, too. Logan's a good man and a good friend to Austin. We can't wait to welcome him to the family," she says as she pets Avery's cheek lightly, a hidden gleam in her eyes, before she slides past Logan and heads toward Joseph.

"Hey, babe. Everything okay?"

Looking up at his handsome face, his chiseled jaw line, two-day scruff, Avery can't help but release a contented sigh; Jameson's comment forgotten for the time being.

"Everything is perfect."

A VERY TRAILS BEHIND LOGAN into the house, her mind seemingly elsewhere. He didn't want to bring up the interaction he witnessed between her and Jameson. Logan could tell her brother said something that upset her, he could see her eyes widen and her chest expand in a sharp intake of breath from the other side of the restaurant, but Austin assured him that Jameson just needed time to adjust to the thought of the man he loved and respected fathering another child.

She follows Logan into the bedroom where she promptly settles on the chair in the corner of the room, shoes left on the floor and her knees brought to her chest. She's in self-protection mode.

Logan walks to the chair and kneels in front of her, bringing her feet to rest back on the floor.

"Tell me what's bothering you. I know you've got something on your mind."

He waits for her to answer, but she continues to look outside, avoiding eye contact with him.

"Avery."

"Fine," she says, taking a deep breath and then turning her beautiful eyes on him. "Do you think I'm destroying their family?"

"No way. Why would you say that?" Logan asks angrily, then after a second he realizes what Jameson must have accused. "Avery, listen to me. You did not destroy their family - *your* family. Jameson just need time to adjust, they all do. But you're their sister and there isn't anything they can do to change that."

She nods solemnly and whispers, "You're right."

"Of course I am."

Logan rests on both of his knees and tugs her hands so that she stands before him; her small frame bringing her pelvis to eye level. He reaches down and trails his fingers lightly up the soft skin of her legs, and over the soft material of her dress. Placing his hands on her hips, he turns her in his arms so that he has a glorious view of her backside. Reaching up, he tugs down the zipper of her tight dress and guides the material down her arms, letting it pool at her feet. Her breath is coming at heavy pants and Logan can hear each intake of hollow breath.

Taking a moment Logan sits back on his heels and memorizes her beautiful body - every curve, every freckle, every divot in her skin.

Kneeling tall once more he traces a path down her slender back, parallel with her spine. When she shivers at his touch, Logan has to suppress a chuckle. As hard as she fought him in the beginning, her body beckons him closer, always responsive to his touch.

He swirls a finger around her hip and maps a route around one of her plump cheeks before trailing the finger up the crease of her behind.

"Logan," she murmurs heatedly.

His finger traces the crease downward and follows through to the moist and heated center that eagerly awaits his touch. Logan's other hand grips her hip harder and he slides his finger across her slick folds, a gasp escaping her lips. A rush of heat expels onto his hand when he grazes against her clit, her body shaking in anticipation. His finger slides down her inner thigh, lightly skimming her delicate skin. Unable to hold back his need to taste her, he leans forward and gently bites the round skin of her cheek before licking it to soothe the wound. Her groan of delight signifies her approval. No longer capable of resisting, Logan removes his hand from her hip and applies pressure between her shoulder blades, silently commanding her to bend forward. She grips the arms of the chair and bends at her waist, showcasing her glistening folds that yearn for more of his touch.

Logan glides his fingertips back up her leg and strokes the skin closest to her hungry core, but makes no move to contact the area that craves his attention.

"Logan," she moans huskily, her body longing for more of his touch.

"You want me to touch you, baby?" he inquires, his voice giving away how turned on he is, seeing her bent over before him, completely bare.

"Mmmm, I want you to feel how turned on I am, Logan. I need you to touch me."

Logan complies, the scent of her desire penetrating through his shield. A finger slides through her wetness, caressing the plump folds and applying pressure to her exposed button of pleasure with his thumb. Logan's other hand, desperate to feel her warmth, glides two fingers inside her warm channel, coating themselves in her heat.

Powerless to control his appetite Logan removes his hand from her core and licks around her center, her desire blanketing his tongue. His hand again takes over and thrusts two fingers deep inside her core, causing more shutters to pulsate along her body. His lips settle around her unprotected bundle and he flicks the sensitive nerves with his tongue, eliciting a few gasps, before sucking the button into his mouth. As he continues to push his fingers in and out of Avery's channel, he can feel her womb begin to quake, her eruption springing forth. Logan doesn't lessen his movements, but he takes his free hand and searches for the untouched area of her body. His thumb finding the puckered skin and he applies gentle pressure to gain a slight entrance.

As expected, the new intrusion of pleasure ignites her fire and she explodes on his fingers, wetness seeping onto his hands and face and as her ripples of desire continue. Logan laps at her sweetness, his need to prolong her orgasm uncontrollable as the screaming of his name echoes around the room.

When the rippling of her inner muscles subsides, Logan pulls her down to sit limply in his arms. She opens her tightly shut eyes and gazes at him hungrily, her craving evident. She cups the back of his head in one of her hands, pulling him close, and seals their mouths together. With her back to his chest, he uses his legs to spread hers wide, exposing her wet center. Logan grips one of her breasts roughly with his hand, pinching her nipple between his fingers. His other hand slides through her folds one more, before sinking deep in her hot dripping channel.

"No more, Logan. I need you inside me," she groans as Logan continues to penetrate her with his fingers.

"I am inside you, sweetness," Logan sarcastically replies as her hips buck against his hand, her sexual need growing by the second.

"I need to feel your cock inside me, Logan. Please."

He spreads her legs wider as he rubs the heel of his hand against her swollen clit. Avery's head leans back against his shoulder and he uses the opportunity to nip at her jaw line.

Against her neck, Logan allows his heavy words to float to her ears.

"One more, baby. One more and then I'll fuck you as hard and fast as you want, for as long as you want. You own my dick, babe. I can't wait to thrust in you - to feel my cock wet with your hot juices."

She bucks faster against his hand, controlling her movements, but when Logan reaches up with his free hand and slides her nipple between his fingers she convulses around him - once again screaming his name.

Logan lifts her into his arms in her unconscious state and lays her gently across his bed. He bends her knees and spread her legs wide, opening her center to his view. Quickly removing his clothes, he tosses them haphazardly towards the corner of the room.

Joining her back on the bed, Logan rests on his arms above her as he takes one of her taught nipples in his mouth, savoring their flavor. Avery's eyes immediately open, gazing at his mouth as he makes love to her breast. He rocks his hips against her core, sliding through her wetness and coating himself in her honey. Every time the tip of his penis passes over her inflamed clit, shutters wrack her body.

Still resting on his elbows, Logan moves up her body and melds their lips together. Unwilling to hold back any longer, he thrusts his erection to the hilt, her body encasing his shaft, as he mimics his movements with his tongue in her mouth. He moves slowly at first, wanting to savor the feel of being inside her tight body. She responds to his kiss, dancing her tongue with his in an intimate tango. Avery wraps her legs around his waist, rocking her hips with the hope of increasing his speed, but he maintains his rhythm, her body quenching his thirst at each plunge.

A tingling begins in his spine and he has to fight to hold off the release building in his body. Logan growls when Avery removes her lips and bites his shoulder.

"Yes, Logan," she cries, her nails digging into his back, her body on the verge of ecstasy. "Fuck me, Logan. Please. I need you to let go and fuck me."

At the sudden outburst, Logan thrusts twice into her deep and hard and then pulls out of her completely. Her howl of disappointment is mirrored by the selfish rock of her hips seeking his cock.

"You want me to fuck you?" Logan inquires, as he slides only the tip of his cock into her greedy center, sliding right back out before she can grip him tight. "You want me to sink my cock in you so deep and fast that you feel me when you walk tomorrow? Is that how bad you want me to fuck you?" Logan asks as he repeats the same movement.

She mewls at each penetration, desperately clawing at his back, wanting him to worship her body.

His need for release is as rampant as her own and he twists her on the bed so quickly she has no time to react before he pulls her hips up, bringing her to her knees, and plunging deep inside.

They cry out in unison - the pleasure overwhelming.

His erection submerges far inside her body; the connection between Avery's body and his own no longer decipherable. He watches as his cock slides in and out of her center, coated in her heat, each movement reciprocated by her body.

Before long they're connecting at a frenzied pace, each of them spiraling towards release. He twists his hand in Avery's dark hair and yanks her head back so that he can taste the sweetness of her mouth. He uses his other hand to graze her nipple before turning his attention onto her clit. Swirling a pressured touch on the exposed nerves, she cries out against his mouth, her core clamping down on his shaft. Logan grips her hair tighter in his hand, his rhythm soon forgotten as he pounds frantically against her backside, using her tensed inner muscles to ignite his explosion. Soon Logan finds himself pulsating against Avery's body, his seed spilling far within the confines of her womb.

As she makes to rest fully on the bed, Logan slides from her core, his essence leaking from her.

"Damn, that's hot. Me dripping from you like that."

"Hmm," she says sleepily. "Reminds me where you've been."

"Fuck yea it does."

Logan steps into the bathroom and grabs a washcloth, running it under warm water, intent on cleaning up his mess.

Lying naked under the covers with Avery is one of the best feelings in the world. Knowing she is safely wrapped in his arms, guarded from the rest of the world.

With her back to his chest, Logan uses the arm that was wrapped around her waist to push the hair away from her delicate face. He leans over and gazes at her closed eyes and her lips that are pursed in sleep.

Damn, she's beautiful.

His lips move on their own accord and he places a gentle kiss below her ear on her jaw line.

"I love you, Avery," Logan whispers.

As he settles back on the bed, she turns in his arms and returns his gentle kiss.

"I love you too, Logan," she responds, pressing her warm body against his.

Her radiant smile is enough to show that she means every word.

"I thought you were asleep."

"I was close, but not quite there yet."

"I'm sorry."

"Don't be," she says as she bends her leg slightly, placing her bent knee over his straightened leg.

In return he bends his leg and places it between hers. She tilts her head grazing her lips over his in a soft kiss, her hand sliding up his shoulder into his hair.

"Logan," she murmurs as she pulls a breath away, "I will be forever thankful that you showed me that I didn't need to be scared of you - or to be scared of love. I can't imagine what my life would be like without you in it."

His heart pounds in his chest and at that moment, with her eyes glazed in desire and love and truth, Logan realizes that his entire life will have meant nothing without her in it, by his side. It doesn't matter that they've barely known each other for a few months. The love he feels for Avery is so vast and all-consuming that he can't believe he had ever considered himself in love with another. *Love.* Logan had planned to spend the remainder of his life in eternal bachelorhood, jumping from one bed to the next. It's astounding how this tiny creature with her big blue eyes and wavy brown hair pulled him in and made him never want to let her go.

Logan leans closer, his hand moving from under her arm to wrap around her shoulder as he fuses his mouth to hers.

"You'll never have to," Logan says before merging their lips together again.

He presses her back into the mattress and slides his hand down her body to find her already soaking wet for him. His erect member slides into her effortlessly and he makes love to Avery, on and off for the remainder of the night.

*L*OGAN HAS MOVED ALL of Avery's remaining items from her apartment into his home, including the small knick-knacks she had purchased with Nikki. At first, she was extremely apprehensive about moving in with him, but it feels so right. And since that vision she had at the swing set, where she saw her sister, Nick, and Declan, she's been less hesitant to move further with Logan. Avery never mentioned the vision to Logan, not that she was afraid of what he'd say, but it felt so personal that she wanted to keep that last part of those she'd lost with her, close to her heart. And so far, by following their guidance, she's been happier, more carefree.

With Thanksgiving around the corner Avery's tried to get closer to her siblings. Each of them has fit her into her life in a different way, Sydney and Everleigh being the most open. She was afraid Everleigh would have the most difficult time with her arrival since Joseph left after Everleigh was born, but she welcomed Avery into her heart and reminded her that the situation didn't reflect on her. Jameson has yet to come around, but Amy and Joseph have spoken to him numerous times and they said he wanted to get to know her. Avery has yet to meet Ryker, but she's told he'll be home for the holiday, which makes her a bit nervous. She's never met a celebrity.

Austin and Avery have a strange relationship. Knowing that she is dating his best friend makes for some awkward situations. He goes into this *protective* mode when the three of them are together, as if learning that she is actually his sibling gives him a different perspective on how Logan should treat her. Not that Austin's concerns have any merit; Logan treats her like a princess.

Nikki hasn't returned to Carson, but Avery speaks to her frequently as she updates her on the development of the baby. Austin still hasn't been told that she's pregnant with his baby, though Avery's tried to change her mind several times. Avery knows Austin is going to be hurt and angry when he finds out, but she knows it's not her place to say anything.

Joseph and Amy have been incredible; so much so as to invest in her pediatric clinic project, not that it needed any upstart capital. They even joined her and Logan at the lawyer's office yesterday to go over the final reading of her grandmother's will. She left Avery a hefty sum of money, along with all of her jewelry and the house. Avery donated it all. The money she donated to a charity that specializes in the inoperable cancer that plagued Declan, and also to an arts program in Asheville. The house is being donated to the Atlanta Historic Society, who is planning to convert it into a museum. She gave the jewelry to Joseph to use in Asheville at an auction to raise money for the fire department in Carson.

Logan and Avery had been blissfully happy since the family dinner four weeks ago. But this week he seemed different, off. Avery can't put her finger on it, but he's always thinking of something else when they're together, his mind straying to a different world. Normally his behavior would worry her, but when they come together at night, he worships her, like he simply can't get enough. If anything, their physical connection is better than before.

She knows Logan is working on a confidential child protection case at the clinic and Avery chalked up his behavior to that, but last night Austin had to bring him home. He was drunk and reeked of Chanel No.5, which Avery recognized because it's the only perfume her grandmother wore. Avery wants to trust him, especially after Austin assured her that he hadn't been up to any trouble, but it's hard to distinguish the truth when a current womanizer is reassuring the actions of a past womanizer.

Avery wakes in the morning, excited to celebrate her first Thanksgiving surrounded by her family and Logan.

Reaching across the bed, she startles when she touches the cold sheets, a clue that Logan left the bed a while ago. Grabbing her robe, she goes to the bathroom to brush her teeth, then moves to the kitchen for a cup of coffee. She stops herself in the hall when she overhears Logan speaking on his phone at the kitchen island. He speaks in hushed tones to a voice that she can easily determine as feminine.

Not wanting to eavesdrop, Avery rests against the wall, urging herself not to cry, having to bite her lip to suppress a sob.

"Alright, I'll be by in a bit. I'm so thankful to have run into you last night."

What?!?

Her mind races in theory, contemplating how he could have been with both Austin and this woman.

Maybe it's someone he's working with? Or an old friend?

But the smell of the perfume fogs her mind and she can't help but jump to the only conclusion her brain can scramble together.

Instantly awakened, Avery turns around and heads to the bathroom to take a shower. She washes her hair and scrubs her body in a complete haze of simmering emotions. Stepping out of the shower, she wraps herself in a towel and sits on the bed, her soaked hair dripping all around her. Avery can't comprehend the thought of Logan with another woman. He was supposed to be her savior, the person she had to live for, how could this happen to them?

Completely lost in her thoughts, she doesn't realize Logan has entered the room until he lifts her chin with his finger.

"Hey, Avery, you okay?"

Gracious that the dripping hair masks the fallen tears, she wipes her face to clear the evidence.

"Mmmhmm. Yep," Avery replies, masking her sadness with false joy.

Logan cocks a brow at her response but doesn't press any further.

"Hey, I know we have your dad's dinner this afternoon, but I need to do a couple things and run by the office so we may be a bit late. That, ok?"

"What do you need to do? It's Thanksgiving."

He holds his palms up in surrender but nervously glances around the room, instantly giving away the lie.

"Just some stuff I didn't finish yesterday. I'll be back soon. I promise."

Avery jerks her chin upward with a huff and makes an attempt to stalk back to the bathroom, but he takes a hold of her hand before she has the chance.

"Hey, I love you, Avery. I promise that I'll be back soon."

And the sincerity in his eyes is enough to cut Avery to the core. She's conflicted at which action to trust - the lie weaving through his every word, or the love pouring from his heart.

Checking his watch he looks back at her and places a chaste kiss on her lips before rushing out the door and down the driveway.

Avery changes into an olive green blouse, dark denim jeans, and brown boots. She blow dries her hair quickly and puts on a smidgen of makeup before grabbing her phone from the night stand.

Avery calls Nikki first but she doesn't answer, Melanie doesn't answer either.

Relegated to the only other people Avery knows in Carson, she calls Everleigh and luckily her sister picks up after one ring.

Avery begs her for advice after disclosing all that has taken place in the past week. Everleigh offers to ask Austin what is going on, but Avery explains that she wants to keep it private. Instead, Avery asks if she can stay with her for a few days, until she can figure out what she needs to do. At first Everleigh turns her down, suggesting that Avery speak with Logan, but after much begging, Everleigh finally relents. She does point out that Avery is not getting out of Thanksgiving dinner and that if Logan wants to speak to her he'll find her there - and then all of the family will be brought into the mess. When Everleigh explains that possible situation, Avery tells her that she'll think on it for a bit.

Going ahead and packing her small duffle bag, Avery is intent on getting some space before she confronts Logan. She grabs a picture from the dresser to toss into her bag: a photo of her and Logan from Halloween, taken by Sydney. They were leaning against the porch column, Logan's arms wrapped firmly around her body, Avery's head tilted back in laughter at something one of the trick-or-treaters said. Logan was gazing down at her as if she was the most important thing in the world, a beautiful smile gracing his defined face.

Avery wipes away a tear as she tosses the picture in the bag with her few day's worth of clothes. Stepping into the bathroom, she adds some small toiletries into her small travel bag. When Avery moves back into the bedroom, she finds Logan standing beside the bed, eyeing her duffle bag.

So deeply buried in her own turmoil, she never heard him enter the house.

"What's going on, Avery? Why are you packing up?" he inquires, panic raising the tone of his voice.

Avery steps closer to him, unable to ignore the pull he has over her; grateful that she doesn't smell the scent of Chanel No.5.

"Why did you smell like perfume last night?"

He steps back, seemingly astonished that she would ask such a question.

"Avery...," he says, reaching for her hand.

"No, Logan. Don't touch me. I'm going away until I can figure out things."

He tries once more to grab her hand and this time he is successful; the warmth of his grasp is a comfort to the hurtful situation.

Logan urges, "Avery, please, I need you to come with me."

"Why?" she questions, hesitating to follow him.

"Because I need you to, okay? Trust me."

Taking a deep breath, she hesitantly follows him to his car and waits for him to sit in the driver's seat. Avery gazes down at her shaking hands, nerves wracking her body. She's both scared and intrigued at wherever it is that Logan is taking her.

He starts the car and heads to the main road, interlacing his hand with her reluctant one over the center console. No words are spoken as they climb the steep roads leading to the top of the mountains, nor when they descend those roads heading towards the valley and lake.

Surprisingly, they turn onto the gravel road that leads to the winery Logan took her to on one of their first dates. When he parks the car, Avery glances at the empty parking lot and turns to him, raising her brow in question. Without any words, he smiles at her and then kisses the back of her hand before releasing it. He assists her in stepping out of the vehicle and then escorts her to the backside of the large barn.

"Logan, I don't think we're supposed to be here."

"Sure we are," he assures her, then continues in response to her apprehensive face. "It's fine. I wanted to show you something."

He leads her down a flagstone pathway, ending at a dock jutting out over the lake. Confidently stepping onto the pier, he tugs Avery in step behind him. She follows him to the end of the wooden planks, protruding them into the middle of the lake.

Logan turns her in his direction and wraps her in his strong embrace, whispering in her ear, "I love you, Avery. You know I'd never cheat on you. Since you've waltzed into my life, I can't even imagine being with another woman."

Avery leans back and looks into his eyes, but she knows he's sincere, mainly due to the overwhelming fact that she trusts him instinctively. She silently berates herself for considering any alternative.

She moves away from his embrace and turns to glance at the water, running her hands through her hair.

"I just don't understand, Logan. I believe you, but you've been so different this past week and you smelled of perfume last night. I just don't know what's going on."

Avery waits a beat and when he doesn't respond she turns around, ready to press him for an answer. Gasps escape her parted mouth when what she finds is Logan bent, kneeling before her, a glimmering ring held between two of his fingers.

"Oh my gosh," Avery quips, her hands covering her mouth in shock.

"Avery, you swept into my life and took me completely by surprise. I was never looking for you and I never knew I was worthy of someone like you. Someone that would show me what it means to be kind, to trust, to love, and to show love. Without you in my life, my world seems meaningless. You are in every breath I breathe, every intake of air. Without you I cease to exist.

"I love you more than anyone can possibly be loved. And you've shown me what it truly means to love someone. So, Avery Poindexter, I would be incredibly honored if you would be my wife," he proclaims, holding the ring higher in his grasp. "Will you marry me?"

It takes her a moment to catch her breath and gain some composure to answer his request.

"Logan, are you sure?" Avery asks hesitantly, certain he has made a mistake.

"More sure than I have been about anything in my entire life."

"Yes! One hundred times, yes!" she exclaims as she falls down to her knees and wraps her arms around his neck, his free arm enclosing her around her waist.

"I love you, Avery," he says into her neck, wetness settling onto the skin.

As Logan pulls back, Avery sees the moistness glistening in his eyes, confirming the tears she thought she had felt on her skin.

"I love you too, Logan," she replies breathlessly as he slides the overly-large diamond onto her finger.

She knows Logan does well financially, but a diamond this size must have set him back a pretty penny.

"I can see the gears turning, the ring is part of the reason I've been so distant the past week, besides the fact I was nervous as hell."

"You were nervous?"

"Of course I was. I can't imagine you not in my life. Anyway, the diamond came from a necklace that belonged to your great-great-great-grandmother."

Avery peers down at the perfectly cut oval diamond - which she's guessing is about five-carats, set in a single band of white gold.

"Do you think that it's bad luck...with my family history and…" Avery begins until Logan cuts her off by placing a kiss on her lips, silencing any more discussion.

"Sweetheart, it's from your great-great-great-grandmother on your father's side. Joseph gave it to me last week when I asked his permission to propose. He has rings set aside for all of his other children, but he wanted you to have this. It brought his family good luck when they travelled here from England to start new life."

"Oh wow," Avery sighs, peering closer at the flawless diamond in awe.

"So I've spent the last week searching for someone – anyone - willing to pry it from the necklace and set it in a ring. Austin ran into someone yesterday and she offered to do it last night. He took me out after to celebrate the end of my bachelorhood, or so he says, and I'm sorry about the perfume. I swear, we talked about how the lady went swimming in it.

Her daughter called me this morning when the ring was finished. That's why I needed to run off. But my plan was propose today all along; I had a backup ring just in case I couldn't find anyone nearby to take care of this one. It looks beautiful on you," he says as he twirls the ring around her finger.

"I can't believe you did all of that for me. You're incredible." Avery breathes out an excited gush of air. "Wow, we're getting married!"

"We sure are. One of the happiest days of my life."

Logan stands and tugs her up into his arms, kissing her senseless, her patchwork heart beating mercilessly in her chest, confirming the notion that Logan is her savior, the only person capable of bringing her to life despite the pile of ashes.

They drive to her father's house, excited to share their news, but nervous of the family's reaction. When they stroll into the house, later than the rest of the family, they find them all seated in the family room watching a football game. No one pays them any mind, except for Austin who shoots a conspiratorial wink in her direction.

She takes Logan's hand in hers and they walk across the room to the large sofa that is occupied solely by Sydney. Logan stops along the way to greet Austin and Jameson, while Avery sits beside Sydney and smiles in her direction. She returns Avery's smile and turns back to the television, but then she returns her gaze quickly as if something caught her off guard. Avery finds her staring at the obscenely large diamond on her small finger.

Unable to control her excitement, Sydney shouts, "Oh my god what is that? Are you?"

Avery nods and then Sydney tugs Avery's hand in her direction, which prompts a high-pitched squeal from her. The noise is immediately followed by more shrieking from the females in the room. Avery sneaks a glance at Logan just as her dad is releasing him from a hug and Austin is patting him on the back. Jameson reluctantly offers him a hand shake.

A knock has Amy pulling away from Avery to answer the door, and Avery makes her way back to Logan where he wraps his arm around her shoulder.

"So I hear good news are in order?" a dark voice echoes from the entryway, his mother obviously filling him in on the news.

"Ryker!" Cassidy exclaims as she rushes forward to embrace her youngest brother.

Joseph steps ahead and hugs his son, tugging him towards the chair where Logan and Avery stand.

"Ryker, please meet your half-sister Avery and you know Logan."

"Avery," he says as he tugs her into a tight embrace similar to their father's, "Welcome to the family." He pulls away and shakes Logan's hand, then lugs him forward to slap him on the back in a manly hug. "You too, Logan. You're officially a member of this clan."

"Thanks, man," Logan replies before once again tucking Avery under his arm.

"Alright," Ryker exclaims. "So when do we eat?" he asks, dramatically rubbing his taut abdomen.

As they erupt in laughter, they follow Amy and Joseph into the dining room. Avery looks around the room, taking in the conversations between her siblings, her father, Amy, and Logan, and then glances down at her sparkling ring.

Avery has never been more thankful for the people in her life.

Epilogue

*C*HRISTMAS MORNING, AVERY INTRICATELY wraps her gift for Logan. She searched and searched for something to get him, but truly, the man never asks for anything. It took her a while, but one day the idea came to her and she couldn't think of a better item to surprise him with.

They've already exchanged a few gifts but were planning to take the remainder to her parents' house when they leave in a few minutes, along with the gifts they purchased for her brothers and sisters. Avery had no trouble shopping for most of them; Jameson was the most difficult since he hasn't tried very hard to communicate with her. Instead, she relied on her sisters to give her ideas. She keeps her fingers crossed, hoping he is happy with her choice.

She stares at the wall where the picture from Aria hangs, and she can't help but question how her sister was able to capture so much of her future in one drawing. As if she knew all along how her life would turn out.

"Hey, sweetheart, are you ready?" Logan asks as strolls in from their bedroom, dressed in dark denim and a fitted maroon sweater, the dark color highlighting the green in his hazel eyes.

Avery licks her lips as she gazes at him.

"Don't look at me like that. You know I would do whatever you want, but we can't be late today."

Following his sly wink she replies, "I know. I know. You just look so handsome."

Grabbing the last of the gifts, Avery stands on her toes and kisses him gently as she passes by to grab her coat. Logan helps her wrap the new scarf he gave her around her neck, the soft cashmere rubbing her cheek. He returns her kiss and deepens the embrace, their tongues dueling against each other. Avery reluctantly pulls herself back and smiles, knowing if they don't stop they won't ever make it to her parents' home.

They arrive at the same time as Cassidy, and Logan and Avery walk with her into the house, Logan helping to carry all the gifts. Joseph and Amy welcome them and usher everyone into the living room around their magnificent Christmas tree. The decorations look like something you would find in a Country Living magazine. The tree and mantle draped in burlap, lace, and soft white ornaments; Christmas music playing gently in the background.

Joseph instructs the entire group to stand around the tree while he sets up his camera. Avery stands to the side between Logan and Austin; Joseph planning to stand beside Logan.

They take a series a pictures, the first formal, and the remainder extremely candid, by use of the remote Joseph hides in his hand. Ryker has them all cracking up as he tells a story about a roadie trying to board the plane in the nude.

After the pictures, they move into the dining room to eat a large meal cooked by Amy herself. The ham is sweet with hints of brown sugar and pineapple. To Avery's surprise, Amy passes her a bowl of Kraft mac-and-cheese. When Avery looks at her in question, Amy shrugs and nods her chin in the direction of Logan who sits beside Avery, conversing with Austin. Kraft mac-and-cheese is Avery's absolute favorite dish, ever. A comfort food Mila made that she never grew out of. The thought Amy put in at making sure Avery had something that she enjoyed amongst the rest of the gourmet meal is enough to bring a tear to her eye and she quickly swipes away the wetness.

After placing a heaping amount onto her plate, Amy pats her hand on top of hers and whispers, "Merry Christmas, Avery."

Avery watches the new members of her family joking and talking throughout the meal. And though her heart aches at the family she's lost, she has never before felt so much at peace.

Dessert moves them to the living room, where Ryker and Jameson spread out the slew of gifts, divvying them out amongst the family. Avery is truly surprised to find such a large amount placed in front of her legs.

Amy and Joseph instruct everyone to go ahead and open their gifts, acknowledging that if they went one at a time they'd be there until next Christmas. From Sydney and Everleigh, Avery receives a gift card for a spa in Asheville, and from Cassidy, a custom designed dress for use at

Avery's rehearsal dinner, though she and Logan had yet to set a date. It's a pale pink, A-line dress with hints of cream colored flowers covering the chiffon – absolutely remarkable. Much to Avery's surprise, the boys chipped in and bought her a Kindle and a $200 gift card to purchase books. Avery had only mentioned once that she loved to read, but that she rarely found time to make it to the library to check out books.

As she finishes her gifts, she turns to find Jameson opening his present from her and Logan. It was hard to come up with something he would enjoy, but with her current project in the works, Avery couldn't think of anything he would want more. As he opens the slim box, Avery glances nervously at her sisters and waits for Jameson's reaction. The girls had let it slip that since Jameson had graduated college he longed to start his own company that designs games and apps. Avery took the idea and ran with it.

"Is this for real?" he inquires as he looks at her.

Avery hears Ryker and Austin asking questions in the background, but the thumping of her heart in her ears drowns out the excess noise.

"It's real," Logan states for her. "We knew you needed the space and she wanted to help."

Jameson's paper states that he will occupy the upper story of the building that will house the pediatric clinic on the lower level. The second story remains un-leased. Jameson will be able to use the space rent free until he wants to move to another location.

"This is…," he begins as he makes his way over to them, "This is awesome. Thank you, Avery."

His strong arms wrap around her shoulders, his frame towering so far over her that it's hard to believe he is only twenty-one.

"Oh my gosh, I need to call Norah. She won't believe this!"

Avery turns to Sydney who sits on her other side and asks if Norah is his girlfriend. She just says that they're close friends who work together.

Once the gifts have been opened, the family begins relaxing with a few drinks and singing along to the music. Avery continues to glance at the door, unsure if a later surprise will go as planned.

Ryker glances at the tree once more and finds the gift Avery hid in the corner for Logan.

"Hey, man, looks like this is for you. Sorry I missed it."

Logan glances around the room, questioning everyone with his eyes, but everyone shrugs their shoulders, unsure of where the present came from.

Logan carefully peels back the paper from the box, pushing aside the tissue paper from the inside. He is admittedly confused when he finds a finely pressed physician smock - the stark whiteness in deep contrast to the red tissue paper.

He pulls the jacket from the box and holds it up, turning it side from side.

"This is great," he says, still confused. "I needed a new one."

Sydney squints her eyes at the smock – Avery can already tell she's the keen one in the family - and inquires, "What does it say above the pocket?"

That's when Logan's face changes from questioning to weary. He pulls the name to his face to read aloud, also noticing the picture in the pocket.

DR. LOGAN CHAMBERLINDADDYOFTWINS M.D.

At first no one in the room reacts, everyone glancing around wondering if they heard correctly. The Logan pulls out the pictures – Avery's twelve week ultrasound.

"You're pregnant?" Logan asks, Avery's family all holding their breath for her response.

She nods furiously, "Twelve weeks as of yesterday."

Logan launches himself over the coffee table and pulls her close, kissing Avery's face all over.

"I thought you couldn't get pregnant?"

"Apparently my doctor now believes in miracles."

"Holy shit! I'm going to be a father. We're having a baby."

"Babies. Two to be exact."

"Holy shit! I love you so much, Avery."

The crowd closes in on their celebration, Avery's siblings all offering their congratulations.

"Joseph, we're going to be grandparents!" Amy says from her perch on the loveseat.

"Three times over apparently," a new voice exclaims from the doorway.

Avery smile widens at her friends arrival.

She turns in recognition and finds Nikki standing in the family room, looking as gorgeous as ever in a figure-flattering green dress that hugs her every curve, including her baby bump.

"Nikki? You're pregnant?" Austin asks as he crosses his arms across his chest in a protective stance, his glare evident towards her barely distended belly.

"Hey, um...yea...I, um....I'm due in five months... You...you're the father," she says nervously, refraining from making eye contact.

Austin rushes forward and takes a hold of Nikki's arm and tugs her out further into the hallway, but not out of earshot.

"And I should believe you? I haven't heard from you in months."

"You don't have to believe me, but you need to know."

"Where have you been? Why didn't you return my calls?"

"I wanted to call, but when I found out I was pregnant I went away for a weekend to think... and then I got sick, really sick. I was severely dehydrated and I spent the last few months in and out of the hospital. I didn't say anything because I was afraid of losing the baby. But now that I'm feeling better, the doctor says I'm mostly in the clear. I'm sorry, Austin. I didn't know where else to find you. I'm sorry to ruin your Christmas, but I just got to town a few minutes ago."

Avery glances at Logan, clearly hearing the evidence of tears in her voice. Avery had spoken with Nikki quite often, but she had no idea she had been so sick.

Amy moves from her seat and enters the hallway. Avery can imagine that she wraps Nikki in her arms, comforting the mother of her grandchild.

Amy sits Nikki at the table and brings her a smorgasbord of food. Avery had already discussed with

Nikki her staying with them since the landlord at the apartment had decided to rent out the place instead of honoring their year-long rental payment.

Austin stalks into the room and hugs them all once more before grabbing his jacket and leaving the house.

Again looking at Logan, both questioning if it was a good idea to suggest that Austin and Nikki be their best man and maid of honor in the surprise wedding they planned to hold on New Year's Eve.

Logan and Avery leave closely behind Austin, her exhaustion from the day catching up to her.

When they arrive at their house, Logan helps to undress her, taking pleasure at placing small kisses on her abdomen, which has started to swell slightly.

"I can't believe you're pregnant with our children. I feel like everything in my life is coming together." He whispers joyfully, "Thank you, Avery."

"Thank you, Logan. For loving me and giving me this miracle - this gift of life."

He rests her back on the bed and tucks her into his chest, the beat of his heart lulling Avery into a deep sleep. Her heart beats in his rhythm, the broken pieces completely sealed in his love.

RENEE HARLESS

Acknowledgements

Coming Alive was a very personal story to write and I felt myself emotionally drained after each chapter. It took a lot of unknown strength to get every word in, but I am extremely pleased with the outcome. There are so many people I want to thank while I was on this journey and if I missed anyone know that I appreciate everything you did for me.

I first and foremost want to thank my readers for their amazing support for the Welcome to Carson series. I have had an outpouring of love over the characters and that means more to me then you'll ever know. I hope that you'll find this series relatable and easy to read. I wanted to write a story where you could completely lose yourself in the plot.

To my husband: you have been my rock through this entire process. Always making sure I get some sort of word count in and checking out all my artistic work when I need reassurance. It's not always easy to be married to a writer that would rather spend their free time huddled in a corner with a laptop, but you made sure I left the house…occasionally. I love you and it's all about the sunglasses.

Emily, I couldn't have done this without you. I am pleased to say you're not just my editor, but my friend. I know you're still mad at me for all the turmoil I put Avery through, but heck it made her stronger right? You keep doing what you do and silently correct everyone's grammar. We will meet one day, and lord help everyone at that moment.

My Betas, what can I say? Some of you hated that I made you cry and some of you threatened me for throwing the characters through the ringer, but in the end you all had the most positive feedback and comments. Your reactions are what kept me pushing through and revising, and doing whatever I could to make this the best story that it could be. Thank you for taking time away from your lives to give me a little piece of yourself.

To my risqué readers: You all are the most supportive team of friends that I could ask for. You're always working to pick each other up and support each other. Many of you I haven't met, but that WILL change. Until then, cheers (as I hold my over-filled glass of wine towards you).

Thank you to Chance Promotions for guiding me through the marketing process for an indie author. Your knowledge and support has been more than valuable and I enjoyed every moment of the experience.

Finally to my kids: you are the reason I do this; why I'm chasing my dream. I want you to always know that you have that opportunity. You can do whatever you want in life and no one can tell you "No." You're worth more than someone else's beliefs. I will always be here to fight for you. Love you both to the moon and back.

RENEE HARLESS

Keep reading for a look at the Book Two in the
Welcome to Carson Series, **Coming Together**,
featuring Austin and Nikki.

RENEE HARLESS

Chapter One

HE HAD RUSHED FROM his parent's house the moment he realized that she was there. Of course, he should have known that she was near when his heart started beating erratically; she had always caused that effect in him. He had all but ignored his instincts, however, since he hadn't seen or heard from her in a long, grueling four months.

Pregnant?

Of course she was pregnant. She had all but lied to him from the beginning: why would she have been truthful about birth control? He couldn't believe he had thought he was in love with her at one time.

Sitting on the steps of Horizon's, the local bar that was currently closed for the Christmas holiday, he cracked open a beer from the six-pack he picked up from the gas station on the way. He reaches deep within the front pockets of his jeans and grabs the delicate metal within before leaning forward and resting his arms on his knees. Twirling the glistening diamond ring between his fingers, Austin sighs heavily and places it back in his pocket, still unsure why he carries it with him. He takes a deep breath and runs his fingers through his hair before shaking his head in confusion and misery.

How did I get here?

Except… he knows how he got here. He had finally succumbed to the pull he had towards her. Austin had been tormented as he spent a year watching her flirt with his best friend, Logan, before she realized that the two of them wouldn't be anything more than friends. That year was complete torture, ignoring their pull and pretending she didn't exist: pretending that he had no desire to strip her bare, twist his hands in her silken gold hair, and bury himself deep inside her petite body. She was his every fantasy come to life, and now she was pregnant with his child, but she announced it at his family's Christmas dinner like it was an afterthought.

Austin shakes his head in agony as he reminisces about the first time he met Nikki. He had walked into Logan's family practice in need of stitches after slicing his hand on a stray piece of metal at a worksite. It was a worksite he had no business walking across, but when his foreman had called, saying that one of the new workers was drunk on the job, he had had no choice. Standing at the empty front desk, he immediately regretted his decision to ask his friend to sew him up, when suddenly the new receptionist returned from the back room to check him in. She had only looked up at him momentarily before aligning her focus back on the computer, but the few seconds when their eyes had met were enough to set fire to his skin. Her pale blue eyes held secrets; secrets he longed to learn.

After having his hand stitched up, Austin walked with Logan back to the lobby and found the mysterious blonde was gone. But fortunately, or unfortunately as the case may be, Austin saw Nikki from afar at Horizon's a countless number of times as she tried desperately to pursue Logan. Even though she was set on snagging his best friend, Austin couldn't help but soak in the image of her in the skin-tight dresses and sky-high heels. She was a vision wrapped in a tiny package.

After months of waiting and passing time with whatever woman landed in his bed, Austin finally got his chance. One heated game of bowling and an explosive night in bed was all it took to leave Austin and Nikki utterly addicted to each other. The chemistry was off the charts - just as he imagined it would be - but they had a lot in common and were able to pass the time between fiery episodes by filling those space with talks of life. He had fallen head-first in love with her and was just waiting until he knew she felt the same. Then she disappeared. Only her friend Avery knew where she was, and even though Avery was Logan's girlfriend - and Austin's own half-sister, he had recently learned - she wasn't breaking her promise to keep Nikki's whereabouts hidden.

All along, she had been home with her cousin Melanie, at least when she wasn't in the hospital, sick and dehydrated due to her pregnancy. A pregnancy he had no idea about.

Tossing his head in disbelief, he chugs the remainder of his beer before cracking open another.

"Thought I'd find you here," Logan's deep voice resonates from within the brick-lined emptiness of the alley.

"Nowhere else to go."

"I hear ya. So, man, what happened?"

"What happened? You mean the woman that had me completely wrapped up in her and left didn't spill all her secrets?"

Logan shakes his head and turns to look back at him.

"You know she isn't like that, Austin. I didn't talk to her long, I wanted to make sure you were okay, but I overheard her tell your mom and Avery that she was really sick and wasn't sure if she'd lose the baby."

Those last words capture his attention.

"What do you mean she thought she would lose the baby?"

"She told Avery that she had some severe morning sickness, couldn't keep anything down, and then she started bleeding. They had her on bed rest until recently."

"She should have told me. She should have let me be there for her."

"I know, man. That's something you'll have to talk to her about. But I'm here for you, and so are Avery and your brothers and sisters."

"I'm just so mad and confused," he says, taking a long pull from the bottle. "I just keep thinking that I must have done something wrong. How could she hate me so much to keep this from me?"

"She doesn't hate you. If she did, she wouldn't have come back."

Austin sits back, taking a deep breath through his nose, then releasing it into the air through his mouth. The swirl of his breath hitting the chilled air filters out around him like smoke.

"I can't be with someone like that; someone that willingly kept something like this from me. I mean, it's my child, too. I should have been told and I should have been able to be there if something had happened."

"Then we'll stand behind you if that's how you really feel. But don't go completely cold on her. She is the mother of your child and Avery's best friend. You're going to be around her for a long time."

Austin nods in agreement, not mentioning that he had previously planned on being with her the rest of his life, then rises from the steps and grabs the plastic loops of the six-pack between his fingers. He steps towards his truck,

Logan following closely behind, and they wave goodbye to each other, promising to meet up for New Year's.

Turning on the ignition, Austin sits in his truck, listening to the engine rumble for a moment, before shifting into gear and driving back to the home he finished building a few weeks ago.

The 3,000 square-foot farmhouse sits on forty-five acres of trees and pasture, with a small plateau overlooking a man-made pond. When he came across the old farm for sale, he knew he couldn't pass it up: it was the perfect property on which to start a family. The old house had been in disrepair, half of the building burnt to a crisp from a kitchen fire, but luckily for him he had the skill to tear it down and build his dream home in its place.

Austin sits in the cab of his truck, staring at the front porch where the swing rocks gently back and forth, the same swing he had pictured himself and Nikki rocking in, enjoy the soft rays of early morning light. Staying in the house since she left had been agony. He had subconsciously decorated every room with her in mind, the colors she liked and the furnishings she always pointed out in magazines. He couldn't help it; this was the house where he wanted to have a family with her.

And now it had all gone to shit.

She didn't seem to want him in her life, and he wasn't about to give her the opportunity to take her second chance and burn him again. He had learned the hard way that no relationship was perfect – heck, Avery, his newly discovered half-sister, was a testament to that.

Deciding not to open the garage, Austin parks the truck in the driveway and makes his way up the steps. His beagle, Duke, is waiting anxiously for him.

"It's just you and me right now, bud, but how would you feel about a brother or sister?" he says, crouching down, eye-level to the dog.

Duke barks in response, happily wagging his tail in excitement.

"Yea, that's how I feel too. You'll be a great big brother," Austin says, rubbing Duke's head before standing and walking towards the back door. "Come on, go do your business."

As he waits for Duke to come back to the door, Austin glances around the living room and where it opens into the entryway, dining room, and kitchen. He can still picture Nikki in this space, her small body tucked in the corner of his couch, reading a book: the same position she was always in at her apartment.

Running a shaky hand through his hair, he sighs as he looks up at the ceiling and the exposed beams over the living room.

"Not again. I can't do it again."

A small scratch jerks his attention back to the door, and he lets Duke return inside before tossing the six-pack into the fridge and heading upstairs to the bedroom.

Exhausted from the day, Austin tugs off his shirt and tosses it onto the floor, then flings his tired body onto the bed.

Adding to his bitter thoughts of Nikki, his dreams are plagued by visions of his past. Ashley, the first woman he ever fell for, haunts his mind as he tries to escape her hold. Her parting words echo through his mind, reminding him why second chances are no different than the first time around.

"You gave me what I wanted when I needed it and now I'm done. I've found someone better and really, did you expect me to marry a construction worker?"

"What are you talking about?" Austin had asked her. "You're the one that wanted to get back together after we broke up after high school."

She had run her hands down his chest to his waistline - and that should have been his first clue that she was up to something.

"Yes, well I was lonely, and you know that we were good together. Granted, it took far more convincing than I expected. But I needed someone to take care of me and now… I've upgraded."

"God, Ashley, I thought we were going somewhere. I was thinking about proposing!"

She laughed and then pushed his chest gently.

"Propose? With what? A piece of plastic? Look, Jeremy can give me the life I want and I'd be stupid to give that up."

Little did she know that he had just made his first million in the three years since he graduated college. His designs were being sought all over the country and he had crews all over.

"Jeremy is your step-father and that's fucking disgusting. How long were you sleeping around behind my back?"

An incessant pounding on the door wakes Austin from his tossing and turning. Nightmares of Ashley had been happening far more frequently since Nikki left, and visions of her always left him on edge.

Yelling from atop the stairs that he's coming, he finally opens the door after the third round of pounding.

"What?" he commands, opening the door and realizing that Avery is standing on the other side. Softening his features, he relaxes slightly before apologizing and ushering her inside.

Avery is his half-sister from an affair his father had while separated from his mother. She was a surprise to him and his five other siblings, but she was loved no less. His parents had been searching for her for years, even since they had learned she existed. Despite the family's determination to show her that she deserved the love they were bestowing on her, she was just now learning to accept it.

She was also pregnant and engaged to his best friend, Logan.

"You look like shit," she begins, crossing her arms over her chest and narrowing her eyes.

"Yes, well I slept like shit and your friend turned my world upside down, so I'm sorry if I'm not quite as chipper as you are this morning."

Tucking her chin to her chest, she murmurs, "Don't be an ass."

Sighing, Austin takes a deep breath and shakes out his arms before reaching forward and wrapping her in an embrace.

"I'm not trying to be an ass. What can I do for you this morning? Do you want something to eat?"

"Not now, but I need a favor and you're not going to like it."

Stepping back, Austin furrows his brow in her direction. "What kind of favor?"

"Well... see, I've moved in with Logan and we left the apartment vacant. Nikki had been paid up, but they evicted her anyway. Mom and Dad offered to let her stay with them, but she doesn't want to impose. To make matters worse, Logan's practice had to replace her while she was away, so now she is out of a job."

"How does this concern me?"

"She's the mother of your child and my niece or nephew. I was hoping that you could use that big heart that I know you have and offer to let her work for you, and help her find a place to stay that she can afford. I've looked all over and all the reasonable places in town have no vacancies."

"You want me to let her stay here." Austin says: a statement, not a question.

"Only if that's what you want. I'm really just hoping you can offer her a job. She's been over to Angie's Diner, but with all the health problems she's been having I don't think waitressing is good idea. And she only has a GED so she isn't qualified for a lot. Please, Austin," Avery says, a loving gleam sparkling in her eye. Had she had the opportunity to use this look on their father, Austin feels sure she would have received anything she wanted.

"Dammit, Avery!" Austin explodes in exasperation, striking a hand through his thick mane of hair. "I will do my best to get her a job and help her find a place, but you have no idea how much you owe me. That woman destroyed me when she left."

Frowning, Avery steps forward and wraps her arms around his waist.

"She left because she was scared. She loved you too much to risk ruining your life with a child. It took everything she had to come back here."

Leaning his chin on her head, he whispers back, "She tell you that?"

She doesn't acknowledge his question, but continues, "Don't be too hard on her. There are a lot of things you don't know, but she does want to be a part of your life and for her, that is a major step."

"Ok, Avery. I'll help her with a job, but I can't promise I'll do much more than that."

"I understand. Thank you, Austin. I'll see you next weekend for New Years. I'll let myself out."

"You know your fiancé would kill me if I didn't walk you out."

She chuckles as he walks her to her car, then watches her leave, a cloud of dust trailing behind her Audi SUV.

Duke sidles up next to Austin and sits back on hind legs, the two of them watching as Avery disappears onto the main road.

"I swear, Duke. That woman can talk me into anything. Let's hope I don't regret this."

The beagle stares up at Austin with soulful brown eyes and barks in reply. Noticing a squirrel, he is suddenly off, racing to the back yard in hot pursuit.

"God, I hope that I don't regret his," Austin whispers to the air before turning and walking back to the house. Before he has time to think, he is dialing a number on his cell phone that he had hoped he wouldn't have to call again.

7 HE POUNDING IN her head wakes her from her restless sleep on the guest bed in Logan and Avery's home. Nikki sits up slowly, making sure

to keep her nausea in check. She has learned over the past few months that certain movements and smells irritate her stomach more than anything she actually eats. Slouching over while perched on the edge of the bed, Nikki gently places her hands on the sides of her slightly-distended belly. The flutters began a week ago, proof that a piece of her and Austin was growing inside her body. Talking softly to the baby deep within her womb, she moves her hands around until she feels the tiny kicks against the side of her abdomen. Of course, the baby liked it best when she talked about Austin – heck, she liked it best, too.

"Hey, sweet one. How are you doing in there?"

Small flutters respond to her question.

"Good. I saw your daddy last night. He looked as handsome as ever, not that I had any doubts. You'll be gorgeous just like him and his family." She sighs, her lower back aching from the weight of the rapidly-growing infant. "Anyway, let's get this day started. I need to find a job and a place for us to stay once you get here. Love you, sweet one."

More flutters graciously respond to Nikki's endearment and she revels in the feel of instantaneous love for her child.

The past four months had been difficult at best. Nikki remembers the panic she felt as she realized that she was two weeks late - the need to rush to the pharmacy in the next town over. She ashamedly took the pregnancy test in the store restroom, then sat in her car crying as she realized that she was going to destroy Austin's world.

They had never talked about kids, marriage, or anything further that their nightly rendezvous, but she loved him fiercely. The pull she had so long ignored in favor of the logical choice of pursing her boss, Logan, spread ten-fold when she finally gave into their chemistry. She had no idea sex could be so explosive: in the moments that their lips first met, the world had halted. It was just the two of them and everything else ceased to exist. They were together for two months before she recognized the early symptoms of her pregnancy.

And then she fled. She fled out of fear, out of duty to her child, and out of love for Austin. Nikki had loved him so much that she couldn't imagine burdening him with a child. He had a career, after all. Owner of and architect for Connelly Construction, Austin had the world at his feet.

Staring at the pregnancy test, Nikki's fears had bubbled to the top of her heart and immediately overwhelmed her. She loved Austin, but she knew he didn't feel the same – no one did. Her mother had left their family in disarray when she ran off with the boss of Nikki's father – thus having her father fired and black listed in the financial world, all at the same time. Her mother didn't care that she upended Nikki's world, or that her father would never recover and lose himself to the bottle. Her father's love for her slipped through the amber liquid, along with his health and his will to live. The only love Nikki felt was that from her aunt Andrea, Melanie's mother. She had taken her in as Nikki's guardian and given her shelter from the cruel world.

Once again, Melanie and Andrea had been her rock as she fled from Carson and needed a place to think. They were with her the time she was rushed to the hospital when she started bleeding while working at a local restaurant, and they held her hand as she heard the baby's heartbeat echoing in the small room. It was at their insistence that she found herself back in Carson. They urged her to tell Austin about the baby, Melanie gently assuring her that everything would work out for the best. And if it didn't, she had added kindly, she could always move back to Georgia with them.

Nikki didn't know yet if she had made a mistake by coming back to Carson, but after her hormonal outburst at the Connelly Christmas gathering last night, she felt she had made the worst out of an already turbulent situation.

Peeking out from the guest room, Nikki glances into the hall before grabbing a pair of leggings and a sweater from her suitcase, attempting to quietly make her way to the bathroom. She only makes it two steps before the hardwood floor squeaks, and Logan's deep voice booms from the kitchen.

"Nikki, is that you?"

Taking a deep breath, she nervously shuffles towards the kitchen, taking great care to make sure that the pile of clothing in her hands forms a protective barrier in front of her body.

"Hey," she responds softly.

"Morning, Nik. Can I make you something to eat?" He asks, flashing a genuine smile in her direction. That same smile in the past would have been something she would have taken as a flirtatious invitation, but now she sees that it is the smile Logan gives to his friends.

She bites the edge of her bottom lip and shakes her head no, saying that she didn't want to be a bother: she would grab something while she went out looking for a job.

"Nonsense. Avery's been craving pancakes, so if you're okay with that, I'll make you a batch as well."

Nikki laughs lightly at his commanding tone, knowing that she will have no choice but to eat those delicious-smelling pancakes, or Logan would tie her to the chair and let Avery force-feed her.

"Hey, I was wondering if you were awake," Avery whispers from behind Nikki, startling her.

"Oh my gosh, please don't sneak up on me like that."

"Not my fault you were in your own little world. Ooooo, Logan are you making pancakes? God, I love you."

"I am, sweetness. I was just telling Nikki that I'll make her a batch, too."

"Good, and make that two for her please," she says, turning to face Nikki once again, "You're far too skinny to be almost five months pregnant."

"I was really sick, Avery. The only nourishment I had was through an IV. I'm just now able to eat real food again, so please keep your comments to yourself," Nikki snaps. A growl reverberates from the kitchen before Nikki notices the wetness swimming in Avery's eyes.

"I'm sorry," Avery whispers, "you're right. It's none of my business." She moves quickly to join her fiancé in the kitchen, swiping at her face to remove the unwanted tears.

"God, Avery. I don't mean to be a bitch. It's these hormones I swear. I just..." Nikki murmurs, shuffling her feet from side to side. "I just was really, really sick. So sick that the IV is the only thing that kept me alive. I couldn't even keep down water. But now I'm fine and the baby is healthy, so I'm trying to forget my time in the hospital. I didn't mean to get angry at you."

"I wish I had known you weren't well. Every time I spoke with you, you told me that you were working and getting yourself together. I had no idea the personal holiday you took was because you were pregnant. You never even hinted at it."

"I didn't know you were pregnant either, but you look beautiful. I've never seen a more radiant mother-to-be."

And truly, she was stunning. Avery and Nikki had formed a close bond when Melanie brought her to Carson. Her back story was a tragic one. A family hell-bent on making her invisible and a fate that so unjustly took her sister and two fiancés. She had also had a hard life, and the two connected immediately. At first, it had hurt when she noticed Logan had taken an immediate liking to her, but it was hard not to like Avery. She was an empty soul with a dire need for love, and once she accepted her place with Logan, everything else fell in line. Which was why Nikki wasn't surprised to find out that Avery was only a month behind her in pregnancy, a large rock balanced perfectly on her delicate ring finger. Logan looked at her as if she was all he could see, and Avery mirrored that look. There was no denying the connection that they had together; a connection that made it all the more evident that Nikki and Austin weren't ever going to find a happy ever after. A lusty haze is all they saw each other through - a lusty haze that had taken over every aspect of their lives when they were together.

And now after Nikki rushed through breakfast and a shower, and riding with the nosy townspeople on their small bus system, she hoped against all hope that she had made the right choice in coming back to Carson. She didn't want to be a burden to anyone, especially her friend Avery, but it seemed that since no one was hiring and all the cheap apartments in the next town were full, Nikki was going to have to rely on others. She hated that more than anything.

Relaxing against the headboard in the guest bedroom, Nikki types furiously away on the keyboard of her laptop until her phone startles her from her trance. She sighs heavily, hating to stop her work when she gotten to such a good part, but after seeing the name that flashed across the screen, she knew she needed to take the call.

Taking only enough time to save the secret project she was working on - a story that had been agonizing her mind for years – she answers the phone.

"Hello?"

"Meet me in twenty minutes at Angie's," he commands.

"Huh?"

"Twenty minutes, Nikki."

Click.

Staring at the phone in her hand, Nikki shakes her head, knowing that if she doesn't arrive in the allocated amount of time, Austin will only come and find her at Avery's, and he'll be spitting mad to boot. Not wanting to ruffle any more feathers, Nikki takes her laptop and plugs it into the charger, then places it on the night stand.

She arrives at Angie's in forty-five minutes, then heaves a deep breath before moving to open the front door. Before she reaches the handle, a strong hand wraps around her wrist and halts her movements.

"Nikki," he murmurs hoarsely, his voice desperately close to her ear.

She gasps in surprise, not from her name, but from the shock she feels traveling up her skin from his contact – something she had forgotten occurred whenever they touched.

She turns her head towards the voice, bringing their mouths but an inch from each other, whispering his name in a single breath:

"Austin."

RENEE HARLESS

About the Author

Renee Harless is a contemporary and erotic romance author. She lives in the Blue Ridge Mountains of Virginia with her husband and children. Renee is a fan of the Washington Capitals and Virginia Tech Hokies.

To say that Renee is a romance addict would be an understatement. When she isn't chasing her kids around the house, or writing, she jumps head first into a romance novel.

RENEE HARLESS

42800660R00177

Made in the USA
Middletown, DE
21 April 2017